YOUR
DEADLY
DECISIONS

K.N.PANTAROTTO

Illustrations by K.N.Pantarotto
Cover Design by K.N.Pantarotto
Published by K.N.Pantarotto
Edited by KZ and Susanna Goldstone
Interior Design:: Jennie Lyne Hiott

Second Edition
ISBN: 978-1-9992389-1-9

WARNING

Dear Beloved Reader,
The Darkness draws you in, I see.
First, I want to thank you for even laying your wonderful eyes on my book. There are a few warnings I should give you before you continue.

This book deals with some heavy themes:

A car crash
Drug addiction
Childhood illness
Mention of domestic abuse
Mention of sexual assault
Light violence
Mention of suicide
And Death

If you are uncomfortable with any of these themes, I urge you not to read on.
If you do anyway, I want you to know that these themes all come from a very personal place of understanding. When reading through these events, you may remember a similar time in your life where the same thing may have happened to you. In that time, if you had no one around to help, I want you to know that I was there with you, and this book will be like we held hands through it together.

The worst times of our lives can become worse when we are forced to go through them alone. If you ever feel alone in a terrible time, please reach out.

Thank you to all the wonderful people in my life who never doubted me when that is all I ever did.

1

HER EYES

SATURDAY, SEPTEMBER 28, 2019

$$02:29_{AM}$$

Three minutes before the crash.

A yawn escaped Trent as he drove. The dirt road ahead of him had become hypnotizing and could quickly put him to sleep if he weren't careful.

"Why'd you make me do that, Trent?" Jeremy asked.

Trent glanced at his drunk brother in the passenger's seat.

"Listen, Jer, I'm gonna give you the talk before Mom does."

"I already got *the* talk–"

"Not the talk, stupid. The talk about rejection. I'm gonna make it short and sweet." Trent cleared his throat. "There are some things which are beyond your control. Rejection fortifies the soul."

Jeremy snorted in disbelief at his brother.

"What do you know? You've never been rejected in your life. I expect lines like that from Mom, not you."

"I did say it comes from Mom, I just made it more poetic."

"That made it worse." Jeremy sighed, then drunkenly stared into space.

Before Trent could continue his life lesson, Jeremy scrunched his nose and wiggled it from side to side with a sullen expression. Trent caught sight of his brother's antics and looked confusedly back and forth between the road and his brother.

Finally, he had to ask, "What the hell are you doing?"

"Her nose is so cute, especially when she does this." Jeremy pointed to what he was doing as Trent rolled his eyes.

As the pair drove home from the party, Jeremy couldn't stop talking about Tala, the pretty girl who had rejected him. All night, Trent had encouraged him to ask her out. Unfortunately, they'd both miscounted how many drinks it would take for Jeremy to sound like an absolute asshat – he had become noticeably drunk after only four – and went in on one too many.

"You know, I'm just impressed you didn't throw up on her. You were so nervous, you looked like a fucking ghost."

"I looked like an idiot."

"I agree, and listen, if it makes you feel any better, I *have* been rejected before.

"It helps a little," Jeremy mumbled. Trent smirked and pushed his brother's face away by ruffling his short brown hair.

Jeremy usually wasn't one to drink, being only

sixteen, but over the past couple of days, Trent had noticed that Jeremy was feeling down; he had been hiding out in his room and telling Trent off when he entered without permission. Trent figured that the seniors' party, thrown to kick off the first month of the school year, would be the perfect setting to loosen him up a bit. In hopes that it would give him enough confidence to talk to Tala – the girl who Jeremy couldn't stop talking about all week.

It was an unfortunate and surprising turn of events, Trent had never thought Jeremy would be this brazen once he got a few spirits in him. As Jeremy continued sadly twitching his nose, Trent shook his head at his brother. He didn't resemble the cute way Tala had done it, but he was trying.

"Yeah, I'm not giving you rum ever again." Trent sighed as his brother settled his head on the window.

"Wait, which one was the rum?" Jeremy's head propped itself right back up.

He looked like a confused kid who'd been asked a challenging math question.

"The one mixed with Coke," Trent answered.

"That wasn't just bad Coke?"

Trent snorted at his brother's question.

"What the hell is 'bad' Coke, dude? Coke is sugar; it's not gonna go bad."

Jeremy scrunched up his face and made a strange whining sound as he searched for the words he was trying to say.

"I meant like, not a brand name, you know – like knock-off Coke. That value brand garbage," Jeremy said before letting out a loud burp and resting his head back on the seat.

Trent shook his head, rolled his eyes again, and reached for the radio to turn the volume up. 'Under Pressure' by Queen had just started playing. There was no reason to glance at the clock; an oldie playing on the station meant that the night had slipped into early morning, their mother would be asleep for sure. She had never been particularly strict, but Trent knew that she'd have something to say about him bringing his underage brother home inebriated. Even though Trent was an exceptionally smooth talker, he wasn't really prepared to talk himself out of this one if he were caught.

As Trent approached a back-road bend, he nudged Jeremy to hum the intro to the song with him.

"Pressure!"

Before the brothers could laugh at their well-timed but poorly sung duet, the earth-shaking sound of crunching metal filled Trent's ears.

Trent instinctively hit the brakes and threw his hands up over his head. He felt like his body had been ensnared by a vicious whirlpool, as though being thrust forward by an astonishing force. Suddenly, a sinking feeling in his stomach told him that he was no longer in the driver's seat. An incredible wave of pain overtook his body. Everything went dark, even though every nerve in his body felt like it had been lit on fire.

In the darkness, he saw a flash of light.

He tried opening his eyes slowly against the flare. When they were able to focus, he saw his brother looking down at him, crying out as he held his phone to his ear. Trent couldn't understand what his brother was saying. There was a blinding pain in his head, a pain so powerful that it was corrupting typical sights and sounds. All he could see for sure was that Jeremy's head was bleeding. Trent wanted to reach out and wipe the blood away, but the pain held him back like cold bars of a prison cell. Everything went dark again.

Another flash.

He opened his eyes and saw bright lights

overhead. They looked like massive shooting stars in a sea of dark – growing brighter, drowning out the black until Trent could make out a bright tunnel. As he watched the lights, he was aware of his body floating. His mind couldn't piece anything together anymore. He was in too much pain. Trent gasped for air as he tried to ask for help. Before any words could escape him, Trent's eyes rolled back into his head as he heard his brother yell his name.

There was one last flash, followed by a terrible darkness. Trent felt like he'd been thrust into a deep, dark hole in the center of his mind. Trent couldn't understand if he was lost or dreaming. His millions of thoughts felt like a dense wilderness engulfing him.

It was quiet here. The world felt heavy and weighed down, as though he was trying to swim through black tar. When he thought he had almost clawed his way out, he was pulled back in. He remembered those times when his friend Adam would hold his head underwater at the pool – there, he'd be able to push him off quickly and swim to the surface. There had been no consequence to that; it was nothing but a kid's game. Here, he couldn't see what was holding him under. He couldn't see where the water ended, which made Trent fear the price of staying under it.

The next time he escaped the endless black, he still couldn't see or feel anything, but he could hear his mother sobbing beside him. As he tried to look for her, his body felt like it was floating through air, but no matter how much he wanted to open his eyes to see whether or not he was actually levitating, he couldn't. *Have I been kidnapped? Where am I, what's happening?* His mother's crying was slowly drowned out as Trent felt himself being pulled into sleep. Or what he thought was sleep. It felt like sinking into that dark hole again. Only, this time, there were no lights or sounds coming through anymore, as if he were descending into a cave deep below the ocean.

Trent felt as though he was at the bottom of a never-ending abyss. He couldn't tell if his eyes were open or closed, and he didn't think it would matter. The darkness was all-consuming. Trent's body no longer felt like his own.

He didn't feel whole.

There was no moon, no stars – the sun was a distant memory. All at once, Trent couldn't remember anything before this dreadful feeling.

SATURDAY, SEPTEMBER 28, 2019

02:53 AM

The white noise of the hospital's television lulled Lynn Avison into an early sleep as she sat next to her sleeping brother's bed. Late last night, she'd turned the TV on, volume low, to distract herself from the nerve-wracking sound of Theodore's ventilator. Her eleven-year-old brother had been diagnosed with leukemia at the age of five.

Lynn's head rolled forward from her shoulder, and she awoke before her chin hit her chest. In a daze, she opened her eyes and blinked tiredly around the hospital room. She was curled up in the chair positioned beside her brother's bed that she had claimed as her throne away from home. An undercurrent of anxiety and overwhelming sadness crept up inside her as she realized that she was still in the hospital. Everything about this place was gut-churning, from the sickening beige colour of the walls to the tiny size of the room.

Her mother was working a night shift, as she usually did on the weekends. Lynn had offered to stay with her brother. Lynn and her mother didn't agree on most things, but neither of them liked the idea of little Teddy in this place alone.

Lynn stretched her arms before rising from her throne, deciding to get a drink from the nearest vending machine to wake herself up. On her way out of the room, she laid a hand on the boy's forehead, checking for a fever. Satisfied, she gave him a quick peck on his head and made her way down the dreary white hallway, which was way too bright for four in the morning. An awful cold sunk in once she reached the vending machine. Brushing off the teeth-chattering chill, she pulled her hoodie over her shoulder-length hair and searched around her jean pockets for some change. Looking down at her feet kept her attention away from the fluorescent hallway light flickering just three feet away from her.

As Lynn fumbled with her quarters, she silently cursed herself as she came up short. The flickering light finally caught her attention, and she shook her head at the faulty system. Her cynical mind wondered how much she actually trusted this hospital to keep her brother alive when they couldn't even keep the lights on.

On her way back to her brother's room, she thought she heard someone's voice call her from the end of the hall. When she turned to look, she could've sworn she'd seen someone walk around a corner and disappear. It was strange though, in the ominous silence, that she hadn't heard footsteps.

A chill ran up her spine.

When she made it back to the room, it took her a moment to brush off that eerie feeling and start rummaging through her small black knapsack. After grabbing enough change, she walked back down the hall to the same vending machine. Silently, she hoped that the busted light hadn't completely switched off.

Otherwise, she'd be even more freaked out.

Now, more nervous than before, she quickly put in her money, trying to ignore the on-and-off buzz of the flickering light and the tickle of bleach in her nostrils. The hairs on the back of her neck stood up; her breath quickened. Battling with the value brand cola button, she clenched her teeth as she impatiently waited for the stupid machine to hurry up and dispense her drink already. When it finally dropped, she opened it and took a sip.

A cold breeze made her teeth chatter again. It wasn't this cold in here during the day. Even in this autumn weather, there wouldn't usually be a breeze like this. In fact, there shouldn't be a breeze at all. She was inside a hospital, not standing on the roof.

It took her a few moments to notice that someone was standing behind her under the flickering light. Slowly, she looked over her shoulder, her eyes locking onto the figure as her heart skipped a beat. Whenever the light would flicker, so would the apparition of the male standing underneath it.

"It's... dark..." the figure said in a strained voice. Then, he disappeared completely as quickly as he had first materialized.

Lynn stood there, her big brown eyes fixed open as wide as her dry mouth. She didn't know what to do next. She'd forgotten her name, why she was even there, and why the hell her hand was so cold.

"Are you all right, hon?" A familiar voice softly interrupted Lynn's thoughts, but she was yet to move.

As Lynn's fingers unclenched around the soda can in her hands, she jumped at the noise the uncrunching metal made and looked over to see a nurse she knew. Lucinda, Cindy for short, a blonde Latina woman who always had her hair tied back, one of the warmest smiles Lynn had ever seen, and barely any wrinkles stood smiling at Lynn. After what Lynn had just witnessed, this smile didn't seem friendly. Instead, it seemed unfamiliar and out of place. *What the hell just happened?*

"Lynn? Honey? Did you need something?" Cindy asked again, and this time Lynn was able to quieten her thoughts.

The nurse walked over and handed her a napkin off a nearby desk.

"You got a little... just..." As Cindy tried to give her the paper napkin, Lynn still stood frozen.

Cindy took it upon herself to carefully wipe the soda that was dripping from the girl's open mouth.

"Come on, dear," Cindy said, gently placing an arm around Lynn's shoulders and leading her back to her brother's room.

"I—sorry, Cindy. I—" Lynn couldn't form the words to describe what she had witnessed, but she so desperately wanted to try.

"No need to be sorry. Get some sleep, alright? Remember, like I told you before, you can use the white room if it gets too hard to sleep in here."

Lynn nodded in understanding. Cindy walked out of the room, leaving Lynn to her thoughts. To Lynn, the world slowly started to make sense again. Her name was Lynn, the nurse who walked her back here was Cindy, and now Lynn was in her sick brother's room. The white room that Cindy had mentioned was a lounge for the families of patients to sleep in when the melancholy of their loved one's hospital room became too overwhelming.

Like now.

But Lynn wouldn't feel right leaving her brother alone. Lynn fell into the chair from earlier and stared at her brother. When her eyes began to well up from seeing his little body struggle to breathe, she looked up at the television, which was still set to white noise. She didn't want to sound crazy, but she felt like she was losing her grip on reality.

Was it just her? Or did that ghostly figure look exactly like a baseball player from her high school? Either she was having a mild hallucination caused by some unknown, deep-rooted desire, or her eyes were playing a *very* cruel trick on her.

2

LUCKED OUT

02:31 AM

Imagine you're floating high above the clouds, and it's so relaxing that you start to smile – giggle, even. You speed up, the momentum picking up so fast that you can't control your direction, and suddenly you hit a brick wall, face first. Pain erupts in your forehead. You can't tell if the ringing in your ears is coming from the now-busted car radio or within your jostled mind.

Jeremy felt like he could throw up. It was hard to open his eyes as he clutched his head in pain. There was an incredibly loud bang, and his chest hurt from how hard the seatbelt had tugged him back. When he could finally open his eyes, they scanned every inch of the car's front seat.

Jeremy's head was throbbing. He couldn't remember falling asleep on such a hard surface. Sluggishly, he struggled to lift his head. As he sat upright, he felt hot liquid running down his forehead. The throbbing felt as though a tiny hammer was battering the front of his skull from the inside, and the pain made it difficult to open his eyes fully. He tried looking down at his hand, and suddenly noticed the tiny shards of glass which were mixed with the blood. In shock, his eyes widened, and his vision was suddenly clearer than it had ever been. Jeremy looked at the windshield's glass that jaggedly hung from the edges of the frame. There was white smoke rising from the front of the vehicle, which was now so banged up on the driver's side that it looked like something from a movie. Everything around him looked unreal in its atrocity. His brain told him that the destruction he saw could only be a result of CGI. He tried to recount what had happened. He remembered a party and drinks – too many drinks – and he had decided to hit on Tala. Trent was in the middle of giving him a terrible pep talk, and suddenly there was a bright light and a jolt. Noise – there was a lot of noise. Everything was scattered. *Wait... Trent, where's Trent?*

"Trent?" Jeremy's voice strained. When everything stopped being so blurry, Jeremy realized his brother wasn't in the driver's seat, and there was no longer a seatbelt attached to the door. His heart sank. Suddenly, the jagged broken glass of the front window was making sense to him, and he felt stupid for not realizing it sooner.

"Trent? Trent! Where are you?" Jeremy bellowed, tasting blood in his mouth as he did so, and his own abrupt change in volume made the tiny hammer in his head hit harder. Jeremy's eyes flew around wildly, trying to adjust to the overwhelming dark of nighttime, which was barely disturbed by the vastly spaced-out streetlamps. He hastily searched around the car's armrest compartment for the spare flashlight he knew was still there from their summer camping trip. When he found it, he shone the light onto the road. The light flew around the darkness like a manic firefly until it landed on Trent. His black sneakers were the only thing Jeremy could see peeking out of the tall grass. Trent lay face down on the road's side.

"Fuck, what the fuck?!" Jeremy screeched before jumping out of the car and running over to his brother.

Panicking, Jeremy began dialling 9-1-1with trembling hands. He couldn't look at his brother on the ground. The sight was sickening, blood slowly pooling out of Trent's head into the grass. Jeremy took note of the mailbox that Trent had landed in front of. There was no car parked in the driveway. No lights had turned on in the house. There was no one around within a few miles who could help them, because houses were spread far apart here. Maybe this house was abandoned anyway. This part of Heatherdale was pretty dead. *What kind of shit fucking luck is that?* Jeremy yelled at whatever God would listen to him in his head. He didn't have a preference for one, but he'd unquestionably believe in any of them as long as they decided to help his brother out at this very moment.

"9-1-1, what's your emergency?" a calm female voice asked.

"Car wreck, my brother was thrown from the car—"

"Where are you?"

"The mailbox says 1975, and I think I'm on... Skylark? Yeah, the end of Skylark! There's a turn where you can't really see past the trees, and then there's a fork that breaks off to Hanger Road? Please come fast, he's bleeding, he—"

"Get an ambulance to 1975 Skylark Road. Is he alive?" When the woman asked the question, Jeremy suddenly couldn't breathe. He hadn't even checked. Jeremy could barely stomach the blood that was now in a muddy pool beside him, or the idea of Trent being thrown from a car. Kneeling down to check Trent's pulse, Jeremy closed his eyes hard, trying not to let the image of his brother on the ground be ingrained in his mind forever. Getting closer to the ever-growing amount of blood made him queasier than expected. Jeremy would bet money on the fact that his liquor intake was making this experience ten times worse.

"He has a pulse!" Jeremy shouted feeling a tiny morsel of relief.

"Good. Now, check to see if he is awake. Talk to him."

Jeremy was trying to understand how she could be so calm during this, but then he remembered that he was the one in the middle of this shitstorm, not this nice lady on the phone.

"Trent, can you hear me, brother? I need you to wake up if you can, dude," Jeremy's voice squeaked. He didn't want to cry, but a sudden rush of realisation suddenly hit him – this was really happening. Another person had hit them and left, leaving Jeremy to clean up the mess *they* had made. A heavy burden fell on his sixteen-year-old shoulders.

Trent's eyes flickered open for a moment, and Jeremy started sobbing loudly on the phone. His unintelligible sobs were ninety percent fear, and ten percent hope that maybe Trent would survive this whole ordeal.

"He opened his eyes, what do I do? Should I do something?"

"Breathe deeply and stay as calm as you can. Do not move him. Try to keep him awake if possible –

help is on the way."

"This is such bullshit. He isn't even drunk, I'm drunk! I can't believe this fucking car took off! Trent, please keep your eyes open!" Jeremy screamed into the air as his eyes darted around for help.

The frosted cloud from his panicked breathing was like a small, useless smoke signal in the still of the night. Jeremy looked down into his brother's eyes, and his heart sank as Trent's eyes fluttered closed again. He was unsure if Trent's eyes were closing because he was shining the flashlight at them, or if his brother was losing consciousness completely.

"Did you see what the car looked like?"

"No! No, I—at least I don't think I did. Fuck, I think he passed out again."

"What's your name?"

"Jeremy Shawking," Jeremy's shaking voice slowly became steadier, but the uneasiness in his stomach and his trembling hands told him that he wasn't ready to calm down.

"Jeremy, what's your brother's name?"

"Trenton. Trent, come on, wake up, dude." As Jeremy pleaded, he looked down at his brother again, and couldn't hold his liquor anymore. He turned away from Trent and unleashed the night's alcohol intake onto the road.

"What happened, Jeremy? Are you okay? Are you injured?"

"No!" He whined like he did when he was a child.

"Jeremy, I won't get off the line with you, but you're going to have to remember whatever you can about who hit you for the police."

"I can't remember anything, I'm fucking drunk!" Jeremy yelled into the night.

"It's okay. Just take any pictures you can of the car and the road."

"This is all my fault. I should've stayed home. This

is all my fault. I'm so sorry, Trent! I should've just told you to fuck off when you asked me to come!" Jeremy started to sob into the phone.

Jeremy looked wide-eyed at the road and caught a glimpse of the flashing lights of an ambulance. He hung up his phone immediately and started waving the flashlight in the air to get their attention. Three different vehicles showed up. The first was the ambulance. Quickly, three paramedics were pulling out a stretcher while another was assessing Trent. They spoke to each other, and even though Jeremy heard English words, it may as well have been another language for all he could understand.

A cop car and a black jeep pulled up behind the ambulance. Two male officers stepped out of the cop car, and before they reached Jeremy, two other people emerged from the black Jeep: a short blonde woman in an officer's uniform, and a taller black man wearing formal attire. Jeremy's eyes were everywhere. He watched as his brother was put onto a stretcher, but the other cars were distracting, and his eyes kept being pulled one way or the other. Jeremy held his breath as the paramedics carried Trent's unmoving body. His teeth clenched; he was ready to throw a fist at anyone who might accidentally hurt Trent more than he already was.

"Hello, my name is Officer Lexington. This is my colleague, Officer Pierce. Are you injured?" a deep male voice asked.

Confused, Jeremy's head swung around to see where the voice had come from. The tall black man, who Jeremy had noticed earlier, was now standing beside him. He gestured to the white blonde woman at his side. In Jeremy's shock, it took him a moment to take them both in. The man was dressed in a crisp pale green button up and black dress pants, while the female wore a full uniform with her blonde hair pulled back into a tight bun.

"I—my head hurts. I threw up, but I'm fine. My brother—" Flustered, Jeremy looked again from his brother who had been whisked away through the ambulance's doors, and then back to the officer. He still felt sick, but lucky for Officer Lexington's fancy shoes, Jeremy had nothing left to throw up.

"Let me drive you to the hospital," Officer Lexington offered.

"I want to go with my brother—"

"They're going to drive really quickly to get your brother back. You don't want to do that, man, trust me," Lexington interjected, and Jeremy hesitated as he saw the paramedics shut the ambulance doors. Jeremy watched with a knot in his stomach as the other two officers started assessing Trent's car and then looked back at Lexington with a nod of agreement.

The black Jeep was an unmarked vehicle. He only noticed the police lights on the mirrors when he got close enough to it. Jeremy got into the back seat, and Pierce had a brief exchange with the paramedics before getting into the passenger's seat of the black jeep.

Once everyone was in the car, Officer Pierce looked to Jeremy in the rear-view mirror.

"What's your name, kid?" she asked.

Her blue eyes scanned Jeremy in the mirror. She looked about his mom's age. Her tone was sweet, but the look she gave him was intimidating. Jeremy suddenly felt nervous, like the car had turned into a moving principal's office.

"Jeremy Shawking."

"Okay, Jeremy, do you want me to ask you questions now or later?"

What kind of questions? Jeremy thought, gulping so loudly that he felt like the whole car had heard it.

"Questions?" he asked aloud.

"About what you saw, who was driving, who was drinking, the technical stuff. I know it might be hard to go over right now, but you're going to want to recall it while it's fresh in your mind."

"I don't—I didn't even see a car coming. We were going around the bend, and I just saw a bright light. I woke up with my head on the dash—"

"Yeah, the airbags didn't deploy, and it looks like the windshield cracked before the kid even hit it. Paramedics didn't see broken glass where it should be," the lady mumbled to the man who was driving, failing to keep her voice low enough so that Jeremy couldn't hear.

"I knew that truck was a piece of shit when Dad gave it to him," Jeremy snarled and looked out the window.

It didn't surprise Jeremy that the hand-me-down pickup truck their father gave them would be faulty. The only thing that worked well in that hunk of metal was the radio.

"Jeremy, did you know the airbags didn't work?"

"No, I'm just not surprised," he scoffed and looked at her eyes in the rear-view mirror. She looked into his, and then down at a phone Jeremy assumed she was writing notes on.

"I think I saw blue. I think the car that hit us was blue. It was a blur coming around the corner, but... I don't know."

"All right, that's something. Was it big? Small?"

"It was a blur. I don't know!"

"Was it at eye-level with you when you saw the blur pass?"

"What do..." Jeremy shook his head out of a slight daze and looked to her eyes in the mirror again.

"Yeah, I guess. Like, maybe it was a truck, too?"

"Is that what you think?"

"I don't know, you're confusing me." Jeremy sighed and looked out the window again.

"Was your brother drinking before he got in the car?"

"No! I'm the drunk one. I—" Jeremy said defensively and then became quiet. He realized he had just admitted in an undercover cop car that he had been drinking. They didn't know he was underage, but it would've been obvious. It would be better if he shut up now.

"Jeremy, we're not going to book you for something like that. You've been traumatized enough," Officer Lexington mumbled as he turned into the hospital and parked just behind the ambulance.

Jeremy jumped out of the Jeep and sprinted over to his brother, chasing behind the stretcher. He managed to follow the paramedics until they reached the hallway before one of them turned to him and put a hand up.

"You have to stay here—"

"Trent!" Jeremy yelled out and then looked to the man who had stopped him. "Why?"

"He's going into surgery. You need to stay out here until a doctor speaks to you. Hang on, you probably need to get that checked out." The paramedic pointed to Jeremy's forehead, where a gash was dripping blood down his face. Jeremy brushed the man off and took a seat on the nearest chair.

"I'll be fine! My brother's unconscious, not me!"

"Yes, but you could have a concussion. Stay here, and I'll get someone to take a look at you, okay?"

Jeremy was getting sick of everyone being so calm.

He understood that they were just trying to help, but why was he the only one losing his mind? Other than the apparent reason of him just being in a car accident. Jeremy ran a hand through his now-matted hair. More tiny bits of glass fell out of it, and he silently cursed his father under his breath.

The officers finally caught up to him, and Pierce took a seat next to Jeremy on the bench, not close enough to be overbearing, but close enough to make Jeremy uncomfortable. He rested his elbows on his knees and chose not to talk. Lexington was about to say something when a nurse came over.

"Hey, hon, you need a once over?" The blonde lady had her hair tied back and a sweet smile on her face. Jeremy felt sick again – more calm people to show him how irrational he was being. He looked up at her in frustration but quickly relaxed and nodded, coming to terms with the fact that maybe he actually needed the help people were trying to give him. She led him to a room away from the officers and sat him down on the room's vacant bed.

"So, what's your name?" she asked.

Jeremy's frustration hadn't really eased up, and the last thing he wanted to engage in was small talk.

"Jeremy," he mumbled.

"Okay, Jeremy, I'm gonna use the stethoscope if that's okay. If at any moment you feel uncomfortable, I want you to yell at me."

That startled Jeremy just a little, and his eyes widened. She grinned back at him.

"What? Are you not the yelling type? Okay, maybe don't yell. Just let me know. Fair?"

Jeremy didn't want to, but he let himself smile ever so slightly. He nodded to her, and she gently placed the stethoscope on his back.

"Breathe in deeply, please."

Jeremy obliged.

"And out." She moved it to another section of his back, and nodded at him to continue breathing deeply. Once she was finished, she gave him a small reassuring pat on the back.

"Okay, now I need you to follow my finger with

your eyes. If you feel any dizziness or an instant headache, tell me. Or yell at me, really, it's whichever you prefer." She smirked and shrugged, then held up her index finger, repeatedly moving it from her right shoulder to her left. Jeremy followed her finger with his eyes and suddenly winced, closing his eyes hard.

"Sharp pain?"

He nodded.

"Tell me if it stops."

"Yeah... it just happened and then went away." Jeremy opened his eyes and looked to her. She grinned back at him again. Man, that grin of hers was annoyingly contagious.

"Now, I know you don't feel like talking, but I do have to ask you some questions to assess you. First, do you know what day it is?"

"It's probably Saturday now, early morning. September 28."

"What year is it?"

"Two thousand nineteen."

"And your favourite colour?"

Jeremy looked confusedly at her. She was grinning that mischievous grin again, and he had to look at his shoes to not give in. This lovely nurse would not cheer him up that easily; he was too stubborn for that.

"I don't know. Green."

"Good choice. If you'll let me, I'm going to wipe this scratch clean. It doesn't look deep, so you won't need stitches. It may sting a little, though."

The nurse took a cotton ball and filled it with an antiseptic. When she put it to Jeremy's forehead, he winced, and she winced with him and stopped. With a look, Jeremy could tell she was asking if she could continue cleaning the small wound. He obliged with a nod.

"Okay, hon, I don't think you have a major concussion, but I'd like to send you to imaging just in case. Sound good?"

Jeremy nodded, unsure if he could even say no.

"You should call your parents if you haven't already. I know it must've all happened really fast, so if you didn't get the chance, now is the time. Your brother is in good hands. I don't want you to worry too much. There's a bathroom right over that way. You should wash up a little, and is there anything I can get you? Something for your stomach? A blanket, maybe?"

Jeremy shook his head.

The kind nurse nodded sympathetically, wrote something on a piece of paper, and then handed it to Jeremy. Then she walked him to a receptionist's desk, where he spent the next hour answering questions and trying to forget about the throbbing pain in his head. He called his mother, but she didn't answer, so he left her a quick voicemail as he was rushed off to imaging.

✝

When Jeremy finally made his way back to the chair in the hallway – after slowly stumbling through the bleak hospital halls – only Officer Lexington sat waiting for him. He took a seat next to the officer and stared at the floor. In his periphery, he noticed the man open his mouth to say something, but a much more familiar voice interrupted him.

"Jer, what the hell happened? Are you kidding me with that voicemail? Just keep calling me next time!" Jeremy's mother shouted to him as she ran down the hall.

A long grey trench coat, which was two sizes too big, covered her slender figure. The teenager jumped up from his chair. His eyes were puffy. Even though the gash on his forehead was clean now, the bright red wound remained visibly painful. He still smelled of vomit and liquor. This wasn't the best way to greet his mother after the frighteningly vague voicemail he'd left her.

When Jeremy's mother approached him, her expression softened. Jeremy's mother cupped his face in her hands and gently stroked his hair away from his forehead.

"Mrs. Shawking? My name is Darren Lexington. I'm the officer who first arrived on the scene. I'll give you a moment, but I'd like to speak with you over here when you're ready." Officer Lexington gave her a curt nod and backed off.

"Jarebear?" Beth questioned him more gently this time. Jeremy gulped, his face still wrinkled with lines of unease.

"We were at a party, and when we were driving back—" Jeremy noticed the sudden shock on his mother's face. "Trent was driving, but he didn't drink anything, I swear!" Jeremy protested, and Beth let out a breath of relief. "I don't even know what's happening. They wouldn't let me go in with him, and they checked me for a concussion. He was—" Jeremy cut himself off before he said anything else.

Closing his eyes as hard as he could, Jeremy suddenly wished this would all stop. He wondered if now would be a good time to explain to his mother that, when he opened his eyes after the crash, Trent had been thrown from the car and was lying on the side of the road. He didn't know when there would ever be a *'good time'* to say any of that. Besides, he didn't even think he could muster up the words. The image kept coming back to him, making him want to vomit again.

"Ma'am?" the officer prompted.

Jeremy sat back in the chair and buried his face

in his hands. He didn't want to talk anymore; all he wanted to do was sleep in the hopes that this was all just a nightmare he'd wake up from.

"I'm going to say it plainly: your son was run off the road. The other car took off. We're treating this as a hit and run, but your son is still alive." Officer Lexington paused as he noticed the woman's eyes widen and her face turned ghostly white. "I just want to tell you that we're going to find whoever's done this. The first thing they test for in situations like this is if the driver was drinking, and Trent was, without a doubt, sober. I can't say if the other driver was yet, but I will find out." Jeremy's mother looked speechless, but she quickly found her voice.

"Officer, can you tell me exactly what happened to Trent?"

"I think it's best you hear that from the doctor once your son is out of surgery, ma'am. They'll be able to explain it far better than I could," Officer Lexington replied. The concern on his face made Jeremy wonder if the officer just didn't know how to tell her the truth either. "I will keep you updated on the situation, Mrs. Shawking." The officer looked to Jeremy and nodded. "You really lucked out tonight, kid."

He said it with a tone of ease that made Jeremy instantly angry again. His anger and frustration over the entire ordeal had never really subsided. It had just been kept at bay by his own injury, and then by the nice nurse with the smile.

"Lucked out? You think I fucking lucked out? Fuck you!" Jeremy stood and shouted at the man, and the officer looked down at his feet for a moment.

"Jeremy!" His mother tried to hush him and put her hands on both of his shoulders, but that wouldn't hold back his wrath.

"No ma'am, it's fine. I'm sorry. You're right, Jeremy.

Those were the wrong words..." With a genuine look of concern, the officer put his hands up for a moment. Then put them down with a sigh.

"I'm just glad at least one of you is all right," he said. "My apologies, really. You'll hear from me again, and if you happen to hear or see something, here's my card." He pulled a card from his pocket and handed it to Beth. With a slight look of embarrassment, she hesitated before taking it from him, and then Jeremy watched as the officer walked down the quiet hospital hallway. His footsteps had a hollow sound to them and followed a precise rhythm. They reminded Jeremy of a clock, ticking away into silence, until it finally stopped.

SATURDAY, SEPTEMBER 28, 2019

03:53 AM

It wasn't a crash or bang which made Lynn jump. Instead, it was catching a glimpse of Teddy, raising his hand to his breathing mask – a simple gesture that had all the power of an earthquake to shake Lynn's world. Lynn hadn't noticed if her brother had been sleeping when he suddenly lifted his hand to pull the ventilator mask away from his mouth.

"Lynny?"

His voice was so soft that she barely heard it over the drone of the machine next to his bed. Lynn stood up momentarily to turn off the television. When she sat down again, her eyes focused on him.

"Yeah, Teddy?"

Lynn found it hard to pay attention while her mind was somewhere else. She was trying her best to forget about the phantom she had seen an hour ago.

"Oh… good."

25

His words were drawn out, having to take deeper breaths between them. The bronchitis he'd caught from having such a weakened immune system had worsened, and because of this, the doctors had given him a comprehensive cocktail of medications which made him constantly tired. It was rare to see him awake for more than several minutes nowadays.

"Good?" Lynn asked.

"You're here."

"Of course I'm here. Where else would I be?" Lynn asked as her mind drifted to the white room for a moment.

She might've been tempted to leave if she wasn't scared of her little brother waking up without her by his side.

"I thought… you left me alone."

Lynn raised a brow at him.

"I never leave you alone, just like you never leave me alone, you little brat," Lynn said with a small grin.

Teddy smirked.

"I had a dream." Teddy struggled to sit up, so Lynn pulled her chair closer to his bedside.

"About?"

Teddy kept his timid eyes on his feet as they wiggled back and forth under his blanket. Lynn cleared her throat, awaiting his answer, and he looked up at her with uncertainty.

"Don't laugh at me," he demanded shyly.

"I'm not making any promises." Lynn said it as a joke, but her heart sank a little when she saw his eyes flit back to his feet.

"I dreamt I was alone. It was dark, and I couldn't find anyone. There was a monster chasing me, something that looked like a shark," he took a deep, staggered breath in, "but it had legs and three heads."

Her brother dreaming about a monster was hardly

a reason to laugh, but Lynn had to admit that she almost did when he described the strangest shark she'd ever heard of. Holding back a small grin, she moved some hair away from his forehead for him, secretly feeling for a fever.

"Do you know where you were?"

"I think I was at school? But it was dark, and it was back in Logan."

"Oh? You haven't been there in a while. Sounds like a weird nightmare, kiddo."

She took a long hard look at him. The little lines in his young face creased in a way that made him resemble a stressed-out elder.

"Lynn." Teddy took a sharp breath in, but his eyes never left hers.

"Yeah, bud?"

"What if I'm lonely? When I die?"

The words hit her like a truck. He'd said 'when', not 'if'. The only other time she'd discussed death with him, he'd used the word 'if'.

Lynn looked into Teddy's eyes, searching them for the liveliness of her easy-going brother, but finding only her own weariness. This boy was hurt and exhausted, and it was the first time she'd ever seen him this defeated. Teddy never asked her things like this. He was the happiest kid in this place, and even though she wasn't very happy, she made sure she was pretending to be, for him. This question made her think his hope had dwindled, that maybe he finally believed what her mother had been trying to convince her to be ready for all this time.

She didn't have a good answer for his question. She didn't want to lie to him, and she couldn't tell him the truth, but she was determined to answer him. Lynn leaned forward to muster up her most convincingly intimidating facial expression.

"When you die, eighty years from now," Lynn

began, "you won't be lonely. I'll remind you again: I never leave you alone, you little brat. Don't say crap like that." She tried to hide the shakiness in her voice.

"It's not crap, Lynn. I—" Teddy stopped to take another agonizing breath.

The sound made her worry. It made her want to demand he stop speaking and relax so that he didn't have to struggle, but she had to be patient.

"I mean it. When Mom told me about heaven, it sounded so boring. She talks about flowers and food and playing games all the time. But who's even there? I won't have any of my friends from the hospital. You won't be there." His stare burned through hers, and she was using every last bit of her strength not to turn into a crying mess. "It sounds lonely."

There wasn't a day that Lynn forgot that Teddy was just a kid, but sometimes she forgot how it felt to be one. She'd grown up so fast, as she'd gone from a child to a second caregiver in a matter of a year when she first found out about Teddy's leukemia. When she was at the age he was right now, she was being told about his cancer and how her life would change.

Now, Teddy wasn't worried about the fact that death could hurt or that maybe Heaven wasn't even real – a thought that very regularly crossed Lynn's mind. She couldn't concern Teddy with the thought of an afterlife not even existing; there *had* to be another place for him. A place better than this one. A place where people didn't have to poke and prod at him with needles that he hated, or inject him with drugs so powerful they could surely knock out a horse, but somehow only made a dent in his illness. How do you tell a kid that the place he's going will be better than this one when all he wants is company? When he knows very well that everyone around him isn't as sick as he is?

"You're not going to be lonely. My dad is up there. He'll stay with you until I get there."

"But I don't know him. Is he like us?" Teddy asked. "That's what Mom says."

Teddy answered with a sigh, and Lynn hoped he was done talking about this. She didn't want him to have to worry about death, but she knew it was stupid to think he wouldn't. Teddy might've been a kid, but he wasn't naive. He knew there was a possibility of dying young; he'd heard doctors say words that he didn't understand, and when he'd asked his mother what everything meant, she'd had to sit down and have the conversation with him. Lynn hadn't been there for it. Her mother had offered to take that burden alone, and it was Lynn's priority to keep him happy, to make sure he was still being a kid while he had time to be one.

"Come on. Lie back down, and I'll play *Mulan* on my phone for you."

It took him a moment, but Teddy agreed with a nod. He laid back down, and Lynn stood to cover him in his blankets. She helped him adjust the ventilator mask back onto his face and took her place in her throne once again.

As she scrolled through her phone to find the movie, she glanced over and noticed him glaring at the ceiling. She wondered if he was silently cursing the Heavens, as she so often did.

Lynn cleared her throat before pressing play, and then turned her phone screen to him. When he looked over, she put the phone up to her forehead and stuck her tongue out while crossing her eyes. It caught Teddy off guard, and Lynn could tell the ventilator had stifled a small laugh. Lynn put the phone down on his bedside. He would end up falling asleep to the sound rather than watching it – he just needed something to drown out the awful noise of that machine strapped to him.

They both did.

3

FIND JEREMY

SATURDAY, SEPTEMBER 28, 2019

02:42 AM

"Ray, what the hell?!" Andrea yelled as she got out and slammed the passenger door of his blue pickup shut.

Charlie Tresser watched from the backseat of the car as Andrea walked over to him, sloppily pulling at her short black dress as she tried to fix the white cardigan slipping off her shoulders. Her long brunette ponytail was flailing around wildly behind her as she yelled.

Raymond Hurley – the dangerously tall, tanned football player she was yelling at – had been driving, and was now frozen in front of his car, staring at the giant dent left on the driver's side of his navy Ford F-150 with his jaw unhinged.

"I thought you were just fucking around! I didn't think you'd actually hit him! Are you fucking braindead?" Andrea continued shouting, her raspy voice so high that it was breaking with every other word.

Charlie sat with her girlfriend Mel in the backseat of the truck. Mel was behind the driver's seat, hugging her knees to her chest and hiding her face in her arms, repeatedly whispering the word 'no' to herself as she rocked back and forth. Her bleach blonde hair was stuck to her face and covered in her tear-streaked foundation. Charlie, still in shock beside her, stared out into the darkness through the car window in a frighteningly calm daze, softly stroking Mel's hair as if she were nothing but a household cat looking for attention.

"I'm so fucking drunk. I fucked up my flares. I didn't want to fuck up my flares. Those things were custom made," Ray said.

"You might've just killed two people, and you're worried about your car?" Andrea shouted.

Suddenly, Ray focused his striking hazel eyes on Andrea. When he stepped towards her, she cowered and shut up. Charlie didn't want to look at them arguing in front of the car, but she could see them out of the corner of her eyes and as they continued, her eyes trailed over to them. She listened in, hiding behind the thin red veil of her hair. She was just as scared of Ray as Andrea was in that moment, fearing Ray's temper even from the shelter of the backseat. She'd never known him to be violent with his girlfriend, but something in his eyes looked lethal. Both Andrea and Charlie knew his words cut like jagged saw blades. He was terribly good at threatening people, and the threats he made were never empty.

"No, Andy, I'm not worried about the car, I'm just

stating facts. Is that okay? Can you stop screaming now?" he answered with a volatile calmness. She scoffed so loudly in frustration, it sounded like she hurt her throat.

"What the hell did you hit them for?! You said you were just trying to scare him as a joke!" Andy's ramblings turned into a soft cry, which she was obviously trying to hold back.

"Mistakes were made. Now we gotta deal with the consequences," he answered in an eerily comforting tone.

For Charlie, everything went quiet. Ray and Andy had intentionally lowered their voices as their conversation continued, but the sound of Charlie's own heartbeat thudding in her head drowned them out completely. The sound was heavy and hard against her skull, like a mountain bear repeatedly ramming into a wall of stone. The sudden slam of the door made both her and Mel jump as Andrea got back into the car and buried her face in her hands. Charlie was unsure if her shock was wearing off, but she wanted to say something. She didn't want to feel trapped, like a wild bear in a stone body, slowly crumbling under the weight of the consequences to come.

"We need to call the police," Charlie said meekly once Ray started the car, though in her mind she was yelling it.

Ray calmly turned the ignition off, swallowing everyone in uncomfortable silence. Andrea and Mel turned to look at Charlie, as though she had suddenly grown a second head, and the monstrous new appendage had said the words for her.

"I'm not calling the police, and don't let me find out that you did, Charlie. You don't want to know what'll happen if you do," Ray said as he glared at her through his rear-view mirror.

Charlie turned to look out of her window again, swallowing down whatever protest she had. "I'm going to drop everyone off, and then get rid of the truck. I can dump it in the back of Dex's place for now, and get my dad to agree on getting me a new car."

"How are you going to convince him to get you—"

"He's not going to want to know, Andy. I'll just tell him he'd be better off buying it without asking questions if he wants to protect his image," Ray spat before starting up the truck again.

The radio started blaring late-night house music, keeping everyone from talking to each other. Not that anyone had anything to say – there was never any arguing with Ray. The power that the Hurley family possessed in the quiet town of Heatherdale was immeasurable.

$$00:00$$

Trent was trying to remember the last time he'd ever been this scared of the dark. When you're a kid, the darkness is debilitating. It makes you sprint through the basement hallway once you turn the light off, scared that someone's hand will come out of the shadows and grip your ankle. It's what blankets you after waking up from a nightmare, making that nightmarish feeling linger.

Darkness is the unknown, the unexplored, and sometimes, the evil. Trent had never been so acquainted with it in his whole life. His upbringing had been pretty average, sure his parents went through a divorce, but he never felt neglected; by his mother at least. He hated his father and wanted nothing to do with him. Regardless, Trent always had a good birthday party, nice family Christmases, and his mother made it to every one of his baseball games. There was nothing to fear for him growing up. Born as a brunette with wavy locks, beautiful blue eyes, and a chiselled face, high school was easy for him – a breeze, even.

Today, Trent couldn't remember which day it was. If he was dying, then it's true what they say: your life flashes before your eyes.

It wasn't all at once, though.

Maybe Trent's experience was different because his death was being prolonged. Who was Trent to question anything, really? He couldn't even tell if he was actually dead, dying, floating in space, or lying somewhere stoned out of his mind.

Wherever Trent was, the darkness had him trapped. Every now and again, a flash of light would bring him to a memory or a dream. In one of them, Trent was standing at his front door, staring out onto the street through the glass. One of his tiny hands gripped a red backpack strap hitched over his shoulder, and the other gripped his little brother's hand. He could feel the warmth of Jeremy's hand, familiar, comforting. It was the first day of kindergarten, and they were waiting for Mom to drive them to school. Trent swallowed his fear and pushed the door open.

Another flash of light, and he could see himself sitting in a classroom, much older than he was a second ago. Trent was snuggling up to his then-girlfriend, Andy. The two were stealing kisses from each other whenever their teacher wasn't looking.

He felt a pain in his heart.

Another flash of light put him in front of a mirror in his bathroom. Staring at himself in confusion, touching his face, Trent was startled to discover that he couldn't feel his hands on his cheeks. Slowly, his olive skin grew paler, and as much as he rubbed at his face, he couldn't stop it changing. His blue eyes seemed to be drained of the ocean they once held, dimming in seconds. When he put his hands down at his sides, he saw the light in his bathroom flicker and go out.

The air became so cold that his teeth began to chatter. When the light came back on, he was standing in a brightly lit, unfamiliar hallway. His eyes fell on a bright white light, shaped like a person, which radiated before him – then, as quickly as he'd seen it, it was dark again. But, as the darkness surrounded him, he could still see a faint glow where the figure had been. Why was he constantly being consumed by this darkness? The light of the hallway turned on again. The figure in front of him was still unrecognizable, but he knew it had to be a person, and all he wanted to do was get their attention. The light of the hallway dimmed slowly. Even though it was blinding, he tried to keep his eyes on the bright white figure in front of him.

"It's... dark..."

Those words were all he managed to get out. He wanted to ask for help – he was going to explain more – but before he could, Trent once again slipped into the darkness he was becoming all too familiar with.

SATURDAY, SEPTEMBER 28, 2019

$$03:43_{AM}$$

"Mrs. Shawking?"

The voice startled Jeremy and his mother who were sitting on a chair outside the operating room. They'd been waiting in a solemn silence for the past however many hours and both jumped up when they heard the doctor.

"Yes? What's happening? Is Trent alive?" Beth

began, each of her words stumbling over the one before. The doctor nodded his head in relief. Jeremy's eyes lit up at the news, and he and his mother both got to their feet.

"He's as stable as he we could hope for, considering what happened."

"What does that mean?" Beth asked. The doctor hesitated before he continued.

"Right now, Trent is in a coma. There is slight brain activity, with the few tests that we've run, but he cannot breathe on his own."

A coma? How did I escape with a scratch, and my brother's in a coma? Jeremy felt like he may just puke again.

"Does this mean he's on life support? How likely is he to get out of this coma?" Beth pressed the doctor further. Jeremy couldn't speak even if he'd wanted to.

"A form of life support, yes, and there's no telling how long it may take for his brain to repair itself. His skull is fractured, and the surgery we conducted was damage control. Along with a few broken bones, he's also had a partial collapse of the lung. I don't want to lie to you. The main thing now is to watch him closely. He's in a state where anything could go wrong fairly easily, but he is stable for the most part."

Jeremy noticed his mother's teeth clench and her jaw sharpen. He watched as she ran a hand through her chestnut hair slowly, a small tick that he and his brother had inherited from her and mirrored when they felt anxious. There were more questions sinking in her blue eyes, but she struggled to bring them to the surface. Jeremy had forgotten how to speak entirely. His mouth wasn't catching up to all of the horrible thoughts in his mind about what could go wrong with his brother.

"When can we see him?" Beth finally let out.

"Follow me," the doctor said before walking back

through the door he'd entered from. Jeremy and his mother followed him down another hallway and into a dimly lit room, where Trent lay on a hospital bed. The least alarming thing about Trent's appearance was that his left arm had been cocooned in a full cast. There were cuts all over his face and neck from the broken glass. Bruising on the right side of his face peeked through the bandages that were wrapped around his head. He was utterly unrecognizable. Shattered, and now held up by sheer will and life support. Beth let out a sob, and Jeremy held her to him as she cried.

00:00

Trent was tired and frustrated. He felt like screaming, like breaking something, but there was nothing to grasp onto in the darkness, and there was no one around who would hear him. Time wasn't linear anymore. Whatever this life was, it was in pieces. There was a moment when he finally thought he'd gotten out of the darkness, back to the world of time and motion, sounds, and colours, only to find out he'd been dreaming.

In his dream, Trent was getting ready for a school dance. He had no idea which one, and he didn't know who he was taking.

Once he was ready, he stood waiting at the bottom of the stairs in his home. Adam appeared, as if from nowhere, to fix his tie for him. Then, he placed a hand on Trent's shoulder and nodded to the top of the steps, where Trent brought his attention. He watched as water flooded down the empty staircase, and the murky water suddenly turn blood red. Slowly, everything around him was engulfed by a pure, bright scarlet, and then the world faded to black again. He was left in the bleak void, feeling nothing but anger and frustration.

Stuck in the darkness, every now and again he would see the light far off in the distance, and because he felt like he was floating, it was hard to move towards it. He tried willing himself towards this strange light and made some progress, but then he'd be pulled back by a feeling of heaviness in his lungs, or from a sharp pain that would suddenly erupt within his mind.

Nothing made sense to him. Slowly, he tried to move towards the light again, imagining his legs walking. It was hard to remember the feeling of gravity holding him down and the strength it took to hold his body up.

Why am I always so fucking tired?

Trent was only a meter away from the light now, and the whole room lit up instantly.

There was colour and motion, and dull sounds filled his ears. It was overwhelming to come from a complete abyss into a room he'd never seen before.

Where am I? The light which had led him to this room suddenly dimmed and took shape. It was a girl... a girl he knew from high school. She was that new girl last year, or had it been two years ago? Time didn't feel real to him right now. All he knew was that she was someone he'd never really spoken to, but he remembered that she'd caught his eye once or twice in the hall.

L... something with an L...

"Lynn?" Trent said as he remembered the brunette from his grade.

She turned around and covered her mouth with her hands. Her eyes went wide.

"You can see me?" he asked.

A memory came to him in a quick flash when her big brown eyes fell on him. He remembered a day when he had been sitting behind her, and he'd tapped her on the shoulder in math class to ask her for a pencil. They hadn't exchanged words before. She'd turned around quickly in confusion. As she'd done so, her short brown hair had flown up, and he'd smelled coconuts on the wind that her hair created. He'd liked it, and wanted to ask if it was her shampoo or perfume, but he hadn't. People don't ask those things in the middle of a math class. In fact, he'd forgotten what he'd even asked her for until she passed him the pencil. Then they'd both gone back to their own lives, ignoring each other, because that's just the way it was. This first real interaction surprised Trent, who had always considered Lynn, infamous for her cold stare, to be unfriendly and isolated. But up close, he found no trace of her stony persona – in fact, her wide eyes glimmered with an endearing vulnerability. He might have even said she looked scared. Like he was now.

Trent snapped back into the present when Lynn jumped back in fear after he said her name.

All at once, the room went dark. He felt like he had been pushed back into a pool, but he hadn't seen her push him. He didn't know what had sent him back. Floating in dark space again, he took a deep breath in, but it felt as if someone was filling his lungs with hot water, and it burned him from the inside out. The pain was unbearable. He tried to scream, tried to pull himself out of the darkness that he'd been sucked back into, will himself back to the light again if only just for a moment – and he did. He didn't know how he did it, but he was thrown back into the light again, only this time, he found himself in a different room.

"Lynn, please." When he said it, the pain in his lungs disappeared, but he was frightened by the small scream that escaped her. All these different

39

sensations were giving him whiplash.

"Trent, are you dead? Or am I imagining you?" Lynn hissed at him, and Trent's heart sank.

Dead? Why does she think I'm dead? She can see me, can't she? How could I be dead?

"I don't know what's going on, Lynn. I don't know where I am, and you're the only one I can see," Trent answered.

As his eyes darted around this new location, he noticed the edges of the room were fuzzy; when he looked out of the window of the room, all he could see was darkness, even though the room was lit up like it was day. The odd contradiction made him fear for the amount of time he had left in the light.

"What the hell does that mean?" Lynn snapped.

Trent didn't understand why she was so frustrated with him. Had he done something to her and not remembered? He suddenly felt nervous.

"I can't find anything or anyone! It's so dark. Can you find Jeremy? I was with him last, that's all I remember!" Trent's eyes darted around wildly as he watched the edges of the room close in on him, swallowing him in his newfound enemy: the darkness.

The features of Lynn's face and body turned into a bright white light, which then started to move away from him, at first slowly, and then all at once. Trent felt tired again.

Why am I always so fucking tired?

SATURDAY, SEPTEMBER 28, 2019

06:56 AM

After what Lynn had witnessed at the vending machine, the thought of sleep seemed impossible.

40

Her eyes asked her for it, her body needed it, but sleeping was not an option. She needed to figure out the extent of her madness. It didn't help that she couldn't stop thinking about her brother's question about being lonely after death and the ensuing stress of deciding whether or not she should try telling her mother about this conversation.

Most of Lynn's night was spent watching her brother for another sign of movement, mindlessly sketching Trent's face in her sketchbook, and sometimes scanning through channels on the small television on the wall. At seven in the morning, her mother finally came in, rushing to her son's side and checking his head for fever, something Lynn had done only an hour before. The two of them would be continuously doing so for the next two days, as the doctor had said to watch out for it.

"Lynn, did you get any sleep?" her mother, Paula, asked her, not even looking at her as she set down her purse and coat on the table at the end of Teddy's bed.

Paula's eyes had big black circles underneath them to match Lynn's. Lynn and her mother looked so much alike, more than usual now that they were both so tired.

"I got enough," Lynn lied.

"Did you want me to get you breakfast? I was going to pick something up before he wakes up." Paula searched through her purse for some money.

Lynn felt like telling her she'd rather throw up, but she stopped herself.

"No, thanks," Lynn answered and then watched her mother quickly walk out of the room. Her mother was never warm to her, only to Theo. Lynn's father had died before Theo was born – she didn't really know him, but her mother had told her stories of him when she was young. Theo was her mother's little

Teddy Bear from her ex-boyfriend. To her mother, Lynn was... well, Lynn had a reputation for being a trouble-making liar, but that's not how her little brother saw her, his opinion was all that mattered.

As she stared at her brother with a cold expression that she really wanted to shoot at her mother, she noticed his thick eyelashes begin to flutter as he slowly woke up. He couldn't move very much; the tubes from his breathing mask and IV drip restrained his little body like vines holding him down. Lynn stood up and walked to his side.

"Hey, little man, good morning. Did you need something?" Lynn asked in her softest voice as she ran a hand through his hair.

Teddy smiled up at her and slowly shook his head. His eyes closed again. Lynn wondered if maybe he'd just heard their mother come in, and that's what had made him stir. Teddy's bronchitis was terrible, and right now, all he could do was sleep through it. It was a miracle that he'd woken up for as long as he did the night before.

The air in the room suddenly became colder, and Lynn pulled up the blanket on Teddy just a bit. She was very unpleasantly surprised when she turned back around to sit in her throne and saw someone else standing there.

She jumped in place and slapped a hand over her own mouth.

There's no way this is real. I'm seeing things. I'm sleep deprived. This is insane.

Trent Shawking stood before her. He was a foot taller than Lynn, with immaculate wavy brown hair, icy blue eyes, a loose grey T-shirt and blue jeans, but his colour was so pale that she didn't know if she'd suddenly become colour blind or if it was the lighting. Lynn turned almost as ghostly white as he was as she stared at him in horror.

"Lynn?" he said.

His voice sounded cold and tinny, like she had heard it through an old telephone.

"You can see me?" he asked as a certain spark lit in his eye – a spark ignited by a hope that Lynn couldn't understand and wanted nothing to do with. What on earth was she hallucinating this for?

"Lynn, why are you standing in the middle of the room?" Her mother's voice made Lynn spin around on her heel and immediately put her arms down at her sides.

"Nothing, I need some air!" she replied quickly and a little too loudly.

Lynn took off out of the room and down the hall to burst into the white room, which was thankfully empty right now.

"Fuck, fuck, fuck, what is happening to me?" Lynn said to herself under her breath as she paced back and forth.

"Lynn, please."

This time, Lynn screamed. It was short but loud. She turned around to see Trent looking just as horrified as she was.

"Trent, are you dead? Or am I imagining you?" Lynn hissed.

Trent's eyes widened at the question, and Lynn realized how stupid the question actually sounded.

"I don't know what's going on, Lynn. I don't know where I am, and you're the only one I can see," Trent answered, his tone desperate.

"What the hell does that mean?" Lynn snapped, still horrified.

"I can't find anyone or anything! It's so dark. Can you find Jeremy? I was with him last, that's all I remember!" Trent asked, his unfaltering desperation making Lynn's heart sore.

Lynn's mouth and eyes were open wide with

confusion. As quickly as he'd appeared in front of her, Trent faded away. Rubbing her eyes, Lynn looked to where he last was, and when he wasn't there, she felt queasy.

Lynn decided how she could find out if she was hallucinating. She would find Jeremy and ask him where the hell Trent was. It was her only way out of this delirium.

With all her might, she wished that Trent would be alive and well so she could finally just call herself clinically insane and get some medication for whatever was wrong with her.

"Lynn, are you okay? I heard a scream." Cindy walked through the door and rushed over to Lynn, placing both hands on her shoulders with a look of grave concern.

"I just... I—"

"Lynn, you know you can talk to me about anything, right? I know things are getting harder with your brother, but you need to take care of yourself too, honey. You're here all the time. You need to be a teenager sometimes. You know?"

"Cindy—"

"Don't 'Cindy' me – I know what I'm talking about, Lynny. Did you even get any sleep last night? You look as tired as me." Cindy pursed her lips, and Lynn knew that any answer she gave wouldn't be believed.

She felt ashamed. Not because Cindy had heard her scream, but because Cindy was the one who had to deal with her. Lynn loved Cindy like a big sister, but she felt like she was a burden on her. Lynn really didn't deserve her help right now.

"I—I saw a spider. Sorry. I hate spiders. Just... I gotta go," Lynn mumbled before she ran out of the room.

I have to find Jeremy.

4

THE REAPER

$$00:00$$

When time or light doesn't exist, all that's left is an unsettling frustration. A frustration that Trent couldn't handle anymore. Trent didn't want to feel like he was dead, but the more he thought about it, the more this void that he was trapped in was starting to make sense. With whatever time was passing, all Trent could think about was getting back to the light, back to his physical body. More than anything, he wanted to get back to the light which he had confirmed was Lynn. It was strange that someone he had never really known was now the only person he could see, even if he couldn't *really* see her.

Trent was experiencing more frequent instances of feeling his own body now, but every time he did, he was overwhelmed by a horrible pain – a fire in his lungs and his stomach, and every once in a while, a sharp pain like a blade thrusting deep into the middle of his head, making him seethe.

It was exhausting.

Finally, Trent found his way back to the light again. Lynn's body took shape, and this time, someone stood in front of her. Looking closer, Trent recognised his brother, Jeremy. The pair were standing in a long hallway, the same dreary white walls of the hospital surrounding them. Behind Jeremy, there was a pool of darkness, like a black hole cut into time and space.

"Jeremy!" Trent called out as he saw his brother turn and begin walking towards the black hole. "Lynn, why is he walking away? Why can't he hear me? What's happening? He's going to—"

Before Trent could warn his brother about the void, Jeremy walked straight into it and disappeared. Trent felt himself being tugged at by an invisible force behind him, and fell backwards, dropping into what felt like the pits of hell. He didn't feel himself slam into anything, but there was a burning sensation which started from inside his head and went down his whole body in endless waves. A terribly loud beeping sound cut through his mind, making his head throb.

"What's happening?"

"I don't know I was holding his hand and then—"

"I need a nurse! Someone!"

Was that Jeremy? And mom? Jeremy, is that you? Can you hear me? I can't stand this darkness anymore, please, I just want to be in the light.

There was a blinding flash.

When he opened his eyes, he blinked a couple of times to fully adjust to the light of the room. Trent was standing at the edge of a hospital bed, in front of himself, as if he were looking through a morbid fun-house mirror.

The version of himself lying in the bed was broken and bloodied. Scared to move, Trent slowly looked down at his new ghostly form and was startled when he could see through his black sneakers to make out the pattern on the tiled floor.

The terrible beeping was still screeching, and he looked to his mother, who was holding back tears beside the broken version of him on the bed as she held his lifeless hand. Jeremy, standing in the doorway, was frantically calling out for help.

Trent could finally see where that terrible beeping sound was coming from. He was flatlining, or at least this was what he supposed after looking at one of the machines. Trent ran over to the side of his body's bed. Examining his own face was a frightening experience. He'd never seen himself so cut up and bruised in his life. Trent gulped and tried to touch his shoulder, but his hand passed through the one resting on the bed. There was a sinking feeling in his stomach.

A few nurses rushed into the room with a crash cart, and when they should have collided with Trent's ghostly form, they instead passed right through him. He stumbled back away from them, feeling like he'd been pushed by a strong gust of wind, though it seemed like the nurses had felt nothing at all. As the nurses began to treat the lifeless body on the bed, Trent looked desperately between his brother and mother.

"Can either of you see me? Hear me? Why can't anyone hear me, at least?!"

SATURDAY, SEPTEMBER 28, 2019

07:06 AM

47

The sound of Lynn's footsteps echoed as she paced back and forth across the landing of the fourth floor of the hospital. She usually found refuge in this staircase, which was an excellent place to get away from the bustle of the busy hallways that were now filling with regular visitors. A million thoughts raced through her mind, but they were all trying to answer the same question: how on earth was she going to get into contact with Jeremy Shawking? She most definitely didn't have his number, both because he was younger than her, and because she had been anti-social since the day she arrived at that stupid school two years ago. Unfortunately, the one person who she thought might have Jeremy's number shouldn't be giving out anyone's information at all – but she still had to try.

> **I know this is going to sound weird, but do you have Jeremy Shawking's number?**

Lynn typed into her phone and hit send. Less than a minute later, she had a response.

Ye, why?

The answer startled Lynn.

> **I need it. Or I just need you to ask him about Trent.**

What about Trent?
Ray was taking care of that.

> **What?**

Really? Like you don't know?

Lynn's hands began to tremble.

What happened to Trent?

**You don't want that in a
text. It has something to
do with last week.
Remember that favour?**

Lynn's stomach turned. The *'favour'*. She'd hoped that would have had nothing to do with Jeremy or Trent, but it was apparent now that it did.

Can we talk?

Where are you?

Liberty.

Are you fucking with me?

What?

**Incoming call from...
Nate**

Lynn's hands were shaking.
"Hello?" she answered.
"I'm going to Liberty around noon. Jeremy asked me to drop there. Are you playing a joke on me or something? What the fuck, Lynn?"
Lynn's mouth went dry. She hung up on Nate with no explanation. She'd text him later. Maybe. Though she still didn't have all of the information, the conversation with Nate confirmed that Jeremy was, in fact, at Liberty, and something had definitely happened. She couldn't wait for Nate to tell her more; she had to see the evidence with her own eyes. She had to know.
Lynn ran to the closest service desk and nearly startled a nurse out of her seat when she slammed her hands down on the desk in front of her, out of breath and eyes wild.

"Is there any way that you could tell me where my friend is in this hospital? His name is Trent Shawking."

The young girl didn't respond with any words, but began to type the name into the computer.

"And how is Shawking spell—"

"S-h-a-w-k-i-n-g," Lynn spat, like an angry kid at a spelling bee.

The girl took a look at the screen, her eyebrows raised.

"He's on the sixth floor, ICU. I can't tell you what room, but if you go to that floor's desk, they can tell you whether or not the room is open to visitors right now."

Lynn took off, not thinking clearly enough to say thank you.

This wasn't the first time Lynn had run through this hospital. By now, Lynn had become accustomed to the fast-paced movements of nurses and doctors, and the slow, steady pace of regular visitors that Lynn had seen in these hallways almost every day. She nearly ran into the mother of Antonio, one of Teddy's friends. Antonio's mother called out to Lynn as she brushed past, but Lynn kept going without a hiccup in her step. Although Lynn felt bad, it was easy enough to ignore anyone and anything as she rushed forward; running through this place was nothing but an obstacle course to Lynn now. Lynn would catch up with her later anyway, hopefully when she wasn't having hallucinations.

When Lynn reached the sixth floor, she startled the two people at that desk as well. This time, it was an older gentleman who gave her a look like she was a prison escapee. Before she opened her mouth to ask about Trent's room, she spotted Jeremy at a nearby vending machine, smacking it in anger. It was as if Jeremy felt her stare, because he almost immediately turned around. When the two met each other's gaze, Jeremy looked confused to see her, and it was apparent that he didn't want to start a conversation. He started heading down the hallway away from her, but Lynn was determined to know the truth.

"Jeremy!" Lynn called out, and he stopped and slowly turned around to face her. "I know this isn't the place for small talk, but what're you doing here?" Lynn asked, her stomach doing summersaults.

Lynn quickly noticed the wound on Jeremy's head, and realized she was asking a stupid question. Jeremy, gave her a strange look.

"Uhh..." he began, and Lynn guessed that he might not know her name.

"My name's Lynn, by the way. You've maybe seen me in the hallway at school."

Jeremy scratched his head and shrugged.

"Yeah, I know your face, I—I'm just—I was in an accident with my brother. I'm not really in the mood to talk to anyone right now." Lynn's stomach dropped, and she gulped down the knot of nerves in her throat.

"Is your brother, okay?"

"He's... I just... I don't really feel comfortable talking about it. I have to go." Jeremy wrestled with the words before turning back around and heading down the hallway again. Understandable, Lynn thought – she was no one to him, just a weird senior – but she needed an answer like a drought needed rain. She needed to know if Trent was alive.

"Jeremy!" Trent called out from behind Lynn, and she jumped at the voice that was becoming all too familiar to her. She spun around and saw the ghostly mirage of Trent Shawking.

"Lynn, why is he walking away? Why can't he hear me? What's happening? He's going to—" Trent asked frantically, his voice breaking, and Lynn watched as he was unable to finish his sentence. Instead, his eyes rolled into his head, and he fell backward. Lynn instinctively ran to catch him, but as his body was about to hit the ground, it disintegrated into a white haze and disappeared entirely from existence.

"What's happening?" Lynn heard Jeremy's voice in Trent's room.

Then a woman's, Lynn assumed it was his mother's, said, "I don't know I was holding his hand and then—"

"I need a nurse! Someone!" Lynn's head whipped around to see Jeremy yelling as he emerged from his brother's hospital room. After the brief panicked exchange, a high-pitched beeping rang from the room. Lynn's eyes widened as she backed into a wall of the hallway and slid down it, inhaling a deep, shaky breath.

This was all happening too fast. Lynn had finally come face to face with the reality that she might not be hallucinating the ghost of Trent Shawking. Lynn buried her face in her hands before suddenly jumping at the sound of Trent's shouting. This time, his voice was nowhere near her – it was coming from the room Jeremy had yelled from.

"Can either of you see me? Hear me? Why can't anyone hear me, at least?!"

Lynn stood up and cautiously walked down the hall, towards Trent's voice, the room Jeremy had just been yelling out of. She stayed close to the wall so she wouldn't disrupt anyone coming in or out of it. When she peeked in through the doorframe, her eyes wide with terror, Trent looked back at her. The look on Trent's face reminded her of the look that Teddy tried to hide from her when he had to take a needle – like a scared kid.

Lynn had never really known Trent, but when she'd seen him at school, he was always confident, smug, and easy-going. Even though she'd only ever seen him from afar, she could tell that, in this moment, he was a different person.

Lynn ripped her eyes away from Trent's and quickly walked back down the hallway before his brother or mother could see her. When she reached the stairwell, she came to an abrupt stop.

"Lynn, please."

A chill ran up her spine. Lynn slowly turned around to look at him, frightened. This had all become too real when she saw two versions of him in the hospital room: one broken and bloodied on a bed, and the other an unearthly phantom standing in front of himself.

"Trent, I don't—I don't know how to help you," she mumbled as she looked down at her feet.

It was hard to stare at him for long. His eyes were the only part of him which held any colour – they were a faint but sharp blue. The rest of his body was washed out and lifeless. Blurry, even. The more she stared at him, the harder it was to focus on the world around her.

"Can you just... stay with me? I don't know if I'll disappear again." he asked.

If ghosts could cry, he probably would have, but Lynn never saw any tears. Lynn nodded her head and took a seat on the stairwell, her eyes darting around to look at anything else but him.

"When you disappear, where do you go?" Lynn asked.

If there was no white noise or distraction to take her mind off of this lunacy, she'd have to try her best to make sense of it. Trent moved to sit beside her, looking like he had forgotten how to sit for a moment, and hesitating before doing so. It became evident to Lynn that Trent was unsure if his body would go right through the ground. When it didn't, and he was seated, he sighed in relief.

"I don't know. It's dark, and it's hard to move when I'm there. The only thing I can see when I'm there is you."

Lynn was taken aback by the answer and looked at him with a strange expression.

"You see me? Like, all the time?" she asked, creeped out.

"No, sorry, no, not like that. I mean... I see this light in the distance, in the dark, and it has no shape, no features, and then if I try to move towards it, I suddenly get thrown into a room. So far, it's been three different places in this hospital, and the light that I see always turns into you. You make the room light up. I don't know what it means or why it's happening."

It was clear to Lynn that he didn't want to seem like a ghostly stalker, but right now, that was kind of how he was coming off. She didn't know how to answer, and she could tell that her silence was scaring him.

"Um... You can still see me, right?" Trent asked Lynn, staring over at her with wide, winsome eyes.

Lynn continued to stare at him in disbelief, taking in his ghostly appearance that was both dazzling and terrifying at the same time. Lynn had never seen a hologram in real life, but she imagined that it would pale in comparison to what she was witnessing right now. She nodded.

"Yes."

Unfortunately.

Lynn stood up from the steps; the cold air around him was making her anxious. Trent stood as Lynn did, and she scoffed.

"You don't have to follow me around like a lost puppy... or look at me like one," she snapped. Her temper had always been volatile, and Trent would learn that quickly if he was going to spend any sort of time around her.

"Sorry... I'm... this is the longest I've stuck around where I can see. I'm wondering if I'm... dead now?" Trent scratched the back of his head with his hand.

Lynn's eyes went wide for a moment, and then she huffed. It seemed like this mess was really happening; it was time to get over the initial shock and go along with it. Lynn had been mastering the skill of just getting on with things: figure out the problem, then fix the problem.

"I'll check," she said, running up a couple of steps and going back through the sixth-floor doors.

When she turned the corner into the hallway, a shouting Jeremy made her stop abruptly and swerve back around the corner to hide. Jeremy's mother tried to calm him down as he yelled at someone on the other end of the phone. Lynn tried to eavesdrop. It wasn't tricky; Jeremy was angry, and his volume proved it.

"Why haven't you shown up yet? Things aren't getting better! What if he dies before you get here? Will you be able to live with yourself?" Jeremy threw his phone down on to a chair with an abrupt clank.

Lynn heard his mother try to soothe him, but the sound of footsteps barreling down the hall told her that Jeremy was incredibly fed up. The breeze that Jeremy created as he bolted past her towards the staircase made her hair fly up briefly, and goosebumps erupted on her skin. Cautiously, Lynn walked back to the stairwell and listened while Jeremy's footsteps became quieter as he ran further down the steps and eventually stopped at the landing where Lynn had just been.

Trent's voice burst out from behind Lynn, and she was startled once again. "Why is he running away? Am I dead? Did it happen? Can you tell him I'm here? That I'm okay... I think?"

This time, though, she hadn't jumped or screamed. She turned to look at him, sighed, and then turned back to Jeremy, who hadn't noticed she was on the steps yet. He was sitting on the last step now, with his head in his hands. She advanced cautiously. Not the type to be tender, she didn't really know how to approach him.

"Uh... Hey, dude. I know you don't want to talk right now, but I just want to tell you that, whatever's happening, your brother will be okay."

Lynn stood four steps above Jeremy, awkwardly pulling at her sleeve and regretting the fact that she'd said anything to him when he looked back at her in anger.

"Would you just leave me alone?" Jeremy snapped and ran off.

"Do you think I'm dead?" Trent asked, his voice wavering as he watched his brother run off.

"I don't think so. I heard him say, 'what if he's dead before you get here?' to someone on the phone. He was yelling, and your mom was trying to calm him down, so I think you're still in that room, but I don't want to be creepy and go look while your mom is there."

Honestly, they had never been friends, and she thought she'd be caught in a lie if she pretended now. They were from two different worlds. He was a King, and she was nothing but a peasant in the land of Heatherdale High School. Lynn stood uncomfortably looking at her feet as Trent shook his head and rubbed his face with his hands. She could see his growing frustration as he began to speak again.

"Why is this happening? Why can't I remember shit?" Trent groaned.

Lynn could tell the question was directed at

himself, but she felt obliged to answer anyway – and in the same frustrated tone.

"You ask a lot of questions that I don't have the answers to, so here's a better one: What *can* you remember?"

Trent looked up at her. His breathtaking eyes were searching hers.

"I—" he began and then furrowed his brows. "I can remember things when I see them, or people, but anything before that is... blank I guess? It's just dark."

"What in the hell does that mean?"

"Okay, like, when I first saw you." Trent moved towards her.

Lynn instinctively stepped back. It was apparent that ghost Trent had forgotten about boundaries.

"I remembered your name and what you smelled like when I first talked to you in math class, and that's all. I don't remember anything else except maybe seeing you in the hallway. But then when I remember that math class, I don't remember anything about it but that one moment, but I know I was in a math class, you know?" Trent rambled on, and Lynn's face got more scrunched up with confusion by the second.

"What I... smelled like?" Lynn was creeped out again.

"Yeah, you smelled like coconuts, in a good way. I don't know why that's the first thing I remembered. I know it's weird." Trent started to stroke his chin in deep thought.

Lynn slowly backed away and, without warning, started down the stairs again.

"Wait! Where are you going?" Trent called out.

This guy is needy.

Lynn slowly spun on her heel to look back at him.

"I wasn't here for you in the first place! My brother is in the hospital, and I have responsibilities! I didn't plan to entertain a ghost!"

"But Lynn, what if I disappear? What if I die?!"

"Well, that's not my problem, is it?"

That was cold. Lynn knew it, but she didn't care.

Trent was taken aback, unsure of how to answer. She rolled her eyes, but it wasn't at his hurt – it was at her own severe lack of sensitivity. She hated the fact that she didn't know how to be warm to anyone else in the world but her brother.

"Listen, dude, as much as I'd like to help you right now, I also have a sick brother who means just a *little* more to me than you do. You dying isn't my biggest problem. Don't take it personally – this is just the most we've talked in... ever?"

Trent looked down at his feet for a moment, and then back up at her.

"You're right. I just got thrown into your life. I can't expect you to help me out of nowhere."

Lynn was a little bit shocked. She didn't expect someone like him to be so understanding; she expected him to meet her insensitivity with anger or dislike. Lynn began to silently loathe that puppy dog face of his, but she could maybe lighten up a bit.

"Look, I didn't mean to say it like that—"

"It's fine, really. You're right."

His sincerity was completely throwing her off.

"Well, okay. I'll still try to help you. I'll meet you back here. I don't know when, but try not to sneak up on me anymore! As much as I'm getting used to your voice, I get this weird spine chill when you're around. You've really got that ghost vibe down," Lynn muttered, and then started heading down the stairs again, leaving Trent to sit on the steps and wait for her. Or, given his current situation, maybe the Reaper.

5

HIGH TOLERANCE

07:25 AM

As Lynn entered her brother's hospital room, she was caught off guard when her mother immediately started in on her.

"Where have you been, Lynn Marie? You can't text me back? I had to leave half an hour ago – you don't have to work at the weekend, I do! And you know how important it is for me to make money right now! Jesus!"

Lynn's jaw locked. She couldn't speak her mind in front of her mother like she had with Trent a few minutes ago. She knew she'd get shit for it.

"My bad. I wasn't paying attention," Lynn mumbled.

"Yeah, not to anything, clearly! Can I trust you to

59

stay here now?"

Lynn nodded and took a seat on her throne. Even after the yelling, she noticed her brother was still out cold. All the drugs being pumped into his little body would keep him tired for a while. Lynn hated being stuck in this room when Teddy wasn't awake. Here she was, trapped listening to the symphony of technology keeping her little brother alive, imprisoned in an endless loop of anxiety.

Lynn rubbed her forehead and covered her face with both hands. She sighed heavily as she felt the hairs on the back of her neck stand up, and she let out a muffled scoff.

"Trent, are you here?" Lynn groaned.

"...Maybe?" Trent answered from the doorway behind her.

Lynn scoffed again. It seemed like he had told a dark joke, but then she realized it wasn't a joke. Trent was genuinely unsure if he was there.

"I told you to wait on the stairs, not follow me."

"Is it really 'following' if I just always know where you are? You shine like a beacon. Believe me, I tried to stay on those stairs, but the room got darker the farther you moved away, and it creeped me out. I felt lonely. I don't know how to explain it, but everything slowly goes dark if you're not around... so I walked towards the light. I walked towards you, and here I am," Trent rambled on. Lynn sighed as she looked up at him.

"Isn't the general consensus to... not go towards the light?" she asked, looking him in the eyes.

"Yes, but *you're* the light, and why would I want to stay away from *you* when you're *so* delightful to be around?" Trent smirked.

Trent walked up to the side of Teddy's bed and tilted his head as he looked down at him. Lynn immediately got to her feet and stepped in between them like a lioness protecting her cub.

"I didn't know you had a brother too. You look alike," Trent mumbled and then backed up a bit.

"Listen, you have to stay back – you have this icy air around you, and I don't want him getting sick. Well, sicker than he already is."

Trent nodded.

"Sorry, I didn't realise the cold was that bad. I can't feel anything right now… Why's he here?"

Lynn was surprised by his empathy. He'd never seemed like this in school. Sure, she'd never really spoken to him before, but his good looks automatically made her think that he was stuck up.

"Cancer."

"What kind?"

"I don't really want to talk about it." Lynn took a seat in her chair again.

Trent sighed and nodded.

"That's okay. Is there anything you do want to talk about?" Trent took a slow, cautious seat on the hospital floor beside Lynn's chair, further away from Teddy.

Lynn observed him in mild disgust. If he were anyone else, she would've told him to get off the ground because it was covered in germs, but the frightening image of him lying in his hospital bed stopped her. He was a ghost; bacteria was the least of his worries now.

"I don't know. I'm not really in the mood to talk about anything."

"That's okay. We can just sit here." Trent rested his elbows on his thighs and his chin on both of his hands.

Lynn couldn't help but be amused at his strangely genuine behaviour when his eyes shifted from Teddy and back to her. He did it several times, and every time he caught her eyes, his small smile seemed to be building into a broad grin, as if he'd forgotten about his dire situation as a ghost and was simply happy to be around other people.

Lynn was always moody and reserved. Trying to make friends was not something she wanted to do in this town, since she wouldn't be here for long – that's why she'd made herself the school's official loner. Her family had planned to move to this place in the hopes that this hospital could change Teddy's prospective outcome. If it did, they'd stay here and work through his remission at Liberty, and then go back to their old suburb, Logan. If it didn't, like it wasn't now, they would end up moving back even sooner. Lynn had friends in Logan, but within the last year, she hadn't been able to keep up with any of them because of the move. What was the use in making friends here if she was certain she'd be moving back to Logan anyway?

"Okay, maybe there's one thing I want to talk about," Lynn began, looking at Trent curiously. "Do you remember what happened to you? You saw Jeremy just a little bit ago. Did you have any memory flashes, like you did when you saw me?"

Trent looked up at her with a brow raised. By the look on his face, that was a good question.

"I think I was thrown from the car. My face felt so cold like it had been laying in wet grass. I remember looking up and seeing Jeremy. He was yelling on the phone. Then everything is a blur. My mother crying, the darkness – I think I saw my life flash before my eyes." Trent shuddered.

Lynn was listening to him intently now. Another question crossed her mind, but she wasn't sure if it was the right time to ask. She was never really good at timing anyway, so she figured she would just do it.

"Trent...um..." Lynn began awkwardly. "If you are, you know, 'dying'..." She tried to tread as lightly as she could, air-quoting the word, but the air quotes hadn't seemed to soften the blow judging by how wide Trent's eyes had become. "…is there something you needed to do? A last hurrah? I can't see why you'd stick around. Especially in a shitty hospital like this."

Lynn knew that if she died young, she wouldn't have much unfinished business. She'd want to make sure that Teddy would be all right, and that was it. Her friends at her old school seemed to forget about her more and more as time passed. They probably wouldn't care if she left for good. School was just a chore, most of the time. When she was there, she was only there to learn – she didn't participate in social events or extracurriculars – and then she'd rush to the hospital, or home, to take care of Teddy, her best friend. Maybe it was embarrassing to think that her only real friend in the world was her little brother, but the world had made her see just how ugly people could really be. Her purpose now was to protect Teddy and make sure the world didn't break him as he grew up – that is, if his body would let him live long enough.

"I don't know. I just know I don't want to die right now." Trent had a fierce look in his eyes.

Lynn wished she knew how that felt.

"There are so many things I haven't done," Trent continued. "I wanna make a junior rep team and play for Heatherdale. I want to know what comes after high school. I want to see if I can ever make a million dollars. I want two dogs, and maybe a family. I'd like to have kids someday who I can build a treehouse for, just so I can play in it more than them. I want to eat an ice cream sandwich again. I really want to go bungee jumping." Trent's ramblings were turning into the whine of a child. "I just want to live a life, you know! I don't want to die now and be the dumb jock who died driving home from a party!"

Lynn suddenly snorted. Trent frowned up at her.

"What? Why're you laughing at me?"

"Sorry, really, I'm so sorry. I tried to hold back, I swear – I just think it's funny that eating an ice cream sandwich made that list."

Dumbfounded, Trent couldn't do anything else but stare at her.

"I really like ice cream sandwiches, okay?"

"Okay." Lynn shrugged and tried to look anywhere else but at him.

She almost laughed again but stopped herself, not wanting to offend him. After a brief moment of silence, she looked at him from the side of her eye, and Trent stifled a laugh. Lynn fought to hold back a smirk and lost. When the room fell quiet again, all they could hear was the constant drone of Teddy's ventilator.

"That sound is kind of awful."

"You get used to it," Lynn lied as they both stared at the machine.

"Ugh... that feels weird." Trent looked down at his hand. He opened and closed his palm a couple of times in confusion.

"What's weird?" Lynn asked, looking to his hand.

Trent mumbled something that Lynn couldn't quite understand, and before Lynn could question him again, Trent disappeared from the hospital floor. Staring down at the tiles where he sat, Lynn suddenly felt like someone had ripped open her gut. She hadn't felt this way before, and it was hard to understand. Like being alone suddenly made her stomach sick. But she had been alone before, for a long time, and it'd never felt this way. Maybe having a ghost around came with side effects.

SATURDAY, SEPTEMBER 28, 2019

11:32 AM

Getting high used to be different for Jeremy. The oxy used to hit him like a soft, pillowy train. A once pleasant and carefree experience now felt like something he needed, because if he didn't get it, his anger would get to him instead. It wasn't about that instance of euphoria anymore; it was about being able to function. Yet, he was hardly even capable of that these days, especially after that run-in with the Reaper this morning. Seeing Trent flatline in real time really got him thinking that maybe his brother wasn't going to make it. What was worse was running into that weird senior, Lynn Avison, who just wouldn't leave him alone.

Crush a quarter, snort. Wait for hours at your brother's bedside while he struggles to survive a coma. Get an urge. Ignore it for as long as you can. Lock yourself in a bathroom. Crush another quarter, snort. Come back to that bedside. Angrily text your father. Get an urge. Everything was happening to Jeremy in pieces. Nothing felt real. Whatever he might feel was numbed out by the oxy, or the need to snort oxy. This may seem like a dependency, but of course, he could stop when he wanted.

He'd read something once about tolerance, and how drugs lose their potency the more you take them. There wasn't time to think about that, though; there was never any time to concentrate on himself anymore. There was only time for oxy and his brother now. He was trying to make time for his mother, but he felt like she would notice that he'd changed. There was too much guilt and shame inside him to have a full conversation with her.

"Jeremy?"

Jeremy's head snapped upright, and his blue eyes fell on his mother. She was sitting on the other side of Trent, opposite Jeremy. Jeremy was suddenly flooded with overwhelming embarrassment, as if his mother had heard all of his terrible thoughts.

"I'm going to leave now, okay? Let me know if you need me to bring anything back."

Beth stood up from her chair and went to Trent. She reached for Trent's hand, but then stopped, and instead brushed his hair back, away from the bandage on his head. As Jeremy watched her hold back tears again, she turned to him and kissed him on the top of his head before she left the room. Jeremy sighed, disappointed in himself. All she did was care about him, and he felt like a failure. If she knew about what he'd done, what he had started, there'd be nothing but worry on her face, but she'd have disappointment behind her eyes. He just knew it. The most important thing was that he knew that he could stop when he wanted – but now was the wrong time. With everything going on... he just needed it for now. That was all. Just for now.

Ding.

Jeremy's scratched phone caught his attention.

Hey Jare, where's Trent?
He missed pitch practice and
isn't answering his phone.

He looked at the message and winced.

The hospital. We got into
an accident after the party.

What?
What happened?

Are you at Liberty?

> **Ye. 6th floor ICU. If you want to visit, just go to the desk and ask for his room. I can't explain over the phone.**

I'll be there in 10.

Jeremy ran a hand through his hair. He had known that if anyone was going to look for Trent first, it would be Adam. He hadn't paid any attention to Trent's phone, as it had been severely cracked in the crash, and the battery had died. Jeremy didn't want to look at it, let alone attempt to turn it on. Now he was nervous. How many other people would start searching for Trent? How many people would show up to this room when he was trying to score? A hospital was the wrong place to be with an addiction, but from his perspective, it wasn't really an addiction anyway.

His anxiety kept him in a state of panic as he uncomfortably stared at the television in the corner of the room. He wasn't really watching it; he was just kind of taking in the colours and sounds as his thoughts spiralled out of control. Soon, he was interrupted by the sound of footsteps running towards Trent's door.

"What the fuck, Jer?!" Adam Wenner, Trent's best friend, and basically another older brother to Jeremy, came storming through the hospital door. "You couldn't call me, man? What the hell happened?"

Jeremy started stuttering, knowing he was going to get an earful. Adam tore his angry gaze from Jeremy to Trent on the hospital cot. His eyes widened and he covered his mouth in disbelief, only now taking a solid look at Trent. After a few seconds of taking in the broken image of his best friend, Adam's dark brown eyes narrowed in on Jeremy.

"I'm not gonna yell at you, but I expected a damn call. What the hell happened? Are you okay?"

Adam opened his arms for a hug, and that's when Jeremy knew he wasn't mad. He was just worried. Jeremy stood and crashed into Adam's arms. This was probably the only person he'd actually be comfortable crying in front of, other than his mother. Even though Adam would make fun of him sometimes, he'd never take it too far. Adam could be described as a comedian on his best days and a sad clown on his worst, but even a good showman or comedian knew when to be serious.

"I'm sorry. His phone is busted, and I've just been stressing," Jeremy said as the pair ended their hug. "I didn't know what to do. After the party, someone hit us on a back road and took off."

"He wasn't drinking, I know he wasn't. If I'd seen him with something in his hand, I would've kicked his fucking ass when he tried to drive home," Adam replied.

"Yeah, don't worry, they know. They tested his blood alcohol level."

"Did you see who hit you?"

"No." Jeremy sat back in his seat. Adam shook his head and walked to the side of the bed, staring at Trent in confusion.

"I can't fucking believe this, dude. What's the diagnosis? Broken from head to toe? Is he just sleeping? What's going on?"

Jeremy took a deep breath.

"Fractured skull, broken arm and some ribs, something about his lung. He's in a coma – they told us they were going to induce it to help with the recovery, but before they could, he just fell into one. They said that's more dangerous. I'm really..." Jeremy trailed off and put his face in his hands. "I'm really scared, man. I don't know what's going to happen."

Adam put a hand on Jeremy's shoulder and squeezed.

"I do. I know he's gonna wake up. The only question is, *when* is he gonna wake up? You know this fucker can sleep for days given a chance."

Jeremy knew Adam was trying to cheer him up, but he wasn't so sure.

"How can you be so—"

"I just, I know it," Adam said, and this time it sounded like he was trying to convince himself more than Jeremy. "If there's anyone who can wake up from this, it's him. And believe me, he's going to want to wake up to the gnarly scar this is going to leave on his head. It'll make him feel badass. I'm sure of it." Adam took a seat in the chair opposite Jeremy. "Isn't that right, dumbass?" Adam said a little more loudly, directing it at Trent.

Jeremy raised a brow at him, and Adam shrugged.

"What? Aren't you supposed to talk to him like he's awake? Doesn't that help or something? I've heard that helps, and just because he's in the hospital doesn't mean I'm going to be nice. He's still my best friend."

Jeremy shook his head as his phone went off again.

Hey Jeremy, sorry to message unexpectedly, I was just wondering where Trent is? He isn't answering his phone when I call.

Here was another person he had to tell. This one, he'd expected the least.

Hi Ray,
He's in the hospital. I can't really explain over

the phone. He's at Liberty, if you want to visit. Go to the 6th floor and ask for his room.

Woah, what?

Adam looked over Jeremy's shoulder to see who was texting him so much, but Jeremy stood as another text came through that he was scared to show Adam.

Where can I drop?

Exit J.

Be there in five. Do you have all of it? I'm not giving you anything unless you have what you owe.

I have it.

Jeremy replied to the text and then nervously rubbed the back of his head.

"I gotta go do something. I'll be back in like five minutes, man."

Before Adam could question him, Jeremy took off as quickly as he could.

Jeremy had finished his last stash unusually fast. He had hoped he could make it his last, but the pain from the crash and the absolute whirlwind of the bad news he was continually hearing about his brother had brought him to his boiling point. He needed more than his usual fix, just for now. That's where Nate came in.

For the past several weeks, Jeremy had been getting a small but steady dose of oxy. He couldn't remember how it had started, or why he kept texting Nate, but now, here he was, in a hospital surrounded by prescription drugs, and he was going out to the parking lot to buy opioids. The irony made him uncomfortable, but he didn't care enough to let that stop him.

†

"You've got balls," Nate said with a pointed look as Jeremy frantically burst out of the exit door.

Nate was leaning against the cement wall, smoking a cigarette. His dark eyes scanned Jeremy from head to toe. Nate's tone hadn't been judgemental, but his stare sure was. Jeremy sighed and looked at his feet. The comment about his balls was obviously due to the fact that he'd called Nate to a hospital for a drug run.

"Here." Jeremy held out his hand with the money in it, and Nate took the wad of bills from him to count them slowly.

"Come on, man, it's all there," Jeremy mumbled.

"I'll be the judge of that. You're lucky you don't deal with my other guy – he hits first, counts money later."

Nate flashed a grim smirk and finished counting. He pulled a small bag out of his hoodie's pocket and slipped it to Jeremy. Before Jeremy could speed away, Nate cleared his throat.

"Hey, uh, how do you know Lynn?" Nate asked, and Jeremy scrunched up his face in confusion.

"Lynn?" Jeremy asked, immediately remembering the awkward run-in from earlier. "I don't, but I saw her earlier, why?"

"Never mind then. By the way, my guy isn't giving you any more rain checks. You pushed your luck, and he was pretty pissed about this one. Consider this a warning." Nate finished his smoke and threw it on the ground before stepping on it and walking away.

Jeremy felt nauseous for a moment. Warning?

What the hell was he talking about? And why would Nate care if Jeremy knew Lynn Avison? Asking drug dealers questions usually didn't pan out well, so he kept his questions to himself and ran back inside, almost straight into Adam, who was standing at the door of the hospital room.

"Where'd you go?"

"Nowhere. I mean, bathroom."

"So, you went to a bathroom in the middle of nowhere, when there's one in your brother's hospital room?" Adam rolled his eyes, but didn't look as if he wanted to interrogate Jeremy further on his strange behaviour. "Cool," Adam continued, clearly unconvinced. "Let's go to the cafeteria and eat some wonderful hospital food. I didn't get breakfast after practice."

Adam grabbed Jeremy by the shoulder, and before Jeremy could protest, was already walking them both down the stairs.

When they made it into the cafeteria, Jeremy took a seat at one of the tables as he waited for Adam to get his food.

"Do you think the food in prison is better or worse than hospital food? I've seen it on shows and stuff, and it looks worse, but who knows what it tastes like, you know? And have you ever seen those prison shows where they make burritos out of the junk food they buy from commissary?"

Whatever Adam was saying, Jeremy really wasn't listening. Instead, he ran his fingers over the scratch in his phone, which had appeared earlier after he'd thrown it in a rage while talking to his father.

"You listening? I'm talking about some interesting stuff here."

Jeremy nodded, but didn't look him in the eyes. Adam scoffed.

"Jer, I know you don't want to talk about anything

that's bothering you. I know you, man, but you gotta let off steam. You bottle up all that shit, and it's gonna come out in a bad way."

Jeremy rolled his eyes. He knew Adam was just trying to help, but he hadn't asked for it. Why was everyone always trying to teach him life lessons? He was learning enough by living through this hell; he didn't need anyone to narrate.

"Don't roll your eyes at me. One day, your anger's gonna blow up in your face and you're gonna get into a fight with someone, and if that person is not me – 'cause sometimes you really make me wanna kick your ass – *they're* going to kick your ass for real. You can't win a fight with arms like that, man."

Adam smacked him on the side of his arm, and Jeremy winced. It didn't hurt, it was just unexpected.

"Are you trying to convince me to work out more or what?" Jeremy looked away from his friend, unable to keep eye contact.

"Yeah, that couldn't hurt, but that's not the only thing I'm saying. I'm saying that anger can get the best of us, and I don't want it to get you in trouble." Adam punctured an orange juice box with a straw. "And maybe I'm just talking out of my ass, but I want you to know that I'm here for you if you need me. Get it?"

Jeremy shot Adam a glance from the corner of his eye and nodded. Here sat another person who could do nothing else but care about him, and he felt guilty. He couldn't tell Adam what he'd started; Adam would tell him how stupid he was being, and he really would kick his ass for real. Jeremy decided that if he couldn't get rid of Adam right now, he'd at least ask him some questions.

"Do you know Lynn Avison?"

Adam scrunched up his face as he took a bite from the deli sandwich. Jeremy wasn't sure if he was making a face at the bad food or at the question.

"Yeah, I mean, I don't talk to her, but I know of her. That new girl?"

"She's not really new anymore."

"Okay, new-ish. She came to Heatherdale like what, almost two years ago? Always keeps to herself. What about her?"

"Do you know if she talks to Trent?"

Adam paused to think, silencing the insufferable noise he made as he sucked the orange juice-box dry.

"I don't think so. Why?" Adam took another bite of his sandwich and then threw it down, detesting it altogether. Jeremy concluded that the face Adam had made before was indeed in response to his lunch.

"I saw her earlier. She asked me about what happened. I don't know why she was here in the first place. It was weird." Jeremy shrugged.

"She keeps to herself. I don't know her." Adam wafted his empty juice box around as he talked with his hands. "All right, I need some real food – this crap isn't cutting it. You want to leave the hospital for a while? Come get something with me?" Adam asked as he stood and stretched.

"No, I can't leave. Mom asked me to stay with Trent until she comes back later."

"Okay, well keep me updated, yeah? As soon as he wakes up, I need to be the first to yell at him, and if you need me to bring you anything, just ask."

Jeremy nodded to Adam, and then watched as he took off. That sudden wave of guilt and shame washed over him again as he stood up to run to the bathroom, oxy at the ready.

6

FAKE FRIENDS

12:41 PM

"I really don't think we should be here," Charlie whispered as she followed behind Ray and Andrea.

Mel was too much of a mess to even show up. Charlie was only there because she was too scared to go home, and she had slept over at Andrea's that night after Mel had told her she couldn't stay at hers as planned. Well, neither she nor Andrea had really slept. They had just laid down, staring up at the ceiling, plagued by their paranoia. This was the first time any of them had dared to speak after Ray had threatened them into silence post-crash.

"No one asked what you think," Ray said under his breath before clearing his throat and approaching the front desk on the sixth floor. "We're here to see

Trent Shawking."

"Okay, let me just call the room. I think he still has family in there," the nurse replied.

Charlie hadn't thought about anyone else being in the room other than Jeremy. She was prepared to deal with Trent's brother – at least she thought she would be – because she expected him to be there, but if his mother or father or cousin or second cousin were there, the guilt would suddenly feel immeasurable.

"No one's picking up. I'd say you're free to go in. It's room 607, that way," The nurse pointed to their left.

✝

Ray made it into the room first. Charlie and Andrea hesitated. Andrea nodded to Charlie to go ahead of her, and Charlie inched closer to Trent. When all three had entered the room, they looked at his broken body, then around at each other. All of them had the same sickly look on their faces.

"Do you think it's serious?" Ray asked, then looked to the two girls.

Charlie and Andrea glared over at him. That may have been the dumbest thing he'd ever said. Andrea shoved past Ray and took a seat next to Trent's bed. She took Trent's hand in hers and squeezed gently.

"Please don't die."

Charlie scoffed under her breath. She wondered if Andrea was saying it because she actually cared, or if she was just scared of going to jail for murder.

"We'll all be dead when he finds out what we did," Charlie answered Andrea's request to Trent.

"Charlie. Quiet, for fuck's sake," Ray seethed.

This wasn't the time or place, Charlie knew that, and now Ray looked like he was about ready to jump her from the other side of the room. He walked to the door and looked left and right down the hallway.

"I'd like to leave before Charlie here calls the fucking cops, or gets the cops called on us. We never should have brought you – I knew you'd say something stupid," Ray scolded.

Charlie felt a nasty twinge, like a rusted knife was sticking out of her stomach, and now that she could see how scared Ray was getting, she suddenly felt like taking that knife out and burying it into his stomach instead. This was technically a public place, and she knew he didn't want to make a scene. She'd say her piece now. Even if she had to pay for it later.

"What're you so scared of, anyway? No one's here. The car is in the junkyard. Dex will keep your little secret. No one will ever know. Right, Ray? All of our problems are dealt with. According to you."

The sardonic tone in Charlie's voice made Andrea visibly uncomfortable. Charlie felt powerful, if only for a moment. Something had taken over her. The bear that had begun pounding against her head last night had yet to let up, and now it was breaking free. She wanted to tell the truth, no matter how hard it was to say, or how hard it was for Ray to hear.

"That's it. We're leaving," Ray demanded.

Andrea roughly wiped away the tears on her face. For a moment, she looked like she wanted to yell at Ray, and then when Charlie met her eye, Andrea looked desperate.

Charlie was reminded of Ray and Andy's screaming match last night, when Andy had said she'd thought this would all just be a joke. Charlie suddenly realized she had made the wrong person cry. She was trying to force Ray to feel something, not Andy.

Still looking as if she were holding back the instinct to scream at them both, Andy released Trent's hand and brushed past Ray at the door.

"This is all your fault," she muttered angrily in

Ray's direction.

Ray's mouth broke into a frighteningly sinister smirk. He chose not to reply to Andy, but silently followed her through the door.

With swelling tears, Charlie stared at Trent's closed eyes, willing them to blink open so she could feel some kind of relief from her guilt.

"I'm so sorry," she whispered, and slowly followed her partners in accidental crime out of the room.

00:00

Trent felt like someone had wrapped a thick cord around his hand and yanked on it hard enough to pull him from Lynn's brother's room and into his own. He landed in his hospital room with his feet planted on the ground, at the edge of his bed – or, at least, his body's bed. Confused, he looked around to see his schoolmates staring down at the mangled figure he'd once walked around in. He still wasn't used to the fact that the body lying there was just a husk now. He was standing over a gutted house, one he used to live in every day. Now, it was vacant and rotting. Trent looked at Andy's hand holding his, and then down at his ghostly hand. Suddenly, he realized the weird feeling he'd felt before was the warmth of her hand on his.

"Please don't die."

The words sounded tender, but felt strange. Before Trent could answer her with 'I'm trying my best not to', Charlie interrupted the thought.

"We'll all be dead when he finds out what we did."

It took Trent a moment to understand what she had said. When the words sunk in, he felt like he'd ingested acid.

"Charlie. Quiet, for fuck's sake," Ray seethed.

Trent looked over at Ray, startled. Trent didn't want Charlie to be quiet. Trent wanted her to say more. The words were confusing and painful, and he needed her to explain what she meant.

"I'd like to leave before Charlie here calls the fucking cops or gets the cops called on us. We never should have brought you – I knew you'd say something stupid."

"What're you so scared of, anyway? No one's here. The car is in the junkyard. Dex will keep your little secret. No one will ever know. Right, Ray? All of our problems are dealt with. According to you."

Charlie's voice went from soft and shameful to merciless. Anyone could tell she was trying to sting Ray with her words – little did she know, Trent was being stabbed with them instead.

"That's it. We're leaving," Ray declared.

"This is all your fault," Andrea whispered.

Her eyes welled up as she glared at Ray before she stood and left the room. Trent wondered what was going through her mind. Ray's smirk caught Trent off guard; he couldn't tell why it seemed so sinister. Why was Ray smiling at the accusation? Was this some sick joke to him? Was he really to blame? It sounded like it.

Ray stalked out of the room, while Charlie stayed rooted by Trent's bedside.

Trent moved slowly toward Charlie, who suddenly fussed with her sweater. When he was close enough, he could see the welling of tears in her angry eyes and the slight chatter of her teeth. Charlie would be sad, sure, but why would she cry over him? Did she have a reason to feel guilty, too? Whose car was in the junkyard? Did Ray hit him? Was Charlie driving? He had so many questions, and even if anyone could hear him, they didn't seem like they'd be willing to answer.

"I'm so sorry," she whispered, but Trent didn't feel very forgiving.

He was bewildered. What was she sorry for? What the hell had these idiots done?

Trent looked past himself on the bed where the infinite darkness cut off the rest of the room. Amid the deep void that was always lurking at the edge of Trent's world, he could still see the light that Lynn emitted. Distant, but there. The only constant in his life right now. He had to get to someone who could hear him. He had to get to her.

As he started off in her direction, the darkness swallowed him whole. It was like walking into a forest in the dead of night with only a small star of hope in the distance: Lynn's light. The moment he started moving, his body felt heavier, and he tripped over some type of elevation he couldn't see. After what felt like several moments of walking in the silent darkness, he looked back to see the room he'd come from. It had vanished from existence. He was stuck again in this loop of seemingly inert time. However, as he kept walking, a mumble of voices slithered around him. He couldn't tell if the sounds were only his imagination or if something beyond this darkness was waiting for him. Dull pain in his muscles bloomed as the voices grew. When he got closer to the light, close enough to Lynn, she took shape, and suddenly her brother's room came into view. The small number of aches in his body quickly receded. It suddenly felt as if someone had flipped a switch for pain in the back of his mind.

The room was dark, and the door was closed. There was a soft light glowing from the white static television. How long had it taken him to walk here? He remembered that it had been early afternoon the last time he saw her, and now it looked like it was late at night.

She didn't jump at his entrance this time. Her eyes seemed to light up, and even though he felt happy to see her again, he was suddenly angry with the gap of time he'd lost.

7

DRUG LORD

SATURDAY, SEPTEMBER 28, 2019

12:41 PM

Loneliness was something that Lynn had become accustomed to over the last two years, but today, for some reason, the loneliness became irritating. From the moment Trent had disappeared from thin air, she'd felt a little emptier than before, as though the cold that he radiated had numbed her to the weight of everything else she was dealing with. When he left, everything was warm again, but not in a nice way – the air seemed thick with a bitter humidity, and her every move felt sluggish and slow.

The rest of the day went by as it usually would before Trent started appearing. Lynn sat in her throne that was starting to feel more like a guard post and mindlessly played a few games on her phone.

Closer to noon, Lynn noticed a small white ball of fluff suddenly appear in the window of the hospital room door, bouncing about in an odd rhythm. At first, Lynn was confused about what it was, but then she realized it was right on time when she heard a small knock. Lynn got to her feet and opened Teddy's hospital room door to grin down at the little boy. He was holding several toys in his arms, which seemed to drown in his usual grey sweater, two sizes too big for him. Lynn gently shifted the beanie on his head away from his eyes which made the pompom and dog ears on it twitch as if they were a real. Antonio – who Teddy called Ant, and Lynn called Bug – was Teddy's age, and currently in the hospital because of a heart defect. Lynn noticed his sunken eyes didn't look as harsh today as they usually did. Teddy and Bug had become fast friends a year ago, as children usually do, and for the past few days while Bug was back in the hospital, he'd been waiting for Teddy to wake up so they could play.

"Hey, Bug, he's not awake right now," Lynn said warily, bracing herself to see his little heart be broken for the third time this week.

"Oh... well... can I leave him something this time?"

"Sure." Lynn nodded and let him past her.

Antonio walked tentatively into the room before looking over at Lynn, asking her with his eyes if he could put the trucks he'd brought down on her throne. She nodded to him, and he dumped them there and grabbed one.

"I'm gonna give you the green one. You can keep it," Antonio held the car up at eye level for Teddy, "because I know you like green, and when you wake up you can bring it over and we'll play."

Antonio left the car on Teddy's side table and slowly picked up the rest of his cars, a little defeated that his friend still hadn't awakened. He flashed a small sad grin at Lynn before leaving.

"Thanks, Bug," Lynn said as she watched him walk out the door and down the hallway back to his room. Her eyes ventured from the floppy little ears bouncing on his hat to the other passersby, wondering if she'd catch a glimpse of the phantom of Trent she'd seen earlier. When he didn't appear after a minute or so, she sat in her chair and went back to a game on her phone.

At exactly noon, her mother feverishly texted her to make sure the nurses were doing their proper rounds – which was Lynn's cue to get something to eat. Her mother never asked about Lynn's wellbeing over call or text. Only her brother's. In fact, even when they saw each other, Lynn's mother hardly asked Lynn about her own life; they just talked about Teddy. Lynn had gotten used to that. She didn't like to complain about it– she knew how important it was to take care of Teddy right now. Though she had to admit, sometimes she felt a little neglected.

As Lynn ventured out for lunch, she was growing worried about the amount of time Trent had been gone. Had he found a way to haunt someone who could actually help him? Or was he lost in that darkness he'd tried to explain to her? By the time Lynn reached the hospital cafeteria, her thoughts were consumed with endless questions about Trent. That is, until she saw Adam Wenner having lunch with Jeremy Shawking.

The hospital was in no way her sanctuary, but it had easily become her home away from home. To see people from her school life start flooding into this place felt like a mistake, as though a pipe had burst in her kitchen. She'd spent so much time trying to hide her private life from these people, only to have them show up around every corner.

She grabbed an apple as she tried to hide from the pair at the table, and then headed back to Teddy's room. At the very least, Adam and Jeremy being here was a good sign that Trent was probably still alive.

After that almost run-in, Lynn took her usual walk back and forth to the vending machine – not to buy anything, since she felt too sick to eat and hadn't even started on her apple, but because this was really her only exercise. She thought about walking over to Trent's room, but then she remembered his brother could have made it back there from lunch by now, and she didn't want to weird him out more than she already had. Instead, she made her way back to her brother and her throne. At the end of the day, just half an hour before visiting hours were over, her mother would make her entrance.

"Lynn, do you need to go home for anything now? Or are we switching tomorrow?" Lynn's mother asked as she entered the room at precisely eight-thirty in the evening. No greeting. No, 'Hey, how are you?' Just a question that felt like a demand.

"I'd rather go home tomorrow morning and then come right back," Lynn answered.

Usually, she would've gone at this time, but she was afraid of what would happen if she left the hospital now. What if she went home and Trent magically appeared in the middle of her doing something embarrassing? What if, when she left the hospital, he couldn't find her anymore? She thought it would be best to let him know that she was going to leave before she did, seeing as she had a little more control over that than he seemed to.

"That's fine, just try not to be more than an hour this time. I'll have to leave early. I'm pulling almost seventy hours this week, so I'm just going to leave and pray that you make it back here on time." Her mother sounded exhausted, but not with work – just with Lynn.

Lynn didn't answer back. She didn't need to. Her mother was here now, and there wasn't going to be a conversation. Her mother would lie down on the sleeping cot by the window, and Lynn would sit in her chair until her mother's phone alarm went off. Both Lynn and her mother would wake up to the sound, but only her mother would leave the room to go home and sleep there. Lynn would sleep here. She often did on the weekends. This weekend wouldn't be any different – at least, not in this sense.

SATURDAY, SEPTEMBER 29, 2019

02:29 AM

Even though the room was dark, and the television continued to hum a quiet, soothing white noise, Lynn just couldn't fall back to sleep after her mother left. Instead, she sat quietly, waiting for the air to become icy, pining for that cold wave of chaos to crash into her life so she could forget about her own.

For the past two years, allowing herself to cry was a foreign concept for Lynn. It had been quite a while since she'd even shed a single tear, but tonight, she could feel the urge creeping up on her, growing stronger. Lynn looked at Teddy, and her eyes welled up. It was almost funny to consider that, with all the terrible things that had happened over the past six years, seeing a ghost was the least of her problems. Unlike all the other times when she'd been able to swallow her sadness, tonight was different, and she reluctantly let herself cry until she fell asleep.

†

Lynn was in the middle of a dream like the one that Teddy had described to her – lost in her high school during a power outage, minus the shark – when she was woken by a spine-tingling coldness. Her heart fluttered. Instantly, her eyes shot open, and the disorientation that lingered from her dream faded when she laid eyes on Trent.

"Where'd you disappear to this time?" Lynn asked, yawning.

The way his face contorted told her that he was just as confused as he usually was.

"I… don't know. I was in my hospital room, and then… what time is it?"

Lynn checked her phone. "Two thirty in the morning," she answered with a shrug, noticing the frown on his face.

"What the hell? Why did it take me so long to get to you?"

"You're asking me? I don't even know how you left, let alone how you came back." Lynn snorted, but then held back a laugh. She was a little giddier than usual, but it was nice to have some company. He seemed terrified though; it was a bad time to laugh.

"It felt like I was pulled to my room by my hand. Like, yanked! When I got there, my ex, Andy, was in the room, holding my hand, and she had two of her friends with her. People I thought were my friends, too. Fucking fake friends. They talked about how it was their fault, and there's a car in a junkyard. They know something. You have to help me find out what the hell they know." As Trent started pacing in front of Lynn, she felt the cold he was giving off. It was oddly relaxing, but she had no time to think about how nice that odd feeling was. She was stuck in her confusion about everything he had just said.

"Woah, what?"

"Lynn, what if they did something? What if they know something? You have to help me. You will help me, won't you?"

"Trent." Lynn looked him dead in the eyes, and

then glanced at her brother. "Stop pacing. Sit down," she commanded.

Trent took a seat beside her chair like a trained dog, and Lynn felt terrible for how strict she'd sounded.

"Who was there, and what exactly did they say?" she asked, trying to sound more friendly.

"Ray, Charlie, and Andy."

Who the hell are those people?

Her face must've given the thought away.

"Andrea Coniglio, Charlie Tresser, and Ray-"

Oh my God.

"Ray? Raymond Hurley? The politician's son? Andrea's boyfriend?" Lynn asked, and her heart sank. This situation kept getting worse.

"Yeah. Him."

"You think he dumped a car in his cousin's junkyard that had something to do with the crash?" She wasn't really asking him anymore; she was just speaking out loud in an effort to settle her nerves. Unfortunately, saying the words only made her even more nervous.

"That's what Charlie said," Trent answered with a wary look.

"I—I know that junkyard. I—" Lynn stopped herself. She could already tell he suspected something, but she couldn't tell him this. She didn't know him well enough, and she was afraid he would be angry with her when she refused to help him.

"Lynn, if you know the junkyard, you have to go there, you have to see—"

"Trent!" Lynn hissed. "Just calm down, please. I can't be loud. I don't want to wake up my brother. Just give me a minute to think. Even if I wanted to help you, I can't go anywhere right now, so just... chill." Lynn rolled her eyes at her awful choice of words. As if he could get colder than he already was. "I need to get some sleep. I need to go home tomorrow and shower. There are other things I need to do. I need to stay with my brother, I have responsibilities. I want to help, really. Just..."

"You're right, I'm sorry. I'm just confused." Trent sighed, and Lynn felt even guiltier.

She wanted him to put up a fight. She wanted him to get angry. Maybe if he'd gotten mad, she could steer the conversation in a way that made her feel pressured by him – so much so that saying no to his request would be understandable, but he was already so understanding. He was backing off when she said to.

"Just get some sleep. I'll try and stay in the corner so I don't make you cold. Sorry," he said meekly, and then sat on the cot near the window furthest from her and Teddy.

Lynn sunk into her chair, the overwhelming weight of her guilt pressing heavier with every passing moment she spoke to him.

"Thanks," she said before closing her eyes.

As she tried to sleep, a terrible storm immediately erupted in her mind. There was so much she didn't want him to know. She usually didn't care what people thought about her, but that was only because she didn't care about others. She was genuinely starting to care about Trent's wellbeing, and that made it hard for her to tell him all the messed-up shit. How was she going to tell him that she knew about that junkyard because that's where she would drop off drugs? How do you explain to someone that you collect stolen drugs from the hospital for the high school drug lord, Raymond Hurley? How does one say that the junkyard he was talking about couldn't have cops snooping around it or she'd probably be thrown in jail?

How the *fuck* do you tell someone that you can't help them because, if you do, you'll be the one who pays for it?

8

WORST TIMELINE

00:00

Trent didn't mean to, but he'd watched as Lynn passed out entirely. When her eyes closed, it was as though her guard had fallen down, and he took a moment to look over her features. He liked the look of her big eyes, calm and rested, instead of being at the ready to cut through him with her glare. There was a moment where she sniffled in her sleep, and her nose scrunched up like a bunny's. Trent caught himself grinning at the cute gesture and then shook his head, taken aback at how adorable he'd found it. Lynn had never been cute to him; she'd just been a girl who sat in front of him in math class with nice-smelling hair.

After a short while, Trent rose to his feet and started pacing in front of the window's cot. So many things were racing through his mind now.

He couldn't keep staring at Lynn, and he wanted to go back to his room to see if his mother and brother were there, or if his father had ever shown up, but he was too afraid he'd get lost in the darkness and lose another big chunk of time. He could feel that darkness waiting for him, like the deepest ocean, ready to swallow him whole if he got too close to the light's edge.

As he continued to pace, his eyes darted around frantically and eventually settled on the doorway of Teddy's hospital room. Through a small glass window in the middle of it, he could see a bit of the light in the hallway. Trent shuffled towards it and peered out of the small pane of glass, trying his very best not to get too close to Teddy as he made his way over. It was upsetting to think that some of the path to get back to his own hospital room was lit, but not nearly enough to get him all the way back there. He was desperate to walk down the hallway to see his brother and mom. Even if they couldn't hear him, he wanted to see if they were all right. Despite knowing he probably didn't have a chance, he figured that, at the very least, he could try. He needed to try.

Trent hesitantly decided to experiment at the edge of where the light ended for him. As he walked through the door, he felt a full-body chill. Passing through objects was not something he wanted to get used to. When he saw where the darkness began, just a couple feet away from the outside of the door, he slowly reached his hand out to touch it, and his hand disappeared like it was being engulfed by flames. Even though it looked like black fire, it felt as cold as ice, and when he pulled back his hand, it instantly reappeared at the end of his ghostly arm.

Feeling dejected at his failed experiment, Trent went back into the room to sit on the cot. He raked his hands through his hair nervously; even though his hair wasn't bothering him, raking his hands through it was a habit he'd inherited from his mother. There was nothing to do now but wait. There was no sleeping. He couldn't even watch the television, which had been left playing barely audible white noise. He waited while hours ticked by. He had nothing better to do but watch Teddy and Lynn sleep, which he was trying very hard not to do.

Every time his eyes fell on her brother, he'd look to Lynn and think about that uncomfortable scene in *Twilight* where Edward watches Bella sleep. He'd been coerced into watching that movie with Andy at the height of their romantic relationship. He had been at home when he received a text from Andy asking him if he wanted to see *Twilight,* as his hometown's movie theatre was playing it especially for Valentine's Day. Trent had immediately texted Adam for advice, but Adam was slow to text back, so Trent had needed someone else's advice. How could he gently say, 'absolutely not'? Sixteen-year-old Trent had walked over to Jeremy's room to step in front of his television as he was playing Call of Duty. After Jeremy's barrage of name-calling had gotten their mother to yell at Jeremy to be quiet from downstairs, Trent had calmly asked Jeremy if he'd ever see a movie just because his girlfriend asked him to. Jeremy detested the idea, and their mother was quickly at the door of Jeremy's room after she'd followed the yelling to give her own advice.

"If your girlfriend wants to see a movie with you, you see a movie with her, and try to enjoy it. You might surprise yourself and end up liking it, and if you don't like it, at least you get to hold her hand… because that's all you're doing, right? Holding hands?"

Trent remembered the interrogating look his mother gave him before walking out of the room.

But when he pictured her disappearing down the stairs, the memory began to disintegrate, like someone had blown out the small flame at the end of a match. When Trent looked back at the memory of Jeremy, who began to push him out of the way of his television, Jeremy disappeared just as easily. Trent never admitted to his mother afterward that he actually had enjoyed the movie just a little bit, although he assumed most of his enjoyment had come from 'holding Andy's hand' the whole time.

He was staring at his hand now, wondering why that memory so eagerly popped into his head, while others were so hard to grasp. His eyes once again went from his hand to settle on Lynn. Even though Lynn was definitely cute, he knew that watching a girl sleep was not something he should be doing. Over the next few hours, Trent ended up repeating *'I'm just a ghost. Not a vampire'*, so many times in his mind that it turned into a strange mantra. Though he would still find himself occasionally glancing at Lynn, at least his mantra was helping him accept the fact that he was definitely some kind of ghost.

Being alone in near total silence left Trent reminiscing about the few memories he had about his life, which were few and far between. He was still trying to remember his father. He knew he existed. Trent knew his name and what he looked like. He just couldn't remember anything good about him anymore. Instead, he was left with only one memory of his father: his old man, in a blind rage, putting his hands on Trent's mother. It replayed like an awful movie in his head, and Trent wanted so badly to make it stop. He tried to replace the scene with something less frightening, but the only other moment he could clearly remember was the first time he had talked to Lynn in math class.

†

Finally, at around seven on Sunday morning, Lynn's eyes fluttered open and landed on Trent. Startled, he jumped, realizing he had been staring at her as she awoke.

"I'm just a ghost. Not a vampire," he blurted out as if he'd been accused of something, before realising that his mantra shouldn't be said out loud.

"Good morning to you, too," Lynn mumbled as she rubbed the sleep out of her eyes. Trent took a deep breath, thankful that she wasn't lucid enough to call him out on his stupidity. He shook his head at himself and got to his feet.

"I'd offer to get you something, but I can't," he said with a smirk, trying to blow past his strange morning greeting.

Lynn raised a brow at the offer.

"Well, thanks anyway." Looking at her phone, Lynn shifted in her chair hastily. "My mom will be here any minute before she goes to work. I have to go home to shower and stuff. You're okay to stay here, right? And not accidentally pop up behind me at home?"

Before he could answer, Lynn's mom pushed the door open like a storm had entered the room.

"Lynn, let's switch now, please. I have to leave for eight-thirty."

"Yup, I'm going," Lynn answered, already standing up.

On her way out of the room, Lynn shot Trent a stern look to stay where he was, but as she left, he felt the darkness slowly swallow him. Lynn was becoming a shapeless beacon of light again, and the light was moving, disappearing down the hallway. The room started to shake, and the edges of the darkness burned the hospital room away like fire on a picture. Trent chased after her, but as the dark caught up to him, he seemed to be moving in slow motion, as if the darkness had become denser than before. He still felt like he was close to Lynn, though – there was still hope. Trent ran as though his life depended on it, but no matter how hard he pushed, the shapeless light was quicker than he was. How much time had passed? Where was he?

Trent felt increasingly weighed down as he continued on, but it wasn't just pressure that was holding him back – it was the feeling of pins and needles running through his arms and legs. The longer he ran, the more painful it became. He yelled, screamed for Lynn, but she didn't stop moving. Suddenly, amid struggling, Trent noticed that Lynn was at a lower angle than him. He had an idea. Even though he couldn't see the ground he was standing on, maybe this would work. It was a split-second decision, based on a wild thought.

He jumped.

A jolt in the pit of his stomach left him unable to scream. He was so scared, the sound caught in his throat. His feet hit pavement, and suddenly the world lit up around him again.

"Jesus Christ, Trent! What the hell? I told you not to follow me!" Lynn screeched as Trent landed right in front of her.

Trent took a moment to figure out his surroundings. When he finally realized he was standing in the hospital's parking garage, he sighed with relief. Lynn was looking every which way, probably making sure that nobody had seen her yelling at thin air.

"If I could hug you right now, I would. You don't know how hard that was."

Lynn glowered at him.

"Trent, you can't just—"

"Sorry, really, I didn't have time to explain! I couldn't stay in the dark, Lynn. Before, the darkness felt like nothing – it felt weightless and lonely. But now, when you leave... it hurts."

Trent took a sharp breath in, noticing her angry eyes soften, as though she were trying to make him feel safe. Like she genuinely cared, even when she pretended like she didn't.

"Let me come with you, please," Trent continued. "I'll give you all the space you need, I just... when you're not around, this fucking darkness swallows me whole. I need you."

Lynn bit her lip. Trent's eyes darted around the parking garage, wondering what else he could say to convince her.

After a moment's contemplation, though, she finally replied, "Fine, but please don't hug me. I don't like to be touched, and a hug from a ghost isn't on my bucket list." Lynn shook her head and unlocked her beige Ford Taurus. "Well, get in then. If you can sit on the floor, I guess you can sit in a car too."

Trent grinned, ecstatic. He hadn't lost any time, and she was a lot more accommodating than she had been the first time he'd scared the wits out of her.

"Nice car," Trent commented, hoping that insignificant small talk might quell the tension after his short dramatic outburst.

"I hate the thing," Lynn mumbled as she put on her seatbelt.

"Aw, come on, it's not that bad. Does it take you from point A to B?"

"Yeah, I guess." Lynn shrugged.

"Has it ever been totalled in a car wreck which landed you in a coma? No? Then it's already better than my truck," Trent said, rolling his eyes.

Lynn snorted. "That was dark."

She pulled out of the garage and onto the road. Trent flashed her a grim smile, and then looked at the world around him through the passenger's seat window. The edge of Trent's world, where the light met the dark, formed a terrifying dome around the car. Lynn didn't shine like a lighthouse when he was right next to her, but it was easy to tell that she was the center of where the world lit up for him. The darkness swirled at the dome's edges, like a thick smog trying to move closer, making him feel like a fish in the world's tiniest moving fishbowl.

"So, where do you live, anyway?" Trent asked.

"You'll see."

Short, but never concise. Lynn was very obviously not one for conversation, while Trent felt like he needed a distraction right now – a chat to take his mind off the lurking dark. Suddenly claustrophobic, Trent moved to recline his seat. As he reached for the adjustment buttons, though, his fingers went straight through them. Lynn watched the short struggle with a smirk.

He sighed. "This is the worst timeline."

"The worst timeline? What other timeline is there?"

"Only this one. The worst one. How useless is it to have hands that listen to my brain, but can't touch anything? And how is it that I can sit in the seat, but I can't touch it with my hands? Who came up with this? What kind of creator could be so cruel?" Trent whined, raking his hands through his hair with a look of exasperation.

"The same creator who made it possible for kids to get cancer," Lynn answered flatly.

"Now, *that* was dark, Trent replied, and Lynn let out a genuine laugh. He hadn't made her laugh out loud yet, and it was nice to hear. He felt like he'd achieved a small victory against her stubborn solemn mood.

A familiar pop song suddenly came on the radio, and Trent reached for the volume knob.

"Oh, I like this song." Trent's hand went right

through the car, and Lynn laughed again at his theatrical display of disappointment. Lynn took pity on him and turned up the song herself.

"So… when your mom gets back tonight, can we go to the junkyard?" Trent asked.

He hadn't known how to lead into this gently, as it had clearly made her uncomfortable last night, but he knew he had to ask again. He regretted it instantly when her smile, the one he had worked so hard for, disappeared.

"It depends," she answered. Again: short, but never concise.

"How did you know it was his cousin's junkyard, Lynn? I don't remember saying that."

"I told you, I know of it."

This time, her tone was defensive. Her voice had morphed from gentle to gloomy – a sudden shift that he didn't like, and regrettably, was the cause of.

"Yeah, but—"

"We're here."

Lynn pulled into her driveway and unbuckled her seatbelt, clearly finished with the conversation. Trent hopped out of the car without opening the door. Lynn got out and looked over at him, brows furrowed.

"You don't have to get out. Just wait here. I'll be down in like twenty minutes."

"I don't think we can be that far apart before we're, you know, *too* far apart."

"What the hell does that mean?" Lynn asked, exasperated.

Trent frowned, knowing he was becoming a terrible inconvenience on her already burdened life.

"Okay, so, um, have you ever driven somewhere at night in thick fog?" Trent asked.

Lynn shook her head.

"It's pitch black, and even though the lights can

cut through the dark, they can't cut through the fog, so the light rays are cut off at a certain point. Like there's this giant bubble around you. Everything inside the bubble is what I can see. Everything outside the bubble is dark and cold."

Trent paused.

He had taken a few steps away from the car and gone to the edge of the bubble to describe it to her, but he didn't want to get too close or put his hand through to the other side. He didn't want to risk disappearing. Trent was vaguely aware of someone saying his name, and when he looked over at Lynn, she had a brow raised at him.

"Did you just say something?" he asked.

"No."

Trent tilted his head as his lips pursed. He could have sworn she'd said something.

"Well… like I was saying, the dark is *freezing* cold. To the point where it's debilitating… I discovered that today, while running after you."

Lynn reluctantly nodded in the direction of the front door.

"Okay then, I guess you're following me upstairs. But if you think for one second that you're following me into the bathroom, Shawking, you can freeze your ass off for all I care," Lynn mumbled.

Trent smirked, holding back a laugh as she unlocked the front door and he followed her up to her room. As Lynn's hand reached for her doorknob, she quickly pulled it back. The quick movement put her sudden nervousness on display.

"Uh, does it matter if I close the door on you for a second? I haven't really been home lately, and I know there's a mess in there."

Trent grinned at the thought of her being embarrassed to show him her room. She usually seemed so nonchalant about everything; to see her worried all of a sudden was unexpected, and he found it slightly amusing.

"I don't think so. I'll start yelling from the other side if I start disappearing into nothing." He broadened his grin, and Lynn shook her head at him before walking through the door.

He waited patiently in the hallway, twiddling his ghostly thumbs and feeling surprised, but also not surprised, that he couldn't feel what he was doing. A few minutes later, Lynn opened the door for him, and he poked his head in like a curious child. He noticed Lynn roll her eyes before walking quickly to her dresser to grab a towel and change of clothes.

"I'm just going to jump in the shower now. I'd tell you not to go snooping through my things, but I'm pretty sure you can't, so... I guess I trust you. On a technicality," she muttered and closed the door to her bathroom.

Trent's eyes slowly ventured from her bathroom door to the rest of her room. Lynn's house seemed bigger than his own from the outside, but the space felt smaller when he stepped into it. It was strangely deceiving. Trent decided to go back to the staircase where he had noticed just one photo on his way up to her room.

The front door of Trent's home opened into a small entryway, which housed at least twenty photos of himself with Jeremy and their mom. These framed memories lined the walls of all the rooms in their home. He'd become accustomed to this, so Lynn's house, with only one visible photo, was a curiosity.

To take a closer look at this lone framed photograph, he plodded down a couple of stairs before the darkness stopped him short. Trent gazed down where he knew there was a staircase, but instead saw the darkness. When his eyes lingered on it long enough, it was almost as if it moved like still water. He had to tear his eyes away from it before he became utterly hypnotized. Trent set his sights on the image of Lynn, who was laughing, with her arms wrapped around Teddy's waist as they stood in front of a tree. Their mother stood behind the tree, poking her head out as she looked over them. Everyone looked happier and younger in this photograph than they seemed now.

After a long, hard look at the photo, he peeked into the bedroom at the top of the staircase – the one just before Lynn's. This room seemed emptier; moving boxes were half-filled and random toys were placed around haphazardly, but there was still a neatly made bed with bright red and orange sheets. Trent realized this was Teddy's room. He felt a bitter pang in his gut. The room reminded him of his own when he was a child, so full of brightly coloured cars, action figures, and other toys clumsily littered everywhere. It made sense that bits and pieces were still packed away, since Lynn and her brother practically lived at the hospital.

As he moved around the space, he noticed one difference between Trent's collection and Teddy's: this room was full of colouring books. He saw one sticking out of one of the boxes, and something in his mind told him to pick it up, but when he reached for it, his hand went right through the pages. He sighed defeatedly. He felt stupid for forgetting that he couldn't reach out and grab the world. Frustrated, Trent walked back to Lynn's room.

In the corner opposite the door was her bed, with dark teal sheets and matching pillowcases. Across from that was a desk. Organized chaos. Piles of paper, only half straightened, were strewn over and around a closed laptop. In front of the desk, plastered on a small section of the wall, there were drawings, mostly of faces – quite nice-looking and nothing that Trent could ever draw. Her dresser sat in the opposite corner of the room from her bed. His eyes fell on her familiar school bag that sat atop it. The school bag made him think of all the school he was missing, and in any other circumstance, he would've been happy about that. It was surreal to be here, and yet, not really be here.

Trent looked back at her desk, enthralled by the drawings. He moved forward to inspect them closely, and was struck by the immense detail in each one. They seemed so real, but had strange proportions, like overemphasized eyes with no pupils, and large mouths. Strange, but beautiful. He'd never had an adeptness for art, but he enjoyed it. His father had forced him into sports, even though Trent had shown more of an interest in carpentry. He'd picked up a hammer and nails on his own before his father put a baseball bat in his hands. It was his father's dream for Trent to become the best pitcher on the team, and that's exactly who Trent came to be. He started young, so even when Trent began to hate his father, he couldn't hate baseball. Fortunately, he actually enjoyed baseball very much, even though it was forced. Not to mention, Adam always made baseball a lot more fun.

When Trent felt like shit because of school or home, he'd go to practice, and Adam would be the first to cheer him up. Trent was the pitcher, and Adam was the catcher. Over their several years of playing together, they had sort of developed a secret language.

Trent carefully took a seat in Lynn's desk chair, unsure if he'd fall through it. When he didn't, he spent the rest of his alone time scanning her drawings with a gaping mouth until a voice startled him out of his trance.

"You okay over there?"

9

STOCKHOLM SYNDROME

SUNDAY, SEPTEMBER 29, 2019

07:37 AM

Lynn kicked aside the pile of clothes she'd stashed in the bathroom just moments ago before getting into the shower. She spent the next five minutes under the running water, zoned out, furiously scrubbing her skin and shampooing her hair as if she were trying to clean herself of some kind of pheromone that attracted ghosts. After she was finished, she stepped out of the shower to grimace at herself in the mirror. She immediately threw on a giant t-shirt and a pair of shorts. It was easier not to look at her body. Today, though, she felt like she had to look somewhat presentable, so she reluctantly turned back to the mirror and stared at herself. She gently pulled at the eye bags she was sporting as she sighed at her reflection. Nothing new to look at; her hair needed cutting, sure, but she was still the round-faced, small-framed Lynn Avison she'd always been. Probably not good-looking enough to ever be found attractive by the athletic Trent Shawking. But wait – why on earth would she even care? She wasn't trying to impress him. He was a freaking ghost, and his body was in a coma. She was just trying to look presentable. Lynn shook her head at herself and put her hand to the doorknob.

I hope he doesn't think I look like shit, even after cleaning up.

Lynn quickly pulled her hand away as if the doorknob had bit her. Why did she just think that? Why was she suddenly caring so much about what he thought of her?

Lynn huffed, attempting to brush off her anxieties about how she looked… and about Trent. She chalked them up to exhaustion, and walked out of the bathroom to find Trent sitting on her bed, staring in awe at her drawings. For a moment, she watched him, wondering what he was seeing in them. When she looked at any piece of art she enjoyed, she was always searching for the technique and revelling in its beauty. Art always invoked an unspeakable wonder in her, and it was fascinating when she saw other people staring at artwork with the same wonderment.

"You okay over there?" she asked, not really wanting to break his concentration but knowing that they had to get going.

Trent shook his head lightly and looked over at Lynn, seeming nervous, before quickly looking away. Her heart suddenly sped up, and she pulled down her shorts a little more, concerned that her giant t-shirt maybe made it look like she wasn't wearing anything underneath.

"You have a tattoo?"

Well, at least he wasn't looking at her eyebags.

"Yup," Lynn answered, hoping that would be his only question, although she was quickly realizing that Trent was not the quiet type.

"Your mom let you get a dagger tattooed on you?"

"Nope."

"Aren't you still seventeen? Isn't it illegal? Which shop let you do that?"

"I did it myself."

"Why?"

"It's my superpower."

"Huh?"

"If a guy gets too close, I can make it real," Lynn glared at him and crossed her arms over her chest, hoping that would scare him out of leering. She knew Trent was asking why she'd tattooed herself, not about her choice of a small dagger just above her knee, but she felt reluctant to comprehensively answer his every question.

He looked back at the drawings. "These are really good."

Is he just saying that to be nice?

"Thanks."

"What else are you into?"

Lots of stuff, but you wouldn't care.

"Not a lot," she lied.

"You don't talk much."

You make me nervous for some inexplicable reason I haven't figured out yet.

"There isn't much to talk about."

"What if I want to get to know you better?"

Yeah, right.

"You don't want to get to know me."

"Yes, I do. Why would I say it if I didn't?"

Because you have no other choice.

"No, you don't, Trent. You're quite literally in a Stockholm Syndrome situation. I'm the only person you can talk to; you've been forced into this by some strange cosmic event. You don't *want* to talk to me. I'm just your only option."

"Okay... you have a point. But what if it's for a reason?"

See, you're just stuck with me. You don't want to be here.

She glared at him.

"So, you're one of *those* people?" she said aloud. "You think tragic events happen because we need to find some kind of deeper meaning in them?"

Lynn felt a sadness in the pit of her stomach, hurt by Trent, even though he wasn't saying the wrong things. If she was honest with herself, Lynn was hurt by the things that Trent hadn't said. She wanted him to say that, if he had a choice, he'd still choose to be here with her. No matter how nice he was being now, her instincts told her that he would leave the minute he got the chance. Not that she could even blame him for that – she hadn't wanted him here in the first place, and it was a little shocking that she was suddenly feeling this way now.

She watched as his jaw clenched, but she couldn't quite read the expression on his face. For a moment, he looked as if he was going to be angry. His brows furrowed, his mouth pulled back, and then she saw him frown slightly. She realized he wasn't angry; he was sad and confused.

"Trent, you remind me of a kid who doesn't know what's best for himself because he hasn't been burned by the stove yet."

I wonder if that's why you're here. Maybe I'm the one who has to burn you.

"Why? Because I'm not a cynic, like you?"

"Exactly."

"So what're we supposed to talk about? The fucking weather I can't feel?"

"I could describe it to you." Lynn shrugged along with her sarcastic remark.

"I don't know why you're so closed off."

"That's just a nicer way of saying that I'm difficult."

"I didn't say difficult. Closed off isn't difficult. It's just frustrating, I'm standing here—" both of them looked down at Trent's transparent body. Lynn raised a brow, and Trent shook his head frustratedly. "...Kind of. I'm kind of standing here, okay. Either way, I'm here for whatever reason, trying to get to know you, and you don't want to let me in. I know I probably have a certain reputation; I'm the dumb jock. My name is in everyone's mouth when they talk about baseball, but they couldn't give two shits if I disappeared. I have, like, one friend who I've known all my life, who is the only guy I trust other than my brother, and my brother hasn't even wanted to talk to me lately. The friends I thought I did have are apparently the cause of all of this. It'd just be nice to maybe make another real friend, before..."

Oh, yeah. You might die, if you're not dead already.

Lynn looked to the ground, her cheeks suddenly red as she remembered the harsh reality of Trent's situation. Great. She was being a total bitch to a guy who was just trying to live out whatever life he had left. She knew she was selfish and stubborn, but she'd never realised it was this bad – seeing her attitude directed towards an actual ghost really put her behaviour into perspective, and it was embarrassing to say the least.

"I'll be waiting on the other side of the door when you actually want to open it."

Trent shook his head before walking out of her bedroom.

"I would close the door to make my point, but I can't," he muttered, and Lynn almost chuckled.

Despite herself, she thought his self-awareness was cute. He was a lot more eloquent than she'd ever thought he'd be, for one thing. And it bothered her that he was right – she'd only ever thought of him as the perfect jock prototype, and she was finding it hard to process that he could be more than that. How strange to finally see him be so human, when he wasn't really human at all right now.

Lynn collected the rest of her things and slipped on a pair of sweatpants. She walked out into the hallway to see Trent sitting with his legs crossed, his head resting back on the wall. He had been glaring at the ceiling until Lynn hovered over him, and he looked up at her miserably. She couldn't tell if his eyes naturally had that puppy dog look to them, or if he was doing it intentionally to soften her up.

"You make a compelling argument, Shawking. I know I can be a real bitch, but I'm not used to someone asking me as many questions as you do. Honestly, I still haven't really processed the fact that you've been dropped into my life for some *'reason'*." Lynn air quoted the word, and Trent grinned slightly. She was trying her best to say this nicely, and she interpreted his smirk as recognition that she was working on it. "Give me a break, okay? I never thought I'd be haunted by a jock. Especially one who was nice enough to ask if he could haunt me."

Trent's grin broadened, and Lynn had to hold back a small smile of her own.

"Come on, in the car, before you make me late." She nodded to the stairs and started on her way down. He followed along like the lost puppy he was.

"So, does this mean we can go to the junkyard later?"

Not fair, you already asked that one. No matter how terrible my answer was.

"My answer hasn't changed on that," she said through clenched teeth.

Soon, they were back in the car and on the road again. Trent stared at her from the passenger's seat. His eyes on her were making her more uneasy than before.

"What? Why're you looking at me like that?" she snapped.

"Do you have a favourite movie, Avison?"

"Um… I guess."

But for some reason, you're stressing me out so much that I can't think of one right now.

"This would be the time to tell me what it is." Although Lynn was looking at the road, she could practically feel him smirking again.

She bought some time to figure out an answer. "Hey, that's not what you asked, and it's hard to narrow it down to one. I have several favourites in different genres."

She glanced over and saw Trent looking at her inquisitively.

"Okay, fine," he said. "What's your favourite kid's movie? And no, I don't mean your favourite movie as a kid. I mean, if you had to watch a kid's movie today, that you would actually enjoy, which one would it be?"

Lynn grinned despite herself.

"It's a toss-up between *Charlie and the Chocolate Factory,* or *Atlantis.*"

"Those are so different from each other. *Atlantis?* So, you're a *real* nerd?

"What makes that movie nerdy? You know what, better yet, why did you say that like it's a bad thing?" Lynn asked, aghast as she held back a grin at his outrageous assumption.

Trent chuckled awkwardly.

"Sorry, it's not a bad thing, but I didn't get into that one as a kid, 'cause I thought it was really weird. And I'm pretty sure I was a wimp – that sea scorpion scene really freaked me out."

The way his voice came to life now that she was talking to him made Lynn want to smile just as much.

He had a way about him. He wasn't just charismatic – his charm was absolutely disarming. It took him almost no effort to change her mood. Or maybe he was putting a lot of effort into it; she didn't really know. All she knew was that she was caught under some kind of spell – a spell that made her want to talk more when she knew she shouldn't, in fear that she might say too much.

In spite of herself, she continued the conversation.

"So, what are yours?" she asked.

"Well, since you said two, mine are The Emperor's New Groove, and *Hercules*."

"Really? You don't seem like a musical kind of guy, but I guess the superhuman strength makes sense." Lynn shrugged.

"You're right. According to my brother, I can't carry a tune to save my life, but I love music…" Trent suddenly went quiet.

"Are you okay?" she asked.

Did I say something wrong?

"I just remembered something," Trent said, almost at a whisper.

Lynn found the closest parking spot in the hospital garage and turned off the car's engine before turning to him with her full attention. She waited for him to continue, not realizing her breath had caught in her throat.

"The night I crashed," Trent said finally, "I think… I was singing? I can remember really bright lights and a song playing."

Lynn glanced down at her phone – they had three minutes to get up to her brother's room before her mother had an absolute fit.

"I don't mean to rush you, but we gotta go. Tell me more in the room?"

Trent nodded before following her into the elevator and then swiftly down the hallway.

✝

"Look at you, being on time for once. That's really nice. Thank you." The condescending tone was a little unnecessary, but Lynn was thankful her mom wasn't chewing her out in front of Trent. That would be embarrassing to explain later. "I'll be back around ten tonight so you can go home and get some sleep. There will be food at home if you don't eat here."

Her mother gave Teddy a quick kiss on the forehead, and she was off. Teddy's eyes fluttered open for only a second, and then closed.

"Hey, Teddy. Good morning," Lynn whispered as she gently stroked his forehead.

He opened his eyes again and managed to smile up at her. The oxygen mask on his face shifted, and the smile faded as he fell back into sleep.

Lynn took a seat on her chair and watched as Trent assumed his place on the cot. How strange, she thought, that he had a designated spot in Teddy's room now. Thankfully, Trent seemed less zoned out than he had in the car; instead, he just looked confused. Lynn tilted her head at him, not wanting to talk right now, as she didn't want Teddy to hear her supposedly talking to herself, or her mother to come barging in again and witness her having a conversation with empty air.

"I think I was singing when I crashed. In the car just now, I had the quickest flashback, and then everything went dark," Trent said in a low tone. Lynn stared at him with a gaping mouth, and he awkwardly flashed a small grin. "Yeah, I don't know. I guess it just came to me. But I wanted to ask if, um, instead of white noise tonight, can you put on a movie? I spent most of last night doing nothing. Plus... I want to watch one of your favourites."

Lynn tilted her head at him.

"Why do you want to watch *my* favourite movies? she whispered.

"Because if you're not going to tell me anything about yourself, maybe your favourite movies can give me some insight."

Why is my mouth dry? Why can I feel my heartbeat in my throat?

Trent flashed her a small, innocent-looking grin, and Lynn fought the urge to keep staring at his smile.

"I'll see what I can do."

Shawking, you're a ghost. You have no business being this charming, and I have no reason to find you as such. What the hell is happening to me?

Caught in a shocked trance, Lynn looked down at her blank phone and felt like she had to interrogate herself. Why was she feeling this way about a boy who had previously wanted nothing to do with her until he was a ghost? She'd never really taken in her surroundings at school, but she was trying to figure out whether or not Trent might have an ulterior motive. What could he possibly want from her other than her help with finding out more about the crash? Or maybe that was all he wanted, and he was just a surprisingly good actor. If he was to get what he wanted, would he turn out to be another Raymond Hurley? All she ever saw Trent do at school was talk to the guys on the baseball team. He barely spoke out in a class, and maybe she'd made eye contact with him three times in the hallway.

But then again, maybe she was overthinking this. There was something equally as scary about the idea that, perhaps, he was just a genuine, kind person who earnestly wanted to get to know her. Suddenly, she felt awful for not doing all she could to help him. Lynn snuck a look at him again before typing a message to Nate on her phone.

Hey

He answered almost instantly. She had hoped he wouldn't answer this quickly, but she had already gone this far – she might as well go through with it.

What's up?

I need a favour.

Another one?

I need to go to Dex's. I just want someone else to be there.

Ye, okay. When?

Tonight, probably around ten or later. I'll text you. I just need a second set of eyes.

Nate wasn't stupid; he understood exactly what she meant. Usually, she never went into the junkyard alone, and technically she wasn't allowed to be there at all. Lynn and Nate usually met up outside Dex's place, where she would give him what she had collected from the hospital – a small bag left for her by Ray's 'friend in the pharmacy' on the roof's fire escape. She'd bring it to Nate, and he would take it into the Lion's Den. She was meant to be an invisible middleman. Lynn was not meant to be seen in the junkyard where the handoff took place. If anything went wrong, and the police were called, someone could get booked, and Ray had explained to her that she would be the source of the drugs to the authorities, and she had the most to lose.

"Is he okay?" Trent asked, seeing Teddy's head

begin to move uncomfortably and his brows furrow in his sleep.

Lynn got to her feet immediately and went to her brother's side.

"Hey, little man, you okay? I'm right here." Lynn put a hand to his forehead and suddenly felt sick. He was hotter than usual. "I don't know if I'm overreacting, but he feels feverish."

She hit the button for the nurse a little too frantically. Cindy, the nurse who never slept, came in at her regular quick pace with a grin.

"Hey, Lynn? Feeling better, honey?"

"Yeah, thanks, but I think Teddy might be getting a fever. Mom said to call a nurse as soon as I felt something."

"Yes, we're making sure to watch that carefully. This current round of chemo is pretty intense. This little guy is very susceptible to infection right now. Hey, hon, wake up for me," Cindy said as she put a hand on his shoulder.

She pulled out a single-use thermometer from the drawer beside his cot. After unwrapping it, she carefully took Teddy's oxygen mask off and tried to place the thermometer in his mouth. Teddy's eyes opened fully, and he looked up at Cindy, slowly shaking his head. Both Cindy and Lynn watched him curiously as Teddy then looked over at his sister.

"Who were you talking to earlier, Lynny?" His little voice was strained, but Lynn was just happy to hear him speak – a rare occurrence these days.

"It was just Mom. She was in here this morning."

"No, after that. There was a boy. I thought..." Teddy muttered, and Cindy looked slyly over at Lynn.

"You—you heard a boy, Teddy?" Lynn asked, stunned.

In her peripheral vision, she watched Trent get to his feet.

"He can hear me?"

"I don't know. I think so," Teddy said as his brows furrowed again.

"Wait, was he answering you, or me? Teddy?" Trent asked cautiously.

"Here, hon." Cindy put the thermometer in Teddy's mouth. Everyone in the room went silent. Cindy checked the number a moment later and winced at what she saw. Trent sat back down after a few moments with no response from Teddy, looking disappointed.

"You're burning up, honey bun. We're gonna get you a heavier blanket and up your fluids a little bit," Cindy said. Teddy nodded in response. "I'll go let the doctor know what's happening and grab him a different blanket," she added to Lynn. "He's going to have to sweat it out. We'll see if it's okay with the doctor to give him some medication for it. It doesn't look like he's got teeth-chattering chills yet, though. Good catch, Lynny." Cindy winked at her and gave her a reassuring pat on the back before leaving the room.

Lynn smiled warily back at her, and then looked to Trent.

"You don't think it's because of me, do you?" Trent asked.

Lynn felt like she had been punched in the gut. She shook her head at him as discreetly as possible, but his frown wasn't so reassuring. Trent sat on his cot with his arms crossed over his chest and looked worriedly over at Teddy. Lynn found herself staring at Trent as she sat back in her chair. The look of concern on his face shone with a passion she hadn't known him to ever have; she always saw him as egocentric because of how flippant he acted at school. To see him now, like this, felt oddly comforting. When Trent looked over at her and caught her staring, his brows went up.

"You okay?"

Not really. Lynn shook her head again.

"That's understandable. Your brother is in the hospital, and you're being haunted. Sorry, not sure why I even asked."

Lynn huffed out a small laugh and looked over at Teddy, whose eyes fluttered closed.

When she looked back at Trent, he was gone, and her heart hurt. She wasn't sure if he'd done it by choice or if something was happening to him – something he couldn't control. Lynn found herself in an unexpected predicament. She had to decide between staying here, when her brother needed her most, or running across the hospital to make sure Trent was still alive.

10

WRONG LEVER

SUNDAY, SEPTEMBER 29, 2019

10:01 AM

The beating in Jeremy's head had intensified, and he barely had time to think between the incessant jolts of pain. He had gone home the night before to try to sleep, but ended up anxiously falling in and out of it for six hours instead of getting any real rest. Not only was he having trouble sleeping, but he rarely remembered to eat anything. He felt like he'd forgotten how to do the bare minimum for his own survival. He was rationing the small amount of oxy he had left, since he could only really sleep when he used, but he knew going into a drugged slumber was a little too deep of a sleep even for him. He figured his declining ability to function was tied to the fact that his mind was totally consumed by anticipation for the miraculous moment when his brother might finally open up his eyes.

While he sat in the hospital chair, he had a short dream where Trent had woken up and tried to shake Jeremy awake from his drugged blackout while Jeremy watched, out of body, screaming at himself to awaken. It was so jarring, and he was unable to shake the feeling of guilt which lingered even after the dream was over.

Now that he was coming off his high, he felt particularly irritable – so much so that he had yelled at an automatic sanitizer dispenser in his brother's room when it hadn't dispensed any for him. He was glad that no one had been around to see the ridiculous outburst. It was a shame, then, that his father chose today to finally show up. He had texted Jeremy earlier that he would actually make it, and as soon as Jeremy got the text, his mother took off and told her son to message her when her ex-husband was gone.

Trent and Jeremy's father entered the room with a commanding presence – a businessman through and through. Predictably, he was dressed in a suit, with coordinating shoes and a complimentary tie. His brunette waves resembled Trent's, only they had a sleek shine to them, like he'd used too much gel. He briefly looked to the bed, where his son lay motionless, before briskly taking a seat. Brian Shawking owned a car parts company, and Jeremy had no doubt that his father would be mulling over the irony in what had happened to his firstborn.

"He hasn't woken up yet? That's a shame. He might miss next year's season altogether at this rate." Brian shot a half-smile at Jeremy, trying his best to be empathetic but failing miserably.

Jeremy grimaced at him. He hated how much his older brother looked exactly like their father. Though, there was one thing that made them different – a sincerity in Trent's eyes that their father distinctly lacked.

"Thanks for finally showing up. It was your trash car that put him in this place."

"Well, I didn't rush because you were being dramatic and made it sound like he was dying right that minute. And you can blame me all you want, but the air bags were working when I gave it to you both. What did you two do? Use them as party balloons?" Jeremy scoffed at his father's answer. It was just like him to downplay something so serious. "Look, give me a break – I'm here now, alright? It was hard enough to get here, and God, he looks rough." Jeremy rolled his eyes at his father's more than obvious statement. "Rougher than I imagined."

"Well, I'm sorry he didn't come out of a crash like you expected, but it's not like he was playing a fucking baseball game," Jeremy mumbled, and his father pretended not to hear him.

Brian walked around the bed. After a moment, he seemed to grow tired of looking at Trent this way; he patted Trent's hand and turned to leave. As Brian moved toward the door, Jeremy felt a sudden chill travel up his spine.

00:00

"Whoa, what the hell?" Trent yelled, and at the same time, he heard his brother say the same words quietly.

Trent had been hurled back to his hospital room and now he was suddenly standing in front of his brother, who was sitting in his designated chair.

"What the hell is going on? Why do I keep being

dragged back here?"

No one answered his confused exclamations. How could they? No one could hear him. Trent turned around to look at his broken figure on the bed and suddenly realised that his father was in the room too, wearing one of his gaudy suits. Trent watched his father awkwardly lift his own hand from the hand of Trent's limp body, and he let out a condescending laugh.

"That's just fucking marvellous – the first time in seven years you want to hold my hand, and you choose now when it's extremely inconvenient for me. Thanks, Pop!" Trent yelled sarcastically at him.

"Well, I think I'm going to take off, Jeremy. Keep me updated, please."

Both brothers scoffed at the same time, Trent more loudly than Jeremy. That didn't stop Brian, though; he was out the door in seconds.

"That's really fucking nice. Now I'm left here? Is the room going to close in? Am I going to have to waste another day trying to get back to Lynn? Goddamn it!" Trent yelled in frustration as he paced in front of Jeremy. He watched as his brother's eyes welled up with tears, and Trent noticed Jeremy shiver before he pulled up the hood of his sweater over his head. Trent sighed sadly and knelt down in front of his brother.

"I'm so sorry, man. I want to stay here. I wish you could hear me. I'm not going to die if I get a fucking say." Defeated by this perpetual silence, Trent huffed again, knowing his attempt was futile.

Then, Trent looked over to the ever-present beacon that was Lynn. He noticed that she was far enough away that the light looked smaller than usual. This was frustrating – what right did his father have to touch him? They were estranged for a reason. Ever since that night, Trent had wanted nothing to do with his father.

Trent was never supposed to see Brian hit his mother, but he did. His little eleven-year-old self walked in on an argument to witness a hard slap across his mother's cheek, and then her quiet sobbing. That's the reason they got the divorce. Trent didn't know if that had been the first time Brian had hit Beth, but she made sure it would be the last.

As Trent rubbed his eyes, trying to erase the image of his mother in pain, more memories of that night flooded in.

Trent remembered being dragged out of his parents' bedroom by his mother, who dashed into a sleeping Jeremy's room. She swooped Jeremy up in her arms and put both of her children in the car with shaking hands. They drove for a good three hours through the middle of the night before arriving at Trent's grandmother's house. In the car ride there, Trent remembered asking his mother why his father had done that to her. The words she had said to him then echoed through his head now.

"Anger is a monster that can get the best of us, and I hope it never finds you boys."

After that night, Trent's relationship with his father became the most painful aspect of his life. For the first few years following the incident, his mother tried not to talk about their father at all. Trent asked his mother once if they would ever see his dad again, and when he saw his mother wince, the way she had done the night Brian hit her, he never asked that particular question again. He did ask why they were living at their grandmother's, and for how long, but he never really got a straight answer. He learned to just go with it; learning to hate his father came naturally because he just wasn't around anymore. Even as time went on, and they would see each other occasionally, his father was cold and standoffish.

A few times during his baseball season, his father would show up at Trent's games. His mother let the boys know that she had issued a restraining order that required Brian to stay away from her and her sons – at least thirty feet away, to be exact, which meant that he could watch the baseball diamond as long as he stood on the road.

And so, Brian did stand on the road. The first few games his father showed up, Trent played like shit. He was preoccupied with worry about his father doing something stupid, like hurting his mother in public. The longer his father continued to spectate, the easier it became for Trent to block him out, and eventually, Trent could block everything out when he was playing baseball. He learned how to focus on the game and not on the world around him. It became like a form of therapy. Not to mention, baseball had become a constructive outlet for all of Trent's aggression towards his dad. Baseball was the ultimate distraction, but now, in this forced limbo, there were no distractions from the anger he felt towards his father. He was feeling both new anger and old buried anger all at once.

His father had just caused Trent more pain by accidentally ripping him away from the one person he could talk to when she needed a friend the most.

At this point, he had to do anything to get back to Lynn. Back to the light, where there was no pain, and the darkness was held at bay. Trent's eyes locked onto the light, with a determination only he could muster, as he prepared himself for a hike through a cold, pitch-black forest for the second time.

†

The minute Trent entered the darkness, the cold nipped at his skin. As he continued on, he began to feel pain, and slowly the intensity grew. He didn't know why, and he wasn't sure he wanted to find out. A small thought in the back of his head made him think that maybe he was feeling more pain in his ghostly body because his real body was... well, he did his best to gulp that thought down and leave it to rot in the pit of his stomach. He refused to think about that. He wanted to wake up one day; he wanted to talk to Lynn without making her cold or scaring the wits out of her. It was strange to him, how much he wished he could just give her a hug. He remembered her saying that she hated being touched, but he wondered if she'd ever been close enough to somebody to be comfortable with them just hugging her. He didn't know why he wanted to be that person so badly, but he knew this was what he felt. Whenever her eyes became sharp and defensive, he wanted to make them gentle again. He never thought someone so standoffish could be this captivating. Her light drew him in, in more ways than one.

Suddenly, every inch of his skin stung like he had been scratched with a wire brush over and over. When he finally reached the edge of the light, Teddy's hospital room formed, and he stumbled into the cot by the window. All at once, the pain he had felt subsided. He looked over at Lynn, who had a small grin on her face. Trent grinned back at her and resisted the urge to run towards her with open arms.

Then he looked over at Teddy, who was now wrapped in even more blankets than Trent remembered. The lights in the room had been dimmed; the last time he was here, it wasn't this late in the day. His grin disappeared, and he stood gaping at her, his brows furrowed.

"It's almost ten at night, so my mom will be here soon. I'll have to go home tonight. But he's not getting any better," Lynn mumbled and looked down at the floor. Trent noticed her eyes were swollen.

"I'm sorry, Lynn."

I wish I could do something for you.

"Where'd you go, anyway? Did I scare you away?" she asked. The small grin on her face told him that she didn't really think that, but he could see the sadness in her eyes.

"No, of course not. My dad visited. The man hasn't had a full conversation with me in ten years but decided to pat me on my hand. Of course, he doesn't know that it's like someone pulling a lever which flings me back to that goddamn hospital room. I just fell into the room like someone dropped me into a pit. It's terrible." Trent shook his head.

"Wrong lever, Kronk?" Lynn tried to smile as she referenced The Emperor's New Groove, but her eyes stayed fixed on the floor.

"Ha, yeah. Wrong lever." Trent smiled sadly back at her.

Every part of him wanted to hold her, but he couldn't. She looked so scared. Whatever cosmic freak event he was living through, it was robbing him of the regular human interactions he wanted to partake in. He shook himself out of that thought when he noticed Lynn open her mouth to say more.

"I thought we could go to the junkyard tonight, but—"

Trent grew excited at the words and stepped closer toward her. When her eyes widened, and she looked worriedly at Teddy, Trent instantly backed off into his corner again and sat down before she continued.

"I'm not getting out of the car if there are people around," she said quietly. "I don't like Raymond or the people he knows." Lynn raised her eyes in realisation, and then stuttered, "I—I didn't mean you, just that his cousin is a piece of work."

Trent shook his head.

"I hoped you hadn't meant me. Thanks for clearing that up."

"Lynn, what the hell happened?"

Both Lynn and Trent whipped their heads around. The question had come from Lynn's mother, who they could hear from the other side of the door. She burst through it and threw all of her things down on the cot – and, unknowingly, at Trent. He jumped up to avoid them.

"Like I texted, fever," Lynn mumbled.

"You're making sure your hands are clean before touching him, right?"

"Yes."

"Making sure all the nurses are handling his meds properly?"

"Yes."

"Then what the hell brought on a fever, Lynn Marie?"

Lynn winced at the use of her middle name and shook her head.

"I don't know. I'm sorry."

"Lynn, I'm not blaming you. I'm just frustrated."

Her mother's face seemed worn. Trent hadn't really taken a good look at Lynn's mother until now. She looked over forty and like she had never discovered what sleep was. Other than the physical signs of exhaustion, Lynn and her mother had the same face, and it wouldn't take much more than one glance to notice that they were related.

"You should go home. You have school tomorrow. Just remember, straight here afterwards."

Lynn's mother tucked the sheets around Teddy tighter and frowned before going over to sit on the cot. Lynn grabbed her stuff and said a quiet goodbye to her mom and brother before heading to the door.

"Hey, come here," Lynn's mother said. Both Lynn and Trent stopped to turn to her. "I want a hug."

Her tone was sincere enough for an exhausted

woman. Lynn hesitated, but went over to hug her. Then, expressionless, she headed out the door.

†

"So, are we going to the junkyard first, or your house?" Trent asked slowly, not wanting to upset her, but this time she didn't seem to be thrown by the question.

"In the car," she whispered, and Trent nodded, suddenly remembering that every time he talked to her, she couldn't just answer him if there were people around, or else it would look like she was talking to herself.

As soon as she opened the door to the parking garage, she did a quick scan of the area, ensuring no one was around them.

"Home first, then junkyard. But I have to make sure someone else comes, or we're not going." She unlocked the car and instantly started the engine as soon as they were inside.

"Why?"

"Because."

Maybe I shouldn't push on this. At least she finally agreed to take me to the junkyard.

"Okay." Trent looked straight ahead through the windshield.

He could see Lynn in his periphery. She scrunched up her face in confusion and mouthed the word 'okay?' to herself as she pulled out onto the road.

"And um... you'll still put a movie on for me tonight when you go to sleep, right?" he asked, feeling like he was asking for too much all at once.

"Yes, I'll put a movie on for you. Sorry, I didn't even think of it the other night. I didn't realize you don't sleep anymore."

"Well, technically, I'm in a deep sleep, so I guess this counts as dreaming?"

Lynn shrugged.

"I'm not completely past the theory of this being one big fever dream. I think we're both in a deep sleep somewhere. Probably in some government lab," Lynn said with a laugh.

"What're you, a conspiracy theorist?"

"Maybe."

"That's not a good enough answer."

"Hey, at least I'm answering you."

"Good point." They both giggled, and when Lynn parked outside of her house, Trent got out and looked back at Lynn, noticing her hesitation to step out of the car.

"You okay, Lynny?" he asked with a tilt of his head, and she glared at him for a moment, but her small grin told him she wasn't angry.

11

LION'S DEN

SUNDAY, SEPTEMBER 29, 2019

10:26 PM

"You okay, Lynny?"

Oh no, don't call me that.

Trent grinned at her, and Lynn's breath caught in her throat. Her glare at him quickly turned into a smile.

"I never gave you permission to use my embarrassing nickname."

"Aw, come on! If anything, I should be the one who's allowed to use it the most. No one else can hear me embarrass you."

Why do the ridiculous things you say make sense?

Lynn unlocked the front door and walked inside, her sights set on the kitchen, but Trent ran in front of her and began moving up the stairs. For a moment, she imagined that he wasn't so see-through, that he was a normal teenager who'd chosen to visit her house so often that he'd grown comfortable just walking in. It was a nice feeling. At least, it was, until Lynn remembered that he was technically haunting her. She cleared her throat.

"Where are you going, Shawking? I'm hungry. Follow me." She gave him a slight, yet somewhat affectionate scorn, and then shook her head before heading down the hallway towards the kitchen.

"What you gonna eat?" Trent asked as he took a seat at the table.

Lynn held back laughter as she watched Trent slowly inch his way into her kitchen chair with a look of uncertainty, as if he'd fall through it if he weren't careful. Lynn opened the fridge and looked at the greasy bag her mother had left her.

"I think my mom left me a burger."

"Homemade or fast food?"

"The wrapper tells me it's from Burger Monk."

"Nice, I love that place," Trent said with a strange passion behind his words.

Lynn placed the burger on the table and raised a brow at him.

"It's just a burger – why're you so excited?"

"I miss food."

Aw. Lynn raised her eyebrows.

"Sorry about eating in front of you, then. But I don't have a choice. You're haunting me."

"That's okay. At least it's not an ice cream sandwich. That'd really hurt me. And haunting is such a scary word. I'm not scary, am I?"

Lynn's eyes widened as she took a bite of her burger.

"You have scared the shit out of me twice, but you as a whole are not scary. You're like a giant puppy half the time."

"A puppy? Are you calling me cute?"

Wait, am I? Oh god.

Trent's sly expression warmed her cheeks, and she gulped down the food in her mouth before he did something else adorable to make her choke on it accidentally.

"I didn't say that. I meant you *act* like one. Like, brand new and innocent."

"Sure, sure."

That was embarrassing. It was still confusing to her how ordinary and attractive he was. Most guys that looked like him acted like real pricks. It was like he had a superpower he didn't know how to use. Lynn raised a brow at him as she noticed him still grinning at her.

"What's that face for?" he asked.

"Nothing, just… you seem so ordinary. It's always surprising to me, how normal you are." Lynn clapped the crumbs off her hands.

It was getting easier to talk to him, even when he made her nervous.

"Thanks, I guess?"

Lynn watched as Trent mimicked her shrug and kept his eyes on hers. There was something about how he looked at her that made her think he was waiting for something. She wanted to ask him what he was thinking, but her phone lit up on the table.

You ready?

Leaving now.

"Okay, back in the car, Shawking." Lynn looked back up at him, and Trent jumped up quickly.

"Man, you really are acting like a puppy who just heard me say the word 'walk.' Why are you so excited about this?"

I'm walking you into a fucked-up truth, possibly two if you realize why I know these people.

Trent's smile faded as quickly as it appeared, and

130

Lynn felt sick to her stomach.

"I'm not excited about it. I'm just… it's been hard not knowing. I feel like this will at least answer one of my questions."

"And are you sure you're ready for the answer? 'Cause I don't want to see you get hurt. I mean, any more than you already are."

Trent suddenly stepped closer to her, and Lynn watched as his hand almost touched hers. She noticed him come to a quick realisation though, and he sadly put his hand at his side. Her stomach did a somersault. The cold lingering around him didn't bother her anymore, but she was scared to be touched by anyone. It was overwhelming. When someone she didn't know touched her, it always reminded her that people could touch you against your will. They can touch you in a way that can hurt you, or make you feel shame. She didn't feel like Trent would be that kind of person, but she still didn't know him well enough. Any tiny motion towards her could make her feel something she didn't want to feel – even if he was a ghost, and his hand would most likely go through hers.

"That's really sweet of you, and thanks, but I really want to know. No matter what the answer is."

Her shoulders untensed. She wasn't going to fight him on this. If he was willing to find out the truth, she'd be right there with him – not just because she quite literally had to be, but because she wanted to be a friend to him. His small smile and nod felt comforting. Like she needed to know that he'd be all right for her to feel all right. She nodded back to him and headed into the car.

Lynn's stomach began turning again – this time, because she was nervous that Trent was about to find out more than she wanted him to know. She had a bad feeling about this, and she couldn't tell if it was just because they were going into a Lion's Den, or because they were going into the Lion's Den at night.

†

The drive there was a short and quiet one. Trent seemed taken with whatever he was looking at outside the window, and Lynn didn't want to disturb him.

"There it is. The lights are out. We should be able to get in and out easily enough." Lynn was trying not to sound nervous, but could hear her own voice shaking at the end of that sentence.

"Okay."

They both got out of the car.

> Are you here?

Ye, I parked a block away.

> I can't see your car.

Believe me, I'm here.
I can see yours.
What's the deal?

> I just need you to keep a lookout. If I don't come out in 5, make sure I'm not dead.

What's in it for me?

> Absolutely nothing.

Shit deal, but ok.

"I won't be talking to you. I've gotta stay quiet. Just make sure you don't lose me; if I have to run, I'm running, Trent."

"Got it, Lynny," Trent replied, and even though Lynn was scared, the nickname had an oddly calming effect on her.

Lynn went to the farthest left side of the entrance and scaled her way up the fence as quietly as she could. Trent walked through the metal like it was nothing. When she landed with a soft thud on the other side, she shook her head at him, and Trent shrugged brazenly in response.

Just because it's easier for you, doesn't mean you have to rub it in my face.

Unfortunately, Lynn didn't know her way around this junkyard, and if Ray had hidden something here, she only knew one place to look. That one spot was a lived-in shack deep inside the junkyard, and breaking and entering twice in one evening was not on her bucket list. She really didn't want to go that far into the Lion's Den anyway, partly because it was trashed, but mostly because Lynn wasn't familiar enough with the layout to move through the shadows. Lynn only knew how to navigate the junkyard by moving down the main pathway in the centre of the lot, but this was not an option, as the pathway was often used and in clear view. If she approached the shack having used the main pathway, she could run into the one person she did not want to see – especially not alone. Well, sort of alone.

As the pair made their way further into the mountains of scrap metal, Lynn checked the time on her phone. They'd entered the junkyard at ten twenty-eight, and three minutes had passed. Good. They were almost at the end of the path where they'd have to turn back, whether or not they found anything.

"Well, look who it is."

Lynn's stomach dropped. How the hell did he get behind her without her hearing? Trent jumped at the voice, and both him and Lynn did a full one-eighty.

"Holy hell, that dude should win an award for

scaring a ghost!" Trent exclaimed.

Lynn would have laughed at that if she wasn't scared for her life.

"What you doing here alone, Lynn? Got a supply?"

Lynn felt a sudden rush of panic at the word 'supply'. She could see the look of confusion on Trent's face and realized he might be about to learn something she desperately didn't want him to know.

"I'm meeting Nate."

"For what?"

"For a meeting."

"You said that already."

Lynn didn't respond but held firm eye contact. Dex scoffed.

"You're in my junkyard. Dealing with my business. I should know what's going on."

"You're telling me nobody told you?"

If I make him look stupid, maybe he'll back off.

Dex paused, and his beady black eyes shifted from left to right. When he laughed in disbelief, it gave Lynn chills. Dex had awful tattoos running up and down his arms – it looked like someone had scribbled on him while they were drunk and blind. If he'd ever wash his greasy black hair, that had been tied back into a low ponytail, he might look somewhat presentable.

"You know damn well nobody told me anything, because you're here alone. Now, tell me why, beautiful."

The word 'beautiful' felt predatory in his mouth. Trent cringed out of the corner of her eye. Lynn tried to swallow the lump of fear that had formed in her throat.

"I'm waiting for Nate. That's all. I just needed a place to talk to him about something." Dex raised a brow.

"And you thought here was the best place?"

Lynn didn't answer. It felt like an hour had gone by, but really it couldn't have been longer than two minutes. Nate was nowhere to be found, and he was usually one to be punctual. As punctual as a drug dealer could get.

After a few moments of silence, as Lynn struggled to answer his question, Dex chuckled darkly before his face hardened into a stony glare. This quick behavioural change was something he was quite good at, along with intimidation, and just like his cousin Raymond, his threats were never empty. Though Dex looked like a junkie, Lynn knew that he wasn't; he was more like Ray's short-fused bodyguard. Lynn had seen him go from calm and cool to absolutely downing a guy two-feet taller and two times bigger than him in seconds.

"Tell me what the fuck you're doing here, Avison," Dex demanded.

"All right, this guy is really starting to piss me off," Trent mumbled.

Lynn didn't want to tell Dex what was happening. It was a catch-22. If she told Dex she was looking for the car, he would wonder what she knew about the crash, and she didn't want to be involved in that situation any more than she already was. But, if she told him she was here for a drop, Lynn would owe him something – not to mention that Trent would figure out who she really was, if he hadn't already. Both of these were things that could absolutely not happen. Not in front of Trent. Not at all. She shouldn't have come here in the first place.

"I'll leave. It wasn't that important, anyway."

Trent suddenly opened his mouth to protest, but quickly shut it when he looked into Lynn's eyes. In that second, Lynn realised that her fear must be written all over face, despite her best attempt to stay cool.

"Excuse me? I asked you a question. You don't leave until I say so." Dex's lips curled into a strange grin, so disturbing that Lynn's stomach turned, but she stayed composed.

As Dex walked closer to her, Lynn backed up a bit and saw Trent step in front of her. Oh, how she wished he was a solid human being right now. As Dex continued to move closer to her, Lynn made a quick decision – she pulled out the switchblade she had stashed in her shoe, and it sprung open.

"Woah, the bitch brought a blade, huh?" Dex stopped in his tracks and put his hands up.

"And an attitude. Don't fucking touch me," Lynn sniped back, adrenaline pumping.

Trent turned to look at Lynn, wide-eyed.

"Where did that come from?" Trent asked, watching the blade, but Lynn had a feeling her words had surprised him even more than the weapon.

"Put that shit away. You wouldn't want to hurt yourself," Dex taunted.

Before Lynn could reply, a familiar voice intervened.

"Is there a problem?"

Looking past Dex, Lynn noticed Nate's umber tone in the dim light. The tip of his cigarette lit up his earth-brown skin when he inhaled from it. When she caught his eyes, he nodded to her. He was standing about ten feet behind Dex, barely visible in the night.

"No problem here. Just wondering what the hell you two are doing on my *private* property."

"Talking," Nate said shortly, and flicked his cigarette in Dex's direction with a smug smile.

Dex stepped away from the cigarette butt, which had almost hit his shoe, and glared at Nate.

"Do it elsewhere. If it doesn't involve paying me, find a different place."

Lynn had never been so happy to see Nate in her

life. Dex slowly retreated down the junkyard path back to his shack in the middle of it. She rushed over to Nate once Dex was completely out of view.

"Lynn, what the fuck are you doing? You got a death wish? What if Alex and Ray were here?" Nate's calm demeanour shifted into genuine concern.

Lynn had to look up at Nate, since he was much taller than her – six-foot-two, to be exact. His cornrows with a fade looked neater than usual. He must've gotten his braids done since she'd last seen him. The most surprising thing she noticed about him, though, was the look on his face. Lynn had never seen him so worried.

"I know."

"Yeah, well, you don't seem too broken up about it."

Lynn lifted her hand to show Nate how much she was shaking. Nate's eyes widened, and then he shook his head at her.

"Alright, so what the hell are we here for, anyway?"

Lynn's eyes shifted to Trent.

"I'm looking for something. A car." Lynn paused, pretending to think. "Hm… What kind of car was I looking for?" Lynn asked Trent, though she intentionally raised an eyebrow to feign thoughtfulness, like she was trying to remember the answer herself.

"Last time I saw Ray's car, he had a navy blue F-150," Trent whispered back, though of course, Nate couldn't have heard him anyway.

"Oh, that's right! A navy F-150," Lynn said.

Nate looked at her with bemusement.

"A whole car? You're not going to find that."

"Why?"

"Because when I came here on Saturday, there was some kind of party. Dex and his friends were smashing up every inch of this place. He got his boys to take hammers to everything, and then he used his machine to crush what was too big."

"Are you serious?"

"Yeah – look around, everything here is gutted or parts. Why didn't you just text me what you were looking for?"

"I didn't want any evidence left on my phone."

Nate shrugged.

"Well, they were probably trying to get rid of whatever you're looking for. Dex seemed pretty angry back there – he really doesn't want anyone skulking around. If I were you, I wouldn't keep looking."

"What do you mean? Why would they be trying to get rid of something?"

Nate nodded to her to follow him back towards the gate as he lit another smoke, continuing his chain for the day.

"It has something to do with that favour," he said.

Lynn quickly followed behind Nate, shoving the blade back into her shoe. She looked over at Trent, who looked sad and confused back at her.

"When the fuck did it get so cold?" Nate mumbled as they walked along.

Lynn wanted more information, but realized that she had to change the subject to keep Trent from learning any details about this favour Nate was referencing. Even though, at this point, she guessed that it was too late, and Trent had already begun to think less of her.

"Are you sure there's nothing here, Nate?"

"Yes. I'm telling you he trashed the whole place."

Lynn sighed.

"Well, thanks for saving me from a felony."

Nate snorted.

"Yeah, you looked about ready to skin him. Glad I could be of service."

†

Nate made sure Lynn was safely in her own car before he jogged down the road to his own, which was parked under a streetlamp. Trent sat down in the passenger seat, still sulking as he stared out the passenger's seat window. When Lynn was sure Nate was out of view, she started the engine and looked over at the back of Trent's head.

"Are you—"

"Okay? No, you almost killed a guy, and I'm convinced you know more than you're telling me! I'm not okay!" Trent shouted, but not directly at Lynn. Instead, his eyes were fixed on the junkyard.

Lynn jumped a little, and was too shocked to speak. She'd never heard him have an outburst. It wasn't scary or anything, it was just startling.

After a deep breath in, Trent spoke again, his voice gentler.

"Are you okay?"

"I'll live, which is a little more than you can say right now," Lynn said quietly, and Trent snorted.

"Thanks for that."

The drive home was tense. Trent wasn't looking out the window anymore, and kept his head in his hands as his elbows sat on his knees. He looked more distraught than ever, and as much as Lynn didn't want to admit it, all she wanted to do was reach out and stroke his hair, or hold his hand to comfort him. But she knew how stupid that sounded.

"Do you… do you sell them drugs, Lynn? Is that how you know them? I'm assuming that's what Dex meant by 'supply'."

Lynn hesitated. She didn't want to admit the truth, but she knew it wouldn't be hard for him to figure it out. All at once, she felt embarrassed, but she wasn't going to let him see that.

"Yes."

"Why?"

"The money is good."

"Is that all, really? You seemed pretty fucking scared of that guy. I can't believe you'd put yourself through that just for a buck."

It was annoying how easily he could figure her out sometimes. She felt as though he wasn't the only see-through one in the car.

"Please, just talk to me," Trent begged, and Lynn took a deep breath in.

He wanted her to talk, so she'd talk. There was nothing else she could do. It wasn't like she could hide from him. Lynn breathed out slowly before she began.

"When I first moved here, I was in and out of school, because Teddy was scared of the new treatments at Liberty and I had to be there for him. One day, Ray asked me why I was gone so much – why I was always missing classes, or whatever. It was a weird question. I talked to no one, and to be honest, I thought he was trying to make fun of me or something, so I just told him the truth. Told him my brother had cancer, and if I wasn't at school, I was at the hospital."

Lynn winced. Another memory she had been trying to forget flashed through her mind. She saw Ray introducing himself for the first time. When she had just moved there, she didn't know of the tyranny which so often accompanied the Hurley name. He really should have won an Emmy for his amazing performance as 'harmless nice guy'.

"He seemed like he was a friend," Lynn continued. "Like he was understanding. At least in the beginning. But after a while, he finally asked me if I could do him a favour. I asked him what the hell he was talking about. He took me to the junkyard, and

I met Dex. At first it seemed like Ray was getting me to join his cousin's drug ring, but the more I became invested in this whole thing. The more it seemed like Ray was the one running it, not Dex. Ray was the one who explained how it would all work – how, if I could get a nurse to trust me, it'd be easier to gain access to certain places, specifically the roof. He has a friend on the inside who steals from the pharmacy. That guy leaves a supply on the roof for me to pick up. I'm a mule, but I don't, like, swallow bags or anything, and I don't use. I'm invisible to everyone at the hospital now, because I'm in and out so often. Nobody would ever suspect me or think to look through my stuff." Lynn scoffed, disgusted with herself.

Once Lynn had found a rhythm, it was easy to let all of this out. Almost too easy – she was scared of just how much she was about to tell him.

"After I pick up the stash, I bring it to Nate outside the junkyard. I avoid Dex as much as possible, because he's made a pass at me before, and I'm pretty sure he's just Ray's bodyguard. I got into all of this because I wanted to help my brother. I wanted to do something for him that I had control over. I—I don't know, it's hard to explain. I don't care what you think about me, I don't care what anyone thinks. I needed to make money for my brother on my own, and this was a better opportunity than a part-time job. This made it easier to be there for Teddy and make money. No one's ever really offered to help me with anything. As fucked up as it sounds, Ray helped me with this."

"You use the money for Teddy?"

"Yes – on his meds, or any other bill when my mom's short. She thinks I'm working with some animator part-time giving him freelance drawings, like he's a mentor. She thinks I make way less than

141

I actually do, like twenty bucks or so a drawing. Meanwhile, I'm making hundreds a drop. I always give her just enough, so she doesn't suspect anything. The rest, if I have any leftover, is tucked away for Teddy. Lately though, Ray has only been giving me so much, and everything's getting so much more expensive."

"And she believes all that?"

Lynn sighed and nodded.

"And why didn't you just tell me this before coming here? Why did you risk running into him or Ray if it's this bad?"

Lynn kept her eyes firmly on the road.

"I didn't think we'd run into him."

"That wasn't my question."

"Your question was loaded, and that's the best answer I have. Haven't I answered enough tonight?"

Lynn heard Trent's sigh of frustration and immediately felt guilty.

"Fine. I didn't tell you before coming here because you're in a shit situation, and you made me want to help you. I didn't realize helping would turn into this! You're right – that guy should win an award for scaring a ghost. I didn't know he moved like a fucking ninja. And, I thought he'd be asleep or something, not outside roaming around the junk!" Lynn practically yelled the words, and then the car went silent again.

12

WHO'S THEY?

00:00

When they pulled up to the house, Lynn's car rolled to a slow stop. Neither of them moved, and Trent heard Lynn sigh deeply before she shuffled inside. Trent followed behind her this time. He was far from his usual self, eyes down at the floor, and shoulders drooped so low that his back hunched. Trent didn't want to talk anymore. He didn't know what else to say or where to start.

As they both stopped just outside her bedroom, Lynn turned to him and said, "I want to change first. Then you can come in, and I'll put a movie on for you. If you still want."

Trent nodded without looking into her eyes and stood next to the wall. He motioned to lean against it, but then, quickly realizing he couldn't, stared at the ground. Suddenly, it hit him that this would be the weirdest sleepover he'd ever had. He was here against his will, sort of, and he wasn't even going to be sleeping. The night just seemed to be getting worse and worse for him. When Lynn came out of her room, Trent heaved a sigh.

"I can stay out here tonight if you don't want me in there," he mumbled.

He knew how strange this entire situation was for her, and the last thing he wanted to do was make her more uncomfortable. Lynn had just revealed so much to him, and on top of that, he was sure that the run-in they had with Dex had shaken her up. If she needed to be alone, he'd give her all the space he could. Even if that meant sitting in this dark hallway all night, staring at the wall.

"Just because I called you a puppy doesn't mean you have to sit outside my door like one. Come on."

Bless your soul, Lynny.

"Do you still want to watch one of my favourite movies or yours? Is *Atlantis* okay?"

Trent nodded, excited to watch something finally, and then looked around her room, unsure of where to put himself. In the hospital, it was easy. Stay away from Teddy. Sit in the corner and keep your cold to yourself. Here, there was only one place to sit besides the floor, and he was pretty sure she wouldn't want him there all night.

"You can sit on my bed. I don't bite," Lynn muttered as she opened up her laptop and searched for a movie.

Trent hesitated before he sat. Not because he was nervous about falling through the bed – he had come to master the art of sitting while spectral. Instead, he felt nervous for a much more human reason: because he was a nervous boy in a girl's room. A girl he was starting to like.

He wanted to be whole again. When he was

whole, he knew how to act around a girl. He knew that he was charming and good-looking and was completely aware of how his physical strength could impress a girl when he picked her up like she was air. But with his body the way it was now, he didn't know how to carry himself, let alone how to flirt with a girl. Once these thoughts started, he couldn't stop them; he lamented everything he could no longer do. More than anything, he couldn't stop thinking about how much he wanted to be whole when he stepped between Lynn and that Dex guy. If he were back in his body then, she wouldn't have felt scared enough to pull out a knife. If he were back in his body right now, he could try to comfort her by making her hot cocoa, or bringing her something she liked. If he were whole right now… well, he would still be a whole mess of nerves in her room, because not even his confidence was impervious to a pretty girl. But at least he'd be whole.

"Is it okay if I lie down?" Trent asked, trying to pry his mind away from this flood of thoughts.

When Lynn nodded, Trent went to the corner of the bed closest to the wall and rested his head on the pillow. Surprisingly, his head did not go through it.

"Do you like… feel uncomfortable?" Lynn asked.

As uncomfortable as a ghost could be? Trent scrunched up his face.

"I mean like, do you feel like you're in pain or tired? Or anything anymore?" Trent thought about the only pain he ever really felt now.

"I don't feel pain unless I'm away from you, in the darkness. I definitely don't feel tired, and weirdly, I don't think I feel temperature anymore. You know when you touch metal, like the end of a seatbelt or something, and it's either really cold or really hot? I don't feel that on anything." Trent shrugged and then put his hands behind his head to rest comfortably on them. "I can't feel the softness of my hair, or your sheets, I just know that it's there. That probably doesn't make a lot of sense. I don't know."

"So, if you touched my hand, would you feel it?"

Are you offering? Because I really want to hold your hand, too. Actually, I'd really like to do more, but I'm literally not all here right now.

"Um..."

Trent, he thought to himself, *you can't use your physical charm here. You have to use your brain. Don't make this sound weird. Don't you dare sound creepy. Choose your words right, you dumb idiot.*

"I think I would feel it. But if I touched you to a certain point where I'm supposed to feel pressure pushing back, I guess my hand would probably go through you? That's what I think happens when I go through doors anyway."

Good. I don't think you fucked that up.

"Hm. Interesting," Lynn mumbled, and then finally found the movie.

She clicked on it and laid down next to him. Trent nervously looked down at her body inching closer to his ghostly figure. She was wearing a big t-shirt and shorts, and no matter how hard he tried to stop himself, his eyes kept falling on her dagger tattoo. It had a new meaning; when he'd first seen it, it was alluring, but now, it was giving him flashbacks of the terrible run-in they'd had hours earlier.

"Did you want to try?" Trent asked.

"Try what?"

"Touching my hand?" Trent smiled, trying to mask his anxiety.

"Uh."

Oh no, you big goof, you did it. You creeped her out.

"If it's going to freak you out like a ghost wanting to hug you freaked you out, then you don't have to."

It was a strange but pleasant surprise when she scoffed and turned to him with a determined look.

When she blew the hair out of her eyes and waited with her hand up impatiently, his face softened. He knew that look well enough by now to know she was going to prove him wrong about something, and he felt perfectly fine with that.

As Lynn impatiently held out her hand, Trent felt like he wanted to do this right. Or as well as he could in his current state. He was scared he wouldn't feel anything, but mostly, he just felt excited.

Trent slowly reached out, and cautiously tried to interlock his fingers with hers. He suddenly felt her warmth, right after he had told her he couldn't feel temperature anymore. He hadn't realised, until now, how much he missed the feeling of warmth. There was something so familiar about the feeling of their hands meeting that he just couldn't understand. Trent looked from their hands to her eyes and flinched slightly at her frown.

"That's weird. I can't really feel anything but cold. I mean, I see your hand in mine, but... it just feels cold."

Trent didn't know what to say, but his eyes never left hers.

"What?" Lynn asked.

I don't want to let go of your hand.

"Um, nothing." Trent looked down and sighed when Lynn took her hand away.

"So, I can't really touch a ghost, and a ghost can't touch me. That's a relief to know, in case I'm ever haunted by a ghost who doesn't ask nicely."

Trent gave a slight grin at her joke, but it was hard to be happy when he missed her warmth.

"Yeah, I guess," he said.

Lynn turned back to the screen, and Trent suddenly felt empty.

"Good night, Trent."

"Night, Lynny."

147

†

As Lynn fell asleep, Trent laid back and tried to get into the movie, but he was distracted when she was lying this close to him. His eyes kept traveling over to her, his focus split between the story playing out on her laptop's screen and the sound of her long, drawn out breaths. Before long, he began looking over at her periodically, watching her body rise and fall in time with the breathing. Trent decided he needed to put a stop to this before he had to start up his 'I'm just a ghost, not a vampire' mantra again, so he stood up and started pacing around her room. He was desperate for something else to look at. He considered her window, but the curtains were closed. As he reached his hand towards them, the curtains shifted slightly, as if they had been moved by a soft gust of wind.

Trent's eyes suddenly widened with an idea. He backed up to Lynn's bed and stared at the curtains quizzically before he took a leap in front of them. He hadn't touched them, and they stayed completely still. He backed up again and this time ran only his shoulder through the curtains and stopped himself before accidentally slamming – or in his case, going through – the door of her bathroom. He immediately turned to stare at the curtains again, and noticed the gentle ripple he'd caused. He smiled at this small discovery. It was nice to know he had the world's most useless superpower. Trent ran a hand through his hair and sighed while he considered what else he could do to pass the time.

The movie was still playing in the background, and he tried to ignore the scene with the Leviathan – the giant robot in the shape of a lobster. Something told him it wouldn't scare him now – at least, not as much as it had when he was a child – but he decided not to risk it. Plus, he had become interested in testing the limits of his newly discovered power.

Trent went over to Lynn's desk and peered over some loose papers. He blew down at them and then jumped back, startled, when he saw nothing move. It was jarring to go through the motion of breathing but have no air escape his mouth. But, of course, it made sense that he wasn't breathing – he wasn't really alive. That thought made him shudder. He put his hand over the papers in an attempt to mirror the curtain tactic. One swipe over them, and the papers shook ever so slightly, but didn't move from their place. He frowned, frustrated, but he wasn't one to be defeated so easily. He tried again performing sweeping motions above Lynn's desk with increasing tenacity, focusing on a piece of blank paper which seemed to be covering up something Lynn had drawn in her sketchbook.

Lynn stirred and turned over in her sleep. Trent watched her wide-eyed, hoping he hadn't disturbed her with the cold breeze he was creating. When Lynn settled again, he focused his attention back on the blank paper, which he'd only managed to move about an inch. Deciding to try something more forceful, Trent moved his hand swiftly across the top of the desk, and it went through it completely. When his hand came back up out of the desk, like a dolphin emerging from water, the blank sheet of paper finally went flying. For a brief moment, Trent attempted to catch the falling piece of paper, but was quickly left sighing in defeat. It was too easy to forget that his physicality was about as dense as a gust of wind. He looked curiously at the drawing he was trying so hard to reveal.

Is that me? The drawing was disturbingly beautiful. He'd never known his jawline to be so sharp or his wavy chestnut hair to be so perfectly placed, but this sketch made him feel quite vain. The way she'd coloured his eyes made them look like giant marbles filled with water, void of any pupils, and for a minute, he thought they might actually look like that now that he was a ghost. His thought was refuted, though, when he looked at her other drawings; the eyes in those were also missing pupils. Clearly, it was a hallmark of Lynn's style.

Trent stood and paced again at the foot of Lynn's bed. When he eventually grew bored of pacing, he went back to his spot in the corner near the wall and sighed deeply. In her sleep, Lynn was facing him, and it was even harder than before to not look at her as she slept. Trent tried to watch the movie as best as he could, but the hair which had fallen over her eyes distracted him. These loose strands of hair were like an itch he couldn't scratch – he wanted to move them away from her face. That was all. He couldn't explain why, he just wanted to. The simplest human interaction, gentle and platonic. Adam had long ago told him that this was a good way to make a pass at a girl, but Trent genuinely just did it when he cared about someone – like when his mother did it to him.

Trent couldn't stand it anymore, and reached out to move the hair away from her face. To his own surprise, his fingers made contact with her hair, and he'd actually managed to tuck her hair behind her ear. For a split second he felt peaceful, but he quickly became panicked when he noticed Lynn's teeth chatter and her brow furrow. Trent immediately pulled his hand away from her. He was learning a lot of things that night, and the rest of it went by quicker than Trent expected.

Eventually, he finally settled, and managed to keep his mind off Lynn long enough to properly watch *Atlantis* – though, given all of the distractions, the credits rolled after only half an hour. To his delight, he noticed that Lynn had secretly loaded two other movies, too: *The Emperor's New Groove* and *Hercules*. He watched them both back to back, and even though time was passing pleasantly, chief among his worries was the terrible thought of being pulled back to his room again. What would happen if Lynn wasn't in the building at all? How would he get back to the light? Being stuck in the darkness was becoming more painful each time. The whole night was spent worriedly waiting for that fateful jolt.

†

Lynn finally awoke at six in the morning, when her phone started blaring the default iPhone siren alarm. As she opened her eyes and slowly sat up, Trent stared at the back of her head. Her tousled hair was captivating, and Trent finally felt a blissful reprieve from his anxiety. He was startled when she looked back at him, and her eyes widened.

"Fucking hell. I forgot I was being haunted for a minute."

Trent looked at her, aghast.

"Wow, I'm offended. I like to think I'm pretty good at this new job I have."

Lynn shrugged and stood, stretching out her arms above her head and then turning to face him.

"Hm, I don't know. On a scale from one to ten of how haunting you are, I'd give you a solid four."

"That's all? What the hell, Avison? I expected a better score than that."

They both laughed lightly, and then Trent's smile disappeared. He had to ask before he forgot.

"If I disappear again, can you go to my hospital room?"

Lynn cocked her head at the sudden question and then shrugged again.

"Yeah, I guess if I can't find you around, I could

go stand outside the room."

"Promise?"

"Promise," she yawned. "I gotta take a shower and get ready to go. Try not to disappear right now."

"I'll try my best," Trent said with feigned seriousness.

Lynn picked up a few things and then vanished into the bathroom. Trent was left alone with his thoughts again, but they were being disrupted by Lynn's phone continuously buzzing. He stood up from the bed and took a look at the messages.

Lynn get here now.

Ding.

**You're not in trouble
I just need you here.**

Ding.

**Why aren't you
answering your phone?**

Ding.

You should be awake by now.

"Uh, Lynn?"

He didn't want to admit that he was looking at her phone like he had been snooping, but it was hard to miss the urgent messages lit up on the screen.

"What? Did you get lonely already?"

Trent could picture the smug look on her face when she yelled back, and any other time he'd enjoy the banter, but right now seemed like the wrong time.

"It's just, your phone keeps going off. It seems urgent?" he shouted back, and could hear her instantly jump out of the shower. He also heard shower products be knocked over. He hoped he hadn't made her break anything.

Lynn ran out with her hair slicked back, dripping with water. Her eyes were wide with shock, and the dark red t-shirt and black sweats that she'd thrown on were clinging to her damp body. Trent tried to look everywhere in the room except at her. It was clear to him that he was starting to find her overwhelmingly beautiful no matter what state she was in. Right now, she was gorgeous, and his feelings for her were becoming unbearable. He didn't know if it was just because she was the only one he could talk to, or if he was feeling something genuine for her – something that transcended the strange situation they'd found themselves in.

All he knew was that he couldn't act on these feelings, whatever they were. Not like this, in this state of limbo, where he didn't know whether he'd be alive or buried tomorrow.

This cosmic joke is getting really fucking old.

Lynn was immediately on the phone, calling her mother, while Trent continued trying not to ogle.

"What's happening? Oh…. okay…. did you need me to bring anything? Okay, I'm coming now, I just have to call school."

Lynn spoke with a practiced calm, but Trent could see the worry in her face. She hung up the call and immediately threw on a baggy black sweater.

"We're not going to school," she said, talking to Trent. "We have to go back to the hospital."

"What happened?"

"I don't know, but it doesn't sound good," Lynn muttered, and then started dialling their school. "Hi, this is Lynn Avison, I won't be able to make it in today." Trent couldn't tell for sure, but he thought he heard the secretary on the other end say Teddy's name. "Yeah, thank you." Lynn hung up and let out a shaky sigh. "Okay, in the car."

Trent nodded and followed behind her. It was funny, he thought, the things he missed now that he wasn't whole. In this form, he was limited in so many ways – it wasn't just that he could only see the world up to certain point, or that he couldn't travel without Lynn. Those things were difficult, but his internal experiences were even harder to grapple with. Trent couldn't smell anything anymore. He'd realized that when he was thrown back to his hospital room, and didn't suffocate on his father's cheap signature cologne. He definitely couldn't taste anything, either but it wasn't like he could eat anyway. Sometimes he felt things in his body, like a phantom racing heart or shaking hands of nervousness or panic, but these feelings were faint – as though they were just muscle memories, and he wasn't really experiencing these sensations in the moment. Right now, the sense he missed the most was smell. He tried to imagine how he'd feel if he could smell coconuts wafting from Lynn's hair like he had the first time he had laid eyes on her in class.

Wow, I actually am an idiot. Lynn is worrying about her sick brother, and here I am, wishing that I could smell her hair. Trent rolled his eyes at himself as he took a seat in the car.

"What was that?"

"What?" Trent asked.

"Why'd you roll your eyes?"

"I was just thinking something stupid."

"Tell me."

"No way."

"I need you to talk to me, please."

Trent raised a brow at her and then realized what she meant by the look on her face. She needed a distraction. She was anxious about going to the hospital right now. She needed white noise, and there was no television around that could provide it. If he was going to haunt her, the least he could do was help her. He took a deep, calming breath, and thought to himself for a second.

"Did you know that Major League Baseball players have admitted to peeing on their own hands?"

"What the hell?" Lynn asked, aghast, as she pulled out of the driveway, though Trent could see the small grin poking through her incredulous face.

"Yeah, during baseball season, they do it to toughen their grip or something. My dad told me when I was nine. I'm sure he wanted me to try it, but he didn't actually say that."

"That's so messed up."

"Yeah."

"So, you didn't—"

"God, no, but Adam almost did."

Lynn laughed, and Trent smiled over at her, pleased with himself that he could take her mind off of her nervousness, even if he had resorted to the weirdest fact in his repertoire.

"You can't talk about the weather that you can't feel, so you resort to facts about people peeing into their hands?"

"Yeah." Trent shrugged, and then stared at her blankly.

When Lynn suddenly let out a laugh, Trent joined in the laughter, noticing that hers was tainted with an underbelly of nerves.

†

The car ride to the hospital was quick. It was so early in the morning that there were barely any cars on the road. As they entered the parking garage, Trent noticed that the fishbowl of the world he could see became brighter for a split second.

"Great, a storm," Lynn breathed and quickly parked in a spot near the elevator before going into it with Trent.

The ding of the elevator reaching Teddy's floor was like the starting pistol at a racetrack, because as soon as she heard the noise, Lynn ran as quickly as she could. In the blink of an eye, she was flying through the door of Teddy's room. As Trent followed in behind her, something felt off to him. The air felt thicker. It was almost like the room's air was muggy from the storm outside, but of course, Trent couldn't feel the heat on his skin. Plus, something told him that this was more than a simple change in humidity. It wasn't painful, but there was a sickening feeling in the pit of his ghostly stomach. To his horror, when lightning flashed again, Trent noticed a small, spectral figure in the corner, sitting on the cot that Trent had sat on several times before.

Little Teddy was seated with his legs crossed, and his chin rested on his hands. When Teddy noticed Trent staring, he lifted his head slowly as Trent looked him straight in the eyes. Trent looked from Teddy to Lynn, unsure if Lynn had noticed yet, or if she would be able to see this Teddy at all. Her little brother's ghostly presence was so much fainter than Trent's; if the flash of lightning hadn't happened as they'd entered the room, Trent may have not even seen him.

"What happened?" Lynn asked her mother, who was sitting beside Teddy's bed, holding her son's hand.

"The fluid in his lungs is building too quickly. He stopped breathing once last night and I haven't been able to sleep since," her mother explained in a panic.

Lynn nodded in an impression of understanding, but her eyes told Trent she wasn't really keeping up with the words.

"Lynn, I don't want to scare you right now, but did you see the corner?" Trent whispered, and Lynn looked to the corner of the room. When she looked back at Trent and shook her head, he felt his stomach sink more. She wasn't seeing what he was seeing.

"I knew there was a boy in here earlier," ghostly Teddy said suddenly, and flashed a little smirk that reminded Trent of Lynn's. "I don't think she can see me. My mom can't either. You look kind of spooky, like me. What happened to you?"

Trent hesitated before answering.

"Lynn, please don't freak out, but your brother is in the corner of the room, and he looks a little like me right now," Trent said quickly.

Lynn's eyes went wide, and her mouth suddenly fell open as she was about to say something, but she cut herself off before she did. Her mother was in the room – Trent knew she couldn't answer. That was fine. He'd be the strange, unanswered interpreter who her mother would never hear. Trent noticed Lynn's eyes well up and watched as she dropped her body like a sack of rocks into her usual chair. Trent turned back to Teddy.

"I, uh, I got into a car crash, and my body is healing. Have you... um, have you tried getting back into your body, little man?"

"Yeah, but it hurts too much. It's easier to sit out here. What's your name?" he asked casually.

"Uh... I'm Trent. I'm your sister's..." *I know your dumb brain wants to say boyfriend, but this isn't the time to tease Lynn.* "...friend. I'm her friend."

"Heh, you mean you're her *booooy*friend," Teddy said with his eyes on Lynn.

Teddy smiled broadly, but his smile faded as he seemed to come to a realization.

"I guess, technically." Trent chuckled at the kid's pizazz, but felt a bitter twinge when he saw Teddy's saddened expression. It was a cruel fate, to be a younger brother who couldn't tease his sister directly.

Teddy was the total opposite of Lynn, with how open he was when he talked to new people. Of course, kids usually are.

"Teddy, I know it really hurts to get back into your body, but you need to try again. For your sister and your mom, okay? They're really worried, and I know how painful it is, but you just gotta hold on."

"I did, but it's broken. So, they asked me if I wanted to go away for a little bit, and wait to see everybody when it's not broken anymore."

"Wait, what? Who's they?" Trent asked as Lynn frantically typed something on her phone and then aggressively tapped it to get Trent's attention.

**WHAT'S HAPPENING?
REPEAT EVERYTHING
HE SAYS**

Trent looked up from the phone and back at Teddy.

"He said someone told him his body is broken, and they asked him to go away for a little bit, where he can wait to see everybody when it's not broken anymore. Teddy, who's they?"

"I don't know who they are. They kind of looked like my dad, but it wasn't my dad. They asked me lots of questions, and I didn't know how to answer them all yet, so I told them I wanted to wait for Lynn, and then I got put over here," the little boy explained with a shrug.

"He doesn't know who they are, but they asked him a lot of questions, and he told them he was waiting for you, and they… they put him over there," Trent repeated to Lynn, and he felt a tug at his heart when he saw Lynn trying her hardest to stop her lip from quivering. "What kind of questions did they ask you, Teddy?"

"Um…" The boy scratched his head as he thought. "First they asked me if I knew why I was here in the first place – like, in the world, not in the hospital, 'cause that's what I thought they meant but they didn't." Trent quickly repeated every word to Lynn as her little brother continued, "So I told 'em, I came to save Lynn, 'cause she tells me I'm her hero all the time. Then they asked me," Teddy rolled his eyes as if this story were exhausting, "if I was okay with leaving, because if I didn't leave now, it would happen later, and all I would feel was a lot of pain. They said if I go now, I can talk to Lynn before I leave."

LEAVE? LEAVE WHERE?

Lynn frantically typed into her phone again.

"Did they tell you where you were going?" Trent asked.

Teddy shook his head.

"But they did say I would see everyone again, it would just be a little while, and I wouldn't feel pain and I thought it would be nice. But I didn't want to leave Lynny, 'cause I'm her only friend in this new place." Teddy's eyes went wide, and Trent's went wide as well.

He kept repeating every word. Lynn listened intently in her chair.

"But if you're her friend now, you gotta take care of her when I leave, okay?" Teddy said to Trent earnestly. "And don't give her any crap." Teddy pointed a finger at Trent, so Trent pointed his own finger at himself while he copied Teddy's words. "Because Lynn doesn't take any crap, and she never gave me any crap. And she lets me say crap, but Mom doesn't."

Trent smiled sadly at the remark and looked over at Lynn. He could tell she was holding back tears, and he didn't know what to do next. He looked back at Teddy.

"Teddy, you're a cool kid."

"Yeah, I know," Teddy responded with another shrug of his shoulders, like he'd heard it before many times. "You seem okay, too." Teddy then looked over at Lynn, but his eyes seemed to drift out of focus. "They're telling me I gotta leave now. They told me I'm gonna ride the lightning—"

"Wait, no!" Trent stopped repeating the words and shook his head furiously. "Who's telling you this? Can I talk to them, Teddy?"

Teddy's head tilted for a moment, and then he nodded.

"They can hear you. They said to talk."

"What can I do to get you to stay?"

For a moment, Trent thought about what he was going to say next. Suddenly, an idea came to him: maybe he could trade places. Maybe that was why Trent was still here. Maybe this was his purpose. Trent didn't want to go, but he knew if that's what it took to keep Teddy here, he would do it. His stubbornness to stay alive had been instantly broken by this kid. Trent had no idea if he was going to make it back, anyway, and if he couldn't save himself, he might as well save somebody else, right? Especially someone as innocent as Teddy.

"Can I go with them instead?" Trent asked quickly.

He thought he would regret it, but once he'd said the words, they didn't hurt like he thought they would. They felt like they meant something.

"They said no. It's not your time to choose yet, but you'll get to choose someday soon," Teddy answered.

Frustrated, Trent walked closer to Teddy.

"Come on, there has to be something I can do," Trent begged, trying not to look at Lynn as she rocked back and forth slightly in her chair, her miserable gaze now set on the window.

It was hard to know what she was thinking when

she couldn't openly talk to him. Trent was ready and willing to jump in front of a train for Teddy right now, for Lynn, but he just didn't how to do that.

"It's okay, Trent. I'm not scared. I don't have to be. Don't forget to tell Lynny I'm okay and that I love her. She's my best friend. I'll see her later, and if I'm going to Heaven, I'll tell her if it's lonely or not, 'cause she promised me it wasn't, so if it is, I'm gonna hold it over her head. Okay?"

"No, wait!"

The room lit up with a flash of lightning, and seemingly shook with a massive rumble of thunder. Teddy's ghostly figure disappeared from the corner. Trent could hear a loud, long beeping noise coming from the machines attached to Teddy. He stood frozen in place, staring at the spot Teddy had been only a second ago.

"No, no, no, what's happening?" Lynn sobbed as she stood, and her mother got to her feet as well, pulling Lynn out of the way of the door, and hitting the button for the nurses.

Trent felt pangs in his heart. He didn't know how to answer her. He didn't know what to say because he barely understood what had happened himself. His brain was still processing what had just happened. Why did he get the last moments with Lynn's brother that he felt she so rightfully deserved?

Nurses rushed into the room with a crash cart, and Trent couldn't move as he watched the scene unfold behind him. He already knew Teddy was gone. He'd seen him disappear right before his eyes. Suddenly, among the shock and grief, a terrible fear sprung up inside Trent, as he realised that one day soon, he'd have his own unimaginable decision to make.

Teddy had told him so.

13

RAIN CHECK

09:09 PM

Lynn couldn't remember how she made it back to her car, but she knew hours had passed. Hours filled with doctors explaining that they were sorry they couldn't do more. Her mother gripping her hand like it was a life ring thrown off a sinking ship. Signing papers in a small stuffy room. Saying goodbye to Teddy's body. The nurse with the beautiful smile hugged Lynn, and both of their eyes filled with tears. When Cindy let go of Lynn, she handed her the green toy car that Antonio had left Teddy. As Lynn stared at it in her hand, it was probably the only moment Lynn had felt something stir inside her. The rest of the time spent with her brother at the hospital, she had been totally numb to all of this constant waiting for death. Then when Death had finally shown up at her doorstep, he had brought her the wrong ghost. But she wasn't angry with Trent – she couldn't be.

The whole day, she was hoping that Teddy might appear like Trent. She kept waiting to see him, an apparition, jump out at her from around a corner and surprise her like he always did for fun. She waited, but all the while, she knew deep down that it wouldn't happen. Through it all, Trent's ghostly figure was the only one by her side.

When it was finally time to leave the hospital, Lynn's mother urged her to come to her aunt's house, but Lynn decided she would go home herself. When Lynn finally ended up in her car with Trent in the passenger seat, it was nine in the evening.

Lynn took the little green car that Cindy had handed her and gingerly placed it into her cup holder. Then she looked at Trent. Trent looked back at her. Neither of them had words to exchange, only a look of mourning. When Lynn couldn't look at Trent any longer, she put both hands on her wheel. Eyes forward, jaw clenched, her knuckles turned white from how hard she was gripping it. She felt like she was going to cry, but the tears never came.

Lynn hit the top of her wheel with her fist so hard that it startled Trent. He jumped slightly, but his face quickly resumed the sullen stare he'd worn all evening. Lynn wiped her eyes roughly with the back of her sleeve. Still, not a tear had dropped, but they had begun to well up. She put the key in the ignition and started the car.

"Sorry," she said.

Lynn was sorry for more than just a small angry outburst. She was sorry for things she hadn't told him yet.

"Don't be. If I could cry like that right now, I would," he mumbled. "Teddy wanted me to tell you he loves you, and you're his best friend... and something about whether or not Heaven is lonely, and if you lied to him, he's going to hold it over your head. I just couldn't say it while I was trying to get him to... you know. *I'm* sorry. I'm sorry I couldn't get him to stay. I hoped that if I could do one thing for you, it would be that."

"What?" Lynn looked at him, absolutely devastated.

She knew what he meant, but she didn't want it to be true.

"If I could've traded places with him, I would have done it. If I could have done one thing before I... leave... I would've wanted it to be that."

That did it. Now he was really going to make her cry.

"Trent," Lynn began with a shaky breath.

He was infuriating in the worst way. He was so sweet he hurt like candy to a cavity. Trent was truly the sugar-coated confection, and she was the decaying rotten tooth. She tried to hold back a broken sob, but it escaped her anyway, and now she was half crying, half talking.

"That's not what I would've wanted at all," she continued. "I knew this day was coming. They've been telling me to expect it since he was five. As much hope as I may have had, it didn't... it never meant anything. I can't tell you how much..." Lynn looked away from him. "How much..." Lynn bit her lip hard – she knew she shouldn't say it, but there were no other words to describe how she felt. "...How much I love you for trying to switch places with him."

Her breathing suddenly slowed, but her heart was hammering against her chest. She'd never said that to anyone else but her family. Not even to any of her friends at her old school. She'd never been close enough to anyone for the words to feel comfortable, or the sentiment to feel genuine. Her sobbing eased up.

"But you're not allowed to die," she finished with a determined decisiveness. "I can't lose another friend."

Lynn held back her tears then, because she knew they would be selfish. Trent had almost traded lives with Teddy because he thought he was doing a beautiful thing for someone he owed a great debt, but he still had no idea what role she had played in his own terrible fate.

Lynn finally worked up the strength to drive out of the parking garage.

"I love you, too, Lynn," Trent mumbled as he looked out the window.

I wish you didn't, for your own safety.

"And I'm not going anywhere. If I can help it," he added.

And if you do, I'll chase you there and try to switch places with you.

The ride home was quiet. Lynn wasn't crying anymore; she was numb again. Truthfully, she was trying to forget that her brother had just died so she didn't have to spend the whole night weeping. What a stupid thought. To think getting through this would be as simple as forgetting. To think she would ever stop missing her brother for the rest of her life. Her father being dead was one thing. She always thought of his absence at pivotal points of her life, but she never really knew him. By all means, it wasn't easy to miss her own dad, but it was easier to handle than this, because she knew Teddy. She knew him better than she'd ever known anyone else. She'd taught Teddy how to talk, go trick-or-treating, and even how to tell jokes. The memories stung like wasps. And each time one would hit, it would bring on another that felt just as painful.

†

Once she'd gotten them home and they'd stepped out of the car, the sky started up again. The rain was coming down in buckets and soaked through her black sweater.

Lynn walked jaggedly through the front door and looked around the house slowly. More wasps started stinging her brain.

"I can't be in here right now."

"Come on, you need to get into dry clothes. You should eat soup or something, you haven't eaten all day," Trent urged her, but Lynn stood at the door looking around the house as if she were a stranger in her own home. "If you just want to put on a movie and try to relax, I'll stay as far away from you as I need to so you can feel warm," he added.

"No," Lynn said, and started walking towards the back door beside the kitchen table. She stepped outside onto the deck and lay down on the worn red wood slats, back on the ground, face to the air. The storm unleashed its madness unto her, and she looked up at the sky with total understanding as the world cried buckets.

"Lynn, you're going to get sick," Trent cautioned as he looked down at her.

The rain was cutting through his ghostly figure. Every drop which fell through him glistened brighter. He looked like a strange refraction of light in the night's storm, like a rainbow with no colour. Everything about him was so innocent and pure. He was everything she wasn't. All that time, she had thought he was just some selfish womanizer from her school. She wrote him off, because that's what she did to everyone – she didn't want anyone to get close to her, so she demonized everyone she came across. Even on that first day which Trent had described, when he'd asked her for a pencil. She remembered that day, and a small voice in the back of her head telling her that maybe she should just try being nice to someone for once. Maybe if she were just nice, this person would be nice back, and for a moment she wouldn't have to be alone. She had wanted to talk to him in that first instance, make a joke even. She remembered wanting so badly to just talk to someone that day to get her mind off everything else going on in her life. But when presented with an opportunity, she hadn't taken it; she'd ignored it, that little voice. Instead, she'd immediately put Trent on a list of all the boys at school who reminded her of Ray, and left him there.

Now that she knew him, he'd effortlessly proven that he was nothing like Ray. Nothing like him at all. She hated herself for ever thinking anything like that about Trent.

"I don't care," she breathed.

Lynn just wanted to lie there for a bit and let the world cry for her. She closed her eyes and inhaled deeply. She patted the deck beside her, inviting Trent to sit. He sighed and sunk down. As soon as he did, she moved her hand closer to him, palm up.

"Please hold my hand."

"I thought it just felt cold?"

"It does, but I… I just need…"

Lynn closed her eyes. She couldn't bear to see his reaction, and she didn't want to. She just needed him right now, and she didn't know how to say it. She hadn't told him that when their hands had first met, she'd immediately felt a chill run up her spine and butterflies take flight in her stomach. Despite the blistering cold of it, she could still feel his hand's shape. When he interlocked his fingers with hers, the gesture was oddly comforting – but so precarious. Like if she wasn't looking at his hand in hers, all it would feel like was a simple breeze or temperature change.

Her face must've been writhing with emotion as she felt him gently put his icy hand on hers, and she was thankful that she didn't have to find the words to convince him.

"If you wanted to go swimming, we could've stopped at the lake."

Lynn could hear the subtle hint of a smirk in his voice, and she finally opened her eyes to look up at him. But he wasn't smirking at all. He was still as miserable as she was. He was just trying to make her laugh, or at the very least, make her want to cry less. All he ever wanted to do was lighten the mood. All he ever tried to do was help. There was no reason for him to be this nice to her. He was trapped and dying, and it had been all her fault. She couldn't live with this lie any longer; she couldn't live with herself anymore.

"If you weren't here right now, I'd probably have driven into it instead of coming home."

Lynn regretted the words as soon as she said them, but only because she could tell what she said had made Trent furious. The words were true. Her brother was dead. She didn't know how to stop collecting drugs for Raymond and Dexter Hurley, even though she wouldn't need the money anymore. She thought she'd be in jail one day, if the Hurleys didn't kill her first.

"Don't say that." Trent's brows furrowed, and it seemed like he tried to squeeze Lynn's hand. When he realised he couldn't, he took his hand away from hers and put it on his chest.

"Why would you say that to me?" Trent said, a solemn anger in his voice. "Why would you want to switch places with me? Do you want to be the ghost? Because it's not all it's cracked up to be, Avison. I'd trade walking through walls to be whole again. To be able to hold your hand for real."

"No, you wouldn't." Lynn sat up as she said it.

"Why would you want to die? Tell me right now – give me one good reason."

"Because something awful happened to me when I was young, and my brother saved me from that. Now he's dead, and I have to live with the fact that you might die, too, and it's all my fault. Everything is my fault."

"Why? Why is it your fault?" Trent didn't sound angry anymore, just demanding, but his face stayed contorted in a fury.

He was probably fed up with how numb she was all the time. How she could say all this with little to no emotion. That would change in the next few seconds.

"Because I'm the one who told Nate to make sure he got my money this weekend. Then he told Ray, and Ray fucked you and your brother over. I didn't think he would do anything this fucked up, but he did. He was supposed to scare your brother into paying what he owed, not kill you. Your brother is the one who owed Nate money, Trent. That means that I didn't get my cut either, and I was pissed. I didn't want to tell you, because it was obvious you didn't even know Jeremy was buying drugs. But now you know. I'm the fucked-up reason you're here. You wanted a reason; this is your reason. You should want me dead. My stupid decision landed you here, and now—" *I'm in love with you.* Lynn stopped herself before she said it. The words confused her as much as they scared her. Being in love is different than loving someone for what they did for your brother, and she couldn't tell if she was confusing the two. There was as much of a storm going on in her head as there was outside. She took a quick shaking breath in. "I—I'm scared. I'm scared of everyone and everything… I just want to die."

Lynn was finally, properly crying now, as she let all of the words she swore she'd never say to him fall out of her mouth. His face evened out slowly as he looked anywhere but at her. She couldn't read his expression, but she already knew that he hated her. She already knew that if he had the choice, he would leave her here right now. Leave her drowning in thoughts, drowning in the rain, sinking into the depths of an ocean as blue as his eyes, like a beaten little sailboat after a storm had swallowed it. When Trent looked back at her, he stared into her eyes with some sort of intense determination, but still, she couldn't tell what he was thinking.

"Lynn..." he said gently, but she was waiting for the sting of his words.

She was waiting for his voice to change, for a loud sound like the crack of thunder in his yell. He was going to be angry with her. She was just waiting for it.

"I could never want you dead," he said. "Never. Please don't say that ever again. Okay?"

Confused, Lynn furrowed her brows and wiped her face with the back of her sweater, even though her soaked sleeve wasn't very effective at drying her cheeks.

"What? Why aren't you yelling at me?"

"Why would I yell at you? You can hear me, can't you?"

"Aren't you angry with me? I'm the reason you're here."

"Good," he replied without hesitation.

Lynn was so flustered at his response that she rose to her feet as quickly as she could.

"What do you mean, 'good'? You might die because of me!"

"I'm not dead yet, and I won't die if I have any say in it. If I die, I'll be mad at you then. Who knows, maybe then I'll come back as a mean ghost and haunt you for real." Trent shrugged and stood up, too. "It's good that I'm here, because according to you, you would have been at the bottom of the lake if I wasn't." Trent ran a hand through his hair, clearly on edge, and then sighed. "I know you weren't thinking straight. You weren't thinking about the consequences. You would never hurt me on purpose. Right?"

Well, obviously, but—

"I'm not angry with you. I have no reason to be. You can't change your decision, but I know you would if you could. Wouldn't you?" Trent looked into her eyes, and Lynn's burned with more tears.

"You can't be... there's no way in hell you're... this perfect," Lynn mumbled as her eyes looked everywhere but at him.

"What was that?" Trent asked.

"What if I said no? What if I said I wouldn't change my decision?" she snapped, and then regretted her words immediately. If she were honest with him, she would just admit that she was trying to find his breaking point. But Lynn was pushing at a non-existent limit. As impossible as it seemed, she couldn't find an angry bone in his body.

"Would you really mean it?" he asked calmly.

Lynn glared at him, but it only lasted seconds. Her face softened and she shook her head. Trent turned to the door and walked through it. He beckoned her to come in, then mimed that he had a towel and was drying off his hair. Lynn sighed and followed him in. The warmth of the house hit her at once, and her teeth started chattering.

"Please get into dry clothes."

"What makes you think that's a good idea?" Lynn said, her words distorted by the chatter.

Trent smirked at Lynn's sarcastic response, and

Lynn felt relieved at the moment of levity.

"Oh, I don't know. Just a hunch, I guess."

As Lynn walked through the kitchen to the stairs, she stopped and swivelled back around to grab a box of Cheez-It crackers from the pantry. She took out the bag and tilted her head back, letting the crackers fall into her mouth like liquor from a bottle. As she chewed on a mouthful of crackers, Trent watched her, smiling.

"You sure that's all you need? You don't want to make a sandwich or anything?"

She gave him a weird look.

"Why?"

"Might make you feel better to eat something that's good for you?"

"These can't be all that bad. I'm sure there's a vitamin in here somewhere."

Trent gaped in disbelief.

"I don't even think those things are made with real cheese, Lynn."

"It says 'made with real cheese' on the box. Man, out of all the ghosts to be haunted by, I had to get Officer Health-Conscious."

Lynn shook her head and opened the fridge to get a can of Diet Coke.

"Any objections to this, sir?"

"Yes, but you know what, ma'am?" Trent said in a dramatized Southern drawl, tipping an invisible hat on his head and slipping his thumbs under his belt, like an officer approaching a car. "I'm going to let you get away with it, just this once, because you're having a bad night."

Lynn half grinned. She wanted to laugh, but didn't. She felt like her laugh was broken. Even though Trent was helping her not dwell on the fact that her brother had just died, she felt like she wasn't allowed to laugh or smile anymore. Like that was some unspoken rule of death.

Lynn headed up the stairs and stopped at the top, where her gaze fell upon Teddy's room. She didn't know how long she'd been staring when Trent stepped into view. She hugged the bag of crackers to her chest as if she were protecting them.

"Hey, Officer Health-Conscious here, reminding you that you should put on dry clothes," Trent gently urged, then watched her carefully. Lynn glared at him for a moment but then looked down at her feet.

She didn't mean to direct her anger at him – she was actually angry at that room.

It was going to be empty now. Forever. Not just while Teddy was in the hospital. Lynn looked into Trent's eyes for a moment. She didn't have the words, but she was thankful that he was here, in whatever strange way he was. Although, while she was grateful for his company, she definitely didn't feel like she deserved it. He was too good. A small voice in the back of her mind told her that he didn't actually forgive her for what she had just admitted to him. That small voice made her think he was just trying to make the best out of a bad situation, and she kept her eyes on the ground as she shuffled to her room.

Lynn walked over to the desk next to her bed and gingerly placed her beloved snacks down.

"Can you—" Lynn began, but Trent had already gone to the far side of her bed, laid on his stomach and covered his head so he wouldn't see her undress.

"Thanks," she muttered.

Once she had changed into a dry baggy sweater and pants, she took a seat on her bed and hesitantly put a hand on his ghostly back. She didn't feel anything but cold, but he raised his head slightly.

"Uh, is that the signal that you're wearing clothes?" he asked, and Lynn smiled slightly.

"Yeah, I'm done. And sorry if the touching freaked you out, I just wanted to see if you could feel it."

"It's okay. You're warm."

As he turned to lay on his back, Lynn noticed that Trent's face looked unnaturally calm.

"I thought you couldn't feel temperatures. And I'm not even warm – my hand is freezing." Lynn shivered unintentionally at the thought of her icy palm.

"That's weird. It felt nice." Trent shrugged and then suddenly sat up, nervous. "Hey, if you're too cold for me to sit here, I'll stand by your door and watch videos while you sleep."

"No, stay where you are," Lynn breathed, and got under her covers beside him.

"Yes, ma'am." Trent saluted her like a soldier and then lay back down.

Lynn chuckled lightly at the playful gesture. He was so cute sometimes that she didn't know how to react – whether he was trying to be or not, he was annoyingly good at it.

"You need to stop making me want to smile when I'm sad. It's confusing my brain."

"I can't stop. I make people happy, effortlessly." He grinned.

Yeah, but what if you die next? Then who will make me smile?

The thought made Lynn's momentary happiness disappear, and she turned to her computer. She put on a playlist of movies, this one different from yesterday's.

"Are we watching your favourites?" Trent asked.

She lay down on her side to face the screen and not him.

"These are Teddy's favourites. This is his happy playlist. He'd make me play it after a bad day of long treatments. Or when he was in pain and needed to take his mind off of... everything. He loves... I mean... he loved this playlist. Never wanted it changed, just movies added. But it always starts with *Mulan*. Because he couldn't wait to hear the song 'I'll Make a Man Out Of You'."

"That *is* a pretty good song."

"Hey, Trent?"

"Yeah, Lynn?"

I can't bear to lose you.

"Please don't die."

"I'm trying my best not to."

Lynn saw the corners of his lips inch up lightly in the reflection of the computer screen, and she closed her eyes hard. The vision in her mind of him smiling now lived alongside the vision of him broken in his hospital bed. Like a ticking timebomb.

"No. Just... don't," she demanded. "Tell me you won't."

Her eyes stung again. She didn't know if she was crying because of the movie and how it reminded her of Teddy, or over the idea of Trent disappearing for good. It was probably both.

"Lynn, look at me."

When she didn't oblige, Trent got up and walked around to face her. He got so close to her face that when he knelt down between her desk and bed, the cold coming off of him made her shiver.

"If I have any say in my own death, you'd better believe I'm gonna say I don't want to die. I never did. If I die, it's going to be for a greater good, not by accident. Not like this." He sighed and looked to the ground. "Now that I know you, I have even more reason to stay here, because I can't wait to get back to you when I'm not so see-through anymore."

Lynn stared into his eyes. She'd never seen such determination. She had so many fears, so many questions for him, but his fiery look was oddly calming.

"I really want to kiss you right now," Lynn whispered.

The words left her on a shaky breath. She was both glad to have told him, and regretful that she wanted to kiss him at all. She didn't think she deserved that. He was far too good for her. Lynn watched as his fierce eyes lit up, and a small grin played across his lips.

"Same here..." Trent looked down at his feet again, then stood up and scratched his chin. "Rain check?"

Lynn smiled, despite herself, and nodded.

MONDAY, SEPTEMBER 30, 2019

11:44 PM

"That's why you called me here this late? Avison?" Ray asked.

"Avison," Dex responded.

"Why the hell would Avison come here? I told her no drops in the yard."

"That's what I'm asking you, fuckhead. We can't have her here, she'll cause problems. You should've picked someone else."

"I was told to pick her," Ray grumbled.

Raymond Hurley had been raised by his father to be a businessman with the thought process of a politician. Networking, networking, networking. It's all about who you know, and who you say yes to. So naturally, he had to say yes to his father's every request. Mortimer Hurley had power and influence, and he also paid for Raymond's extravagant lifestyle. As conflicted as Ray felt about his father's choices sometimes, he knew blindly saying yes to him would get him further in life than pushing back ever could.

He could still remember the day his father came to him, asking about the moody new girl at school. Ray was confused about how his father had even heard about her, but somehow, she came up in conversation around the dinner table.

"Yeah, I still think your dad's an idiot for that one. I think she was here looking for something."

"Looking for what?"

Dex pursed his lips, and Ray suddenly realized what he was alluding to.

"Why the hell . . . ?" Raymond's voice trailed off, and then his eyes widened with concern. "She doesn't know anything about that. Does she?"

"She comes here after the weekend it happens to skulk around in junk? She has to know something, Ray. Like you said, why the fuck else would she be here? And I think she brought your gofer with her to help. I told that fag to stay out of here unless he had business when he showed up. With that skin colour, he'll bring cops here faster than I would if I was waving a gun around."

Ray internally recoiled at Dex's bigoted comments. It wasn't Ray's place to critique Dex, so he kept his disdain to himself. Compliant with his older cousin, as usual.

"Okay, okay – fucking cool it, dude. I'll talk to her."

"Yeah, good luck. She barely talks."

"Whatever. I'll talk, she'll listen. She doesn't want to fuck us over. I know what kind of state her brother is in. She has too much riding on this."

Dex shook his head and waved Ray off before turning into his old home in the middle of the junkyard. Ray sighed and headed back to his car, where Andrea was waiting in the front seat.

"Did he get rid of it?"

"Yes, Andy."

"But like, *really* get rid of it? He's not selling parts, is he?

"Andy, when I tell you he got rid of it, I mean it. He got rid of it. Now stop asking. Find Avison's number, and text her from *your* phone, not mine. Tell her we're coming to her house."

Ray demandingly threw his phone onto Andy's lap.

"What the fuck? Why?"

"She's the reason Dex called. I need to have a talk with her."

"Why do you even have her number in your phone?" Andy sounded jealous, and Ray rolled his eyes.

"She's the source, Andy! Just text her. Why do you have to argue about everything?"

"Because you give me a fucking reason to," she mumbled as she searched through his call list.

Ray sighed and sped off down the road to Lynn's house.

TUESDAY, OCTOBER 1, 2019

12:09 AM

Ding.

Pick up your phone Avison

Ding.

Come to your door.

Ding.

I can stay out here all night

"What the hell?" The words slipped out of Trent's mouth as he jumped, startled.

The ringtone had caught him in the middle of watching the movie Up. A pleasant experience quickly turned into a traumatic flashback. His heart sank. The last time Lynn's phone went off like this, it wasn't for a good reason, and now it was happening all over again. Trent looked down at Lynn, who had managed to fall asleep after a few hours of restless tossing and turning. She was facing him now, and he could see that her eyes were puffy from all the crying. He watched her stir but not wake at the sound of her phone. Her exhaustion had proven strong. Trent considered letting her sleep, but couldn't shake the anxiety of what bad news might be waiting for them in those messages.

"Lynn? Lynn, it's your phone," Trent said.

He raised his hand to her face and stroked her cheek with the back of his finger. The movement gently brushed her hair away from her face and Trent sighed when she still didn't wake. He took a quick look at the clock beside her bed. The time changed from twelve ten to twelve eleven as soon as Trent's eyes fell on it.

Who the hell would need something at this hour?

Lynn finally opened her eyes slowly and looked to Trent. Groggily, she turned over to grab her phone off the bedside table.

"Whose fucking number is this? I don't know this person... Why are they at my door?"

Lynn muttered hoarsely as she sat up in bed.

Trent looked over her shoulder to check the phone number. It was oddly familiar, but for some reason, he couldn't place it.

Lynn started down the stairs pretty loudly, and Lynn and Trent slowly inched their way to the front door.

"What the fuck is he doing here?" Lynn seethed.

Ray's face was distorted but visible through the shaped glass of the front door. Trent couldn't answer that question.

"What do you want, Ray?" Lynn called out.

"Open the door."

Lynn and Trent both snorted in disbelief at the same time.

"That doesn't answer my question, and whose phone are you using? That's not your number," Lynn shot back.

Trent had noticed that she had Ray's number saved on her phone under 'asshole'. She clearly wouldn't have come down if she knew it were him.

"Open the fucking door, Avison."

"If I shank you on my property, it's self-defence. I don't think you want that."

"Jesus, you're violent. I just want to talk."

"Why are you so angry then?"

"Because you did something that you agreed you'd never do. Don't come to the junkyard again. Nate picks up. We have a system. Don't break it, or I'll half your cut."

Trent watched Lynn's face as she thought about what she wanted to say next. She seemed conflicted. She looked like she wanted to chew his head off, but she was holding back. That was unlike her.

"He's using Andrea's phone... I knew I recognized the number," Trent whispered to Lynn, grimly.

He knew that Andrea didn't want to get caught, but he wasn't aware that she was capable of letting Ray get away with this much. It burned him to know that he'd once wanted to give her the world, only to have her keep the world from knowing the truth of his tragedy.

"I won't be there again," Lynn finally answered Ray.

"Good. I'll be texting you soon for another drop. If you fuck it up, I'm taking your whole cut just for fun. So be careful. Wouldn't want to miss a prescription for your brother, now would you, Avison?"

Lynn closed her eyes hard, and Trent inched closer to her, wanting so badly to be able to hold her, wanting to mend an open wound which Ray was intentionally rubbing salt into.

"I already told Dex, I won't be back. Get off my porch!" Lynn shouted back at him.

Ray was quiet for a second. Then, suddenly, he hit the door with his fist. Lynn and Trent both jumped at the loud bang, while Ray sniggered and retreated into the night. Ray had always been a hothead, but in public, his aggression was usually passive – that way, when he blew up on people, it seemed out of character unless you knew the guy. Trent had always brushed Ray off as a football player with too much testosterone, but now he was realising that Ray's violence was much more sinister than that.

"Are you okay?" Trent asked Lynn.

Her eyes never left the door. They didn't look sad, though. They were sharp. She looked angrier than she ever had.

"I'm going to turn myself in and give them everything I have on Ray," Lynn said plainly.

"Wait, what?" Trent did a double-take to the now-empty porch, then back at Lynn. "Are you crazy? You can't. He's got insane lawyers – you know who his father is, right? You give them anything, and they'll throw *you in* juvi! You're walking on thin ice here. If they try you late enough, you're legally an adult and could go to jail! Everything is against you! You're the one who took drugs out of the hospital, whether or not someone else stole them, and whether or not he planned it, they'll spin that on you!"

Trent looked her in her eyes, and the anger scared

him – not for himself but for her. She seemed to be working on impulse and nothing else now.

"I don't care anymore…"

"But—"

"Trent, stop."

BUT I CARE!

He yelled in his mind, not wanting to yell at her.

"I can't live like this, Trent. Teddy's not alive, I'm being threatened. Once Ray asks me to do another pickup, I'm going to have to tell him I won't, because Teddy is dead. I never wanted to keep doing this once… well, once I didn't need the money anymore. And I know they won't let me go easy. Ray will hold this over my head. They'll force me to do something else for them. It was my plan from the beginning to turn myself in if Teddy died, or get the hell out of here if my mom says she wants to go back to Logan. Just because you were dropped into my life under a faulty hallway light doesn't mean I can change those plans now."

"Lynn, please! There's another way, there has to be!"

When Lynn remained quiet, Trent was struck with a bold idea.

"Let's go back to the junkyard, we'll take video of a deal happening or something. Get some other kind of evidence, you know?"

Lynn scoffed and pointed to the door.

"You did see that lunatic, right? What do you think they'll do to me if they find me anywhere near that place again? I can promise you it won't just be taking money from my cut, Trent."

He was a little taken aback by the comment, but at the same moment, he was stunned as another idea came to him.

"Wait! What about Charlotte, or my brother? Remember? I told you she was acting really guilty when she visited, and we could convince my brother that you really are talking to me so he could help us!"

"Charlie? And you really think your brother is going to believe me if I tell him I'm talking to a ghost? I've already freaked him out enough."

"What if she could help us? What if you could get both of them to help you find something in that junkyard?"

"How?"

"I don't know, but I really feel like we need to talk to her."

"I thought you said you couldn't feel anything?" she shot back in a bratty tone.

Trent frowned. She was trying to deflect, but she wasn't going to get away with it.

"I'm serious, Lynn. This, I can feel. I swear. I can feel the pain when the darkness hits. I can feel the warmth of the sun when you touch me, and I can feel *this*. I don't know how, but I just know I'm right, Lynn. I know we have to talk to her. This is what I'm here for. Before I either wake up or…" Trent looked at the floor, struggling to finish the sentence. "Before… before I die. We have to talk to her, and you have to try to talk to my brother."

Lynn's anger faded slowly. He knew if he'd said that word, she'd seriously consider his suggestion. Trent watched as her eyes softened in that way he liked. Like when you poke a fire, and it jumps and sparks, then eases out to a steady burn.

"Okay, I owe it to you to at least try."

Trent slowly started to grin.

"So, I'll call out of school tomorrow. I'll tell them I'm taking a week off for bereavement, and then I'll talk to Charlie. Do you know where she lives?"

"Yeah, I've been there with Andy a few times." Trent shrugged.

"Okay, whether or not that goes well, we'll find Jeremy after, and try to convince him to help us. Good?"

"Yes, sounds great to me. For now, you should go back to sleep. Ray's a fucking asshole."

He'd heard her crying quietly in her sleep earlier and had tried his best not to wake her, only to have her awoken by the dumbest man alive.

"You can say that again."

"Ray's a fucking asshole."

"Thank you," she said, and started heading up to her room with Trent following behind.

"You're welcome, Lynny."

Lynn turned to Trent with a hurt look on her face, and Trent winced at the mistake he'd made. As much as he liked that nickname, he knew that it was a hallmark of her relationship with Teddy.

"I was going to tell you to stop calling me that… but I'm starting to like it. Just, everything that reminds me of him hurts right now, you know?"

Trent nodded at her in understanding, glad that he hadn't ruined the nickname altogether.

14

GOLDEN TICKET

09:41 AM

Tuesday morning. Exactly four days after the incident. Charlotte Tresser sat up in her bed and was immediately met with her reflection in the giant mirror hanging on the wall across from her. She grimaced at herself. The person looking back at her was barely recognizable. Her long, auburn hair was greasy and sticking out in every direction. Her green eyes were so sunken from sleep deprivation, and her body so weak from hunger, that she was actually worried for her health today. She hadn't eaten or slept properly for the entire weekend. The only 'real meal' she had eaten was pizza. The rest of the weekend, she was powered exclusively by booze, cigarettes, and value brand diet cola.

It didn't matter how hard she tried to focus on something else – whenever she was awake for more than four seconds, her mind kept pulling her back to Friday night, like some kind of sinister time machine. She would be transported to Ray's backseat again, where she could feel the terrible crash jolt her entire body, she could hear Mel's panicked scream and the sound of screeching tires as Ray fled the scene. The worst memory of the night came back to her as an image: Trent's sneakers, sticking out of the grass on the side of the road. She hadn't seen him be thrown from the window, and closing her eyes in time was one thing she was grateful for. But then again, that cowardice made her feel even more disgusted with herself – especially since her girlfriend hadn't been so lucky. Mel had about twelve breakdowns on the phone as she described seeing it happen over and over again. Charlie missed being able to talk to Mel like she once had; they'd been dating for two years now, and nothing had ever shaken them both up this badly.

She rubbed her face hard and groggily rolled out of bed. As she made her way up to the bathroom, she glanced at the clock on her bedside table and noticed that it was almost ten. She'd slept in. There were already three missed calls from school and two unread text messages from Mel, but she didn't have the strength to answer either. She had called out yesterday, and the school should've just figured out that she wasn't coming in today either. As for Mel… she just didn't know what to say to make things better.

A gentle knock on the door spooked her, and she paused in place.

"Hon? Did you want some breakfast? I made eggs and toast. Is your stomach still feeling icky?"

Her mother's voice was kind, but Charlie knew it

was only because she had no idea what her daughter had done. Charlie usually told her mom everything. Four days ago, she had told her mom she was going to a party, and that there was going to be drinking. But she'd never told her that she was in the backseat of a car during a hit and run that night. She wanted to tell her, though. She wanted to tell her mom everything; she especially wanted to tell her how she couldn't live with herself right now.

"I might come down soon, just leave me some, please," Charlie answered, and then heard her mom sigh on the other side.

Charlie felt like she was starving, but she didn't know if she'd be able to keep anything down. She hadn't stopped feeling queasy since Friday.

Another knock on her door made her almost slip and fall; she was in the shower this time.

"What?" Charlie barked, and her mom hesitated before answering.

"I'm sorry, hon, it's just, there's a girl from school at the door. She said she needs to talk to you. Are feeling up to it?"

"Sorry, sorry I yelled. Who is it?"

"She said her name is Lynn."

Lynn? Avison? What the hell could she possibly want?

"Uh, did she say what it's about?"

"No, hon, just that it's very important."

In an instant, Charlie's stomach twisted into a labyrinth of knots. Lynn had never spoken to her, so what could possibly be so important today? This couldn't be about the accident, could it? How would she know anything about that? Charlie racked her brain, but she couldn't think of a single topic which would warrant a visit from Lynn Avison. She hoped Lynn wanted to talk about school – a midterm or something – even though that was the least of her worries right now.

Charlie threw on a pair of oversized sweatpants and a sweater and tied her hair up into a messy bun before heading to the front door. When she looked through the window. She could see Lynn standing there – her lips were moving, and her eyes were fixed on something to her left.

Is she talking to herself on my front porch? Great.

Charlie opened the door with no change to her facial expression. She seemed to startle Lynn, but she didn't really care right now. She just wanted to get rid of her so she could wallow in bed for the next sixteen hours.

"Are you going to tell me why you're here, or are you just going to stare at me?"

"Uh, hi?"

Lynn looked less scared now and more annoyed. Charlie crossed her arms over her chest and waited for Avison to keep speaking.

"I need to ask you something, but I need you to not freak out."

Lynn's eyes kept moving to the left like she could see something there. Charlie raised an eyebrow in confusion.

"What?" Charlie snapped.

"I know what happened to Trent, and I know you were involved, but before you close the door on my face, I want to explain something to you."

Charlie's eyes went wide, and suddenly her whole body started to shake. Charlie instantly shut the door and slammed her back against it – she was scared that Avison had already called the cops, who would start tearing it down right this second.

"I don't know what you're talking about!"

"You're a really terrible liar. Slamming the door in my face doesn't help your case, either. Look, I'm not going to the cops – this isn't about that. Can you just open up? I really need to talk to you."

"I—"

Charlie, you're an idiot. You could've played that a little cooler.

"I'm not feeling well, could you just go away?" Charlie shouted through the door, and her mother came out into the foyer with a concerned look.

Charlie immediately went wide-eyed and started shooing her mother away into the living room. It figured that Lynn would choose today, of all days, to spring this on Charlie. Tuesday was the one day of the week her mother worked from home and could accidentally listen in on this conversation.

"Really, Charlie, I just need to talk to you face to face," Lynn pleaded.

"Honey, what's going on?" Charlie's mother whispered, as Charlie began escorting her away with a gentle pull of her hand.

"Nothing, Mom, it's just something about school. Don't worry, mind your own business."

"Charlie, sweetie, you know you can let them in to talk," her mother whispered, and Charlie closed the door to the living room before she could say anything else.

Once Charlie was finally alone, she returned to the front door and swung it open with a force of strength she was surprised she possessed. She pulled Lynn to the end of her driveway by her arm.

"Listen, I don't know what you know, but you can't just come to someone's house and do this. What do you want? Money?"

Charlie's eyes were wild, and she couldn't understand how Lynn was so calm – what did she want from her? Was this going to turn into some kind of blackmail situation? She couldn't take this right now. She was already being threatened by Ray and his disgusting cousin, Dexter. The last thing she needed was one more person from her high school driving her crazy.

"I'm sorry, I just didn't know how else to do this," Lynn began. "This is going to sound crazy, but I need you to be open-minded."

Charlie looked at Lynn with an alchemy of disbelief and frustration. She'd never talked to this girl before, but now she was really getting on her nerves. She'd never been blackmailed so calmly before.

"I can...um, I'm...I am seeing Trent. As a... well, as a ghost. And he knows you visited his hospital room. He knows you said you were sorry. He knows everything. Now... he needs your help."

Charlie swayed in place. The world seemed too big for a moment, yet simultaneously, she felt the walls closing in. She felt like she couldn't get any air even though she was standing outside on an autumn morning. Charlie became vaguely aware that there was a light breeze. Her eyes followed a small leaf which slowly danced in the wind before hitting the ground. Even though Charlie could see the air moving, all she could feel was her throat closing up and her knees turning to jelly. She would be that leaf in a moment, falling to the ground, if it weren't for Lynn's arm gripping her elbow. In an instant, Charlie stopped swaying.

"You...what?" she said slowly.

"Trent, he's..." Lynn's eyes trailed to the left again, and Charlie glanced where she was looking, but nothing was there. "He's see-through, but he's here right now, and he can hear you, and he wants to forgive you, but he needs your help first. I can tell you haven't slept in days. No offence, but you look like hell."

A chill ran down Charlie's spine. She closed her eyes and breathed deeply for a moment.

"Is this some kind of sick joke? Are you trying to

trick me or something?"

"What in the world would I have to gain from playing this type of trick on you, Charlie?" Lynn asked with a shrug.

Charlie didn't have an answer for her, but this was all too strange. She'd never talked to this girl; who was to say she wasn't the kind of person to pull a stunt like this?

"Trent is convinced that you know more about that night," Lynn continued after Charlie's prolonged silence. "He thinks you might be able to help us put Ray away for what he did. All we're asking for is help. He can see how you're taking this. He knows you're sorry, and he's a pretty forgiving guy."

Charlie began to cry suddenly. For a moment, Lynn frowned and shuffled awkwardly, but then opened her arms for a hug. Avison had never seemed like the hugging type, but for some reason, Charlie accepted the invitation. Maybe she had just grown too tired of holding this in. She wasn't one to keep secrets at all, let alone hide something like this. She had wanted to turn herself in the minute it happened, and everyone in the car knew that. Especially Ray. That's why he was threatening her every hour by calling her. He left no texts or voicemail, but she knew it was a reminder to stay quiet. After a long, strange minute, Charlie let Lynn go, and Lynn looked down at her feet.

"So, do you think you could help us? Nate told me there was some party at the junkyard, and Dex had his guys wreck everything. We doubt we're going to find anything now, but we thought maybe you could help us record something happen to use against them."

Charlie took a deep breath, and then looked around as if she were being watched.

"I know Dex ruined the parts at a burning party the next night, but I also know that he kept a piece.

He was bragging about keeping it to hang over Ray's head, in case he ever fucked him over."

"Woah, what? What piece?" Lynn said as she stepped closer to Charlie with burning curiosity.

"The front fender."

Charlie walked up her driveway to her steps where she took a seat and buried her face in her hands.

"Charlie, are you sure?"

"Yes," Charlie groaned. "I was there that night. Ray left early, but I wanted to keep drinking so I stayed behind. Dex and his boys were wrecking the car, and Dex paraded the fender around and then put it in his house. He said, 'this is to keep his mouth shut'. And I knew exactly what he was talking about. The whole time they were ripping that car apart, I just wanted to... I don't know. Run away. I couldn't breathe. It felt like my stomach was filled with rocks." Charlie sighed and then looked up at Lynn. "You know, Trent was always really nice to me. He didn't deserve this."

"He says thanks."

Lynn flashed her a small grin, and Charlie shook her head.

"This is all really weird. How do I know if you're really telling the truth?" Charlie stood and shook off the weight of her guilt, determined to focus on the present, just for a second.

"Well, we did come up with an idea to convince you if you didn't end up believing us."

Charlie tilted her head in curiosity.

"Guess we gotta try it now," Lynn said. "Okay, I'm going to close my eyes. You put up fingers behind your back, and he's going to tell me how many fingers you're holding up."

"Are you shitting me right now?" Charlie asked, Lynn shook her head before closing her eyes.

Charlie cleared her throat then obliged. She held

up ten.

"Ten," Lynn answered, and goosebumps erupted up and down Charlie's arms.

Charlie glared at Lynn, then quickly turned around to the hedge behind her and shook it furiously. There had to be a camera somewhere. When nothing fell from the rustling bushes, Charlie looked back at Lynn and fixed her hair as if she'd been embarrassed by the sudden outburst.

"Beginner's luck," Charlie whispered, though she barely believed the words herself.

She stood up straight and put her hands behind her back again, holding up three.

"Three," Lynn said, stifling a laugh.

Charlie's eyes darted around the front of her house, and she started to run around the area looking for what she presumed was a hidden camera.

"Trent says you're not going to find whatever you're looking for. He's standing right here, watching you flail around, and you're just going to tire yourself out."

Charlie looked back to Lynn, waving her hand in front of Lynn's eyes, which were still closed. It took a moment for this information to sink in.

"Okay, I'm sufficiently creeped out. I believe you."

Lynn opened her eyes and frowned.

"Sorry, he didn't want to creep you out. He's trying to be a nice ghost."

Charlie stared at Lynn with a gaping mouth.

"What does that even mean?"

"I don't know, ask him," Lynn said, gesturing to the empty air. "He came up with it."

After a moment, Lynn began replying to a suggestion that Charlie hadn't heard.

"Trent, you're crazy, he'll kill me if he sees me there again. Why don't we just send the cops in now? Considering what Charlie said, they'll probably find something right away."

"No!" Charlie suddenly chimed in. "We can't have cops there. I know Dex. He won't. He'll have plan B. If you guys really want to get that fender turned in, we'll have to get in there ourselves. Now, we can't steal it – Dex would notice straight away and immediately go to his backup plan – but we could take pictures."

Lynn looked worriedly from Charlie to that invisible spot in the air. She felt a strange tingling down her spine every time she looked at the space beside Lynn, as though a sixth sense was picking up on something that her eyes couldn't see.

"I can't go back there," Lynn said. "Dex will kill me. And isn't it illegal to be on private property, either way? I'm rethinking even getting video of something... like, if we get something from the property, even just a picture, it wouldn't hold up in court? Or it would incriminate us, too?"

"Technically, it's not private property, there aren't even any signs – Dex just likes to say it is. It's a public junkyard, and Ray's dad just owns it. Dex doesn't even pay rent. I've heard him say that a million times, too," Charlie said, rolling her eyes at the thought. "I know how to get in without him noticing; Ray has taken Andy and I there before. When Ray is short on cash, he goes through Dex's window. I could... I could help you get in and out easily."

Lynn stared at Charlie in disbelief.

"Are you one hundred percent sure we could go unnoticed?" Lynn asked.

Charlie nodded and watched as a small grin crept onto Lynn's face.

"Charlie, you are the golden ticket."

"Yeah, whatever that means. I just don't want to live like this. Ray will blackmail me for the rest of my life." Charlie paused for a moment, and when

194

she spoke again, her voice was softer. "I swear to you, Trent, I wanted to turn myself in the minute it happened."

"Don't worry. Trent believes you. Anyway, you didn't hurt him as badly as I did. I'm the one who started this whole shitstorm in the first place." Charlie furrowed her brow in confusion, and Lynn shook her head. "Just, never mind. Okay, what's the plan? When can we go?"

"Well, every time I've gone with Ray and Andrea, it's usually pretty late – like sometime after eleven. Dex stays at his girlfriend's—"

"That disgusting man has a girlfriend?"

"That's what I said." Charlie smirked at Lynn's response, and the girls shared a knowing look. "Anyway, he's usually gone by then, and there's a way to get in without anyone seeing – if anyone is even still around that late. The fence in the back is broken. You can peel a section open and get inside. Then, there's a tunnel which leads straight to the back of Dex's place. Ray usually goes that way to meet him, and once when Dex was late, Ray found out he could get into Dex's place through the basement window. I think the last time he went through there was last week, so I doubt that dumb fuck has fixed it by now."

"Okay, got it – fence, tunnel, window. And you know where the fender is?"

"That's the hard part. I know he took it into his place, but I don't know where he put it. I mean I have a guess but…" Charlie bit her lip as she heard Lynn sigh. "Yeah, sorry…"

"No, don't be – it's a better start than we had before. I think this could actually work. I'll come back here at around ten-forty tonight, and we'll head over."

Charlie blinked her eyes a few times, as though she had just been blinded by a bright light. Lynn was making plans to come to her house tonight. They were working together. Everything was happening so quickly, when just minutes ago, Lynn was the outsider she'd never even talked to.

Charlie looked at her new ally, and noticed that she seemed to be listening to... well, to Trent. Suddenly, she felt like Lynn had it worse. At least Charlie didn't see ghosts.

"Yeah, sounds like a plan. So, did you get three phone calls from school today for not showing up, too?" Charlie raised a brow, realising now that this would've been a strange conversation if they'd just bumped into each other in the hallway.

"Uh, no... I called out. They know I won't be there all week. Bereavement."

"Wait, Trent died?" Charlie asked, her breath catching in her throat.

"No." Lynn snorted, for some inexplicable reason, but then she breathed out, and her face looked sullen. "My brother just died."

"Woah... I'm sorry to hear that."

You're grieving one loss and being haunted by a separate, unrelated ghost? Talk about a bad day.

"Yeah, it's... it was expected. I'm fine. Okay, I'm not fine, but it's not the time to not be fine. I'm being haunted, and we actually have a chance to screw Ray over, so I'm fine enough for this," Lynn rambled on, and Charlie nodded in agreement.

Ray was an asshole, and she was ready to be rid of him.

"Here, take my number. Text me when you get here later. I'll tell my mom I'm staying over at your place, if that's okay?"

"Yeah, sure." Lynn shrugged and handed Charlie her phone.

After Charlie saved her number, she gave it back.

"Hey, you... you can text me anytime. If you need someone to talk to about your brother. I know

I came out here like a tornado with legs," Lynn looked awkwardly at the ground, clearly trying to be polite by not vigorously disagreeing, "but I'm not usually like this. You seem cool. Really – if you need anything, let me know."

Charlie did her best to smile, though it looked more like an unintentional mouth twitch, before turning back into her house.

She closed the door gently this time, and was immediately met with her mother.

"Are you okay, honey?"

"Yes, Mom. Don't worry. Okay?"

Charlie's mom looked her over carefully, and then nodded. Charlie immediately ran upstairs and into her bathroom. The faucet screeched to life, and she threw cold water on her face. After only two seconds, she grew sick of looking at her reflection in the mirror which hung over the sink. She decided to look out of her window, instead, to see if Lynn had left yet. She saw her sitting in her car, talking to thin air.

Her mind started to race. What if she was going to walk into the Lion's Den on a crazy girl's word? A crazy girl who guessed two numbers in a row correctly. The more Charlie thought about it, the less convincing that whole encounter became. What if Lynn was just having a lucky day? Two numbers weren't impossible to guess. But whether or not Lynn was lying, Charlie knew that Ray deserved to pay for what he did to Trent. Even if Lynn was a crazy girl, she was a crazy girl who knew about that night when nobody was supposed to, and with her help, Charlie was not going to let him get away with this so easily.

15

FREE THERAPY

10:01 ᴀᴍ

Lynn and Trent watched as Charlie retreated back into her home. The pair exhaled in unison – a collective sigh of relief.

"What did I tell you? Didn't I tell you?" Trent started to laugh, and Lynn sighed at his overconfidence; it was cute, sure, but it was also slightly annoying.

"Okay, I know when to admit that I'm wrong. Let's get out of here before a neighbour sees me talking to thin air," Lynn quipped as they both stepped into the car.

"Hey, if we're going to get Jeremy, we need to do it at night."

"Why?"

"Well, he might be in my hospital room right now

198

if he's not at school, and... I just don't want to see myself there anymore. You know? I'd rather catch him at home, before he goes to sleep."

Lynn nodded in understanding and started up the engine.

"Nighttime it is."

"Thanks, Lynny."

†

The car ride to Lynn's house had been fairly quiet after Trent had mentioned not wanting to see his mangled body in his hospital room, and his attention seemed to drift off to something else. The route passed Heatherdale Lake, and Trent's eyes lingered on it longer than usual this time. As they both avoided eye contact, Lynn felt increasingly embarrassed; she wished she had never told him that she had thought about driving into that very lake if he weren't here. When Lynn pulled into the driveway, Trent finally broke out of his daze.

"We're going to convince Jeremy, and we're going to that junkyard to get evidence. We're going to make sure you don't get blamed for this," Trent said.

Maybe he could see the uncertainty on Lynn's face. Or maybe he was just trying to convince himself.

"You don't have any doubts?"

"Doubts?" Trent scoffed. "What makes you think this won't work?"

"So many things could go wrong."

"How? You know what, don't answer that. Trust me, this is going to work. I told you Charlie would know something, and I know exactly how to convince my brother when we have to. This is the best timeline now, Lynn. There's no way it isn't."

Lynn shrugged as she turned off the car.

"I guess that conversation with Charlie did go better than I expected, but I'm just not as sure as you are."

"I get it. Dex and Ray made some big threats, and we're going to go parading into their territory again. I'm scared of getting caught too, but the reward outweighs the risk. Knowing I might be able to get them into trouble, and protect you at the same time, is all the reason I need."

"Yeah, but you aren't the one taking a risk, Trent. You're not going to be the one getting caught."

Lynn shook her head at his carelessness as she got out of her car and went to the door. Trent followed her with his eyes at first, frowning. For once, it seemed he was at a loss for words. After a moment, he also jumped out of the car and rushed closer to Lynn – she assumed to stop the darkness from swallowing him up.

"Okay, you have a point, but it's either try this or sit around waiting for them to win. I'm not the type to do that, and you shouldn't be either."

Lynn didn't feel like answering him yet and pushed past the door, locking it swiftly behind her and going straight to her room.

†

Lynn sat on the edge of her bed, folded arms splayed across her desk, her head resting on them. Trent stood at her door with his arms crossed and his brow raised as he interrogated her with his eyes.

"Tell me what you're thinking."

"Isn't it enough that you're haunting me? Now you want to read my mind, too?"

Trent huffed a laugh and took a seat beside her.

"Come on, Lynny. Let me reassure you. It's what I'm good at."

Lynn looked up at him, and sighed at the sight of his signature grin – that smile which instantly sped up her heartbeat and made her breath catch in her throat. Lynn couldn't keep looking at him, so she tore her eyes away, sat up, and stared at the drawing of him on her desk instead.

"What if you forget everything? What if you wake up from this and don't even remember my name?" In her peripheral vision, she could see how these questions startled him at first, but his grin never let up.

"Well first off, that's impossible because I knew your name already, and... I won't. I know I won't."

"I don't think you can know that. No one in a coma has ever woken up and talked about their life as a ghost. I think this is why; I think they just forget."

Lynn finally gained the strength to look him in the eyes, though it didn't last long.

"How long have you been thinking about this?" he asked with a soothing tone.

"Since the day I finally started believing this was actually happening." Lynn folded her arms on the desk again and buried her face in them.

"Well, I don't think it will happen, but if I forget you... make me remember."

Lynn felt the cold of his hand on her arm for a second.

"You'll think I'm crazy," she mumbled.

"Ease me into it."

"There's no way you'll believe me."

"I don't care. You have to promise you'll at least talk to me. I'm going to want to fall for your undeniable charm all over again, Lynny. No matter what."

You're such a smooth talker.

Lynn could feel her cheeks go red.

"Don't say that." He didn't say the word love, but she assumed he was admitting that he'd fallen for her just as she had fallen for him.

"Say what?"

His smug tone told Lynn he knew precisely what

she meant. She frowned, peaking at him from the corner of her eye. He was smirking back at her. Like he always was.

"Promise me you'll at least talk to me," he asked again.

Lynn felt like she'd hurt him. She didn't return the compliment. She didn't tell him she'd fallen in love with him, too; she hadn't said it when she'd first felt it, and she knew she couldn't now. No matter how much he made her heart skip a beat with his smile, or how nervous he made her with every perfect word. She just couldn't say it back to him. She knew she was the reason he was here in the first place, and every time she remembered that, she felt sick to her stomach.

"Okay, I'll promise to talk to you, but how can you be so sure? I don't know how you can even say that. I don't… you know you won't be trapped by darkness when you wake up. You could easily find someone better than me to say those words to. Someone who didn't almost get you killed."

"Sounds boring if you ask me."

Lynn finally sat up straight and glared at him, but it quickly turned into a frown when she caught sight of his wistful grin. She wasn't angry, though she could tell she looked that way. It wasn't anger, but frustrated sadness. She wasn't convinced that he'd fallen for her organically. She was convinced that he was trapped with her, and she was being forced to face him as some kind of punishment for a decision that she'd made on a whim. She didn't know how to explain it to him, or to herself, but this felt wrong, and she wasn't so sure it was just because of her guilt. When she didn't say anything else, Trent's eyes started to search the room, probably looking for more sweet words that he could magically pull out of thin air.

"You know, I don't see this as a trap," Trent began slowly. "Maybe you're the light in the darkness because I couldn't see you before. The world just needed to point you out. Kind of a funny way of getting me here, but how's that for a cruel cosmic joke?"

He smiled that smile of his, and Lynn couldn't help but smile back, even if hers was sullen. That smile could make almost anyone swoon. It didn't help that he was actually smart and sensitive too. But even with all his reassurance, Lynn still had her doubts. His smooth words and genuine grin weren't enough; she was still scared. Scared that she'd become nothing to him when he wasn't like this anymore. Forever convinced that she deserved exactly that, for the situation she had put him in. Before Lynn could say anything else, a knock on the door made them both jump, as if they were about to be caught doing something they weren't supposed to.

"Holy crap, it's cold in here, Lynn Marie," Lynn's mother breathed as she hugged herself. "Sorry for barging in. I just... I wanted to talk to you about everything that's going to happen. Your Aunt Marie is coming tomorrow. We've made all of the plans. Everything's ready, it's just about showing up at five o'clock sharp. Oh, and I need your help looking through some albums."

Lynn looked worriedly at the floor.

"I thought we were just going to use the blue photo album?" Lynn mumbled, and her mother sighed.

"We were, but I want to talk to you, and I want to look at some pictures while doing so."

Lynn hesitated for a moment. How could she say no?

"Fine. I'll be out in a minute."

Lynn's mother closed the door, and Trent looked to Lynn.

"Why does she always use Lynn Marie? Isn't Lynny easier?" Trent asked to break the silent tension, and Lynn smiled sadly over at him.

"That's what Teddy used to say." Lynn stood and suddenly looked nervous. "I guess you gotta come and see some embarrassing pictures with Mom and me." She hesitated for a second. "Hey, if there's one thing you can forget once all this is over, please choose to forget this."

"No way. This is my favourite part of getting to know anyone: embarrassing childhood photos." Trent beamed. "I just wish I was seeing them for some other reason," he added as the smile faded.

"You and me both," Lynn breathed as she opened the door and headed over to her mother's room.

She knocked lightly before she went inside to find her mother sitting on the bed, surrounded by old photo albums and a large Tupperware box with piles of scattered pictures.

"Jackpot." Trent ran over to the end of Lynn's mom's bed to peak over the photos, like a kid looking through the window of a candy shop.

Lynn inwardly rolled her eyes at Trent, being careful not to react to him in front of her mother.

"I think we should use all the ones from that day camp," Lynn's mother began as she shifted through the blue photo album, the one that had Teddy's first baby photo on the front, with a painful smile.

"Yeah, he looks really happy in those," Lynn agreed, and shifted closer to her mother just a little bit to lean on the bed.

Lynn looked at the pile of photos up close and felt like she was going to pass out. She had been trying to keep her mind off of this overwhelming feeling, but here it was, pulling her in like an ocean tide. Her face contorted with grief, and she recoiled slightly from the pile.

"Lynn, I don't like this either," her mother said. "Start looking."

The tone was sharp and demanding, and Lynn knew it wasn't just her who thought that, as Trent also recoiled.

"I'm sorry, I'm having trouble looking at his pictures right now."

Her mother scoffed. "And you don't think I am?"

"I didn't say that, Mom."

Lynn's mother stopped for a minute and squeezed her eyes shut.

"I'm sorry. I didn't mean to—"

"I know," Lynn answered quickly, brushing it off, and then slowly picked up a couple of pictures from the Tupperware pile.

She could already feel the hot sting of tears in her eyes when she saw the first picture. Halloween. Three years ago. When Teddy still had the energy to put on a costume and walk around the old hospital. Before living in Heatherdale, they had lived in Logan, two hours away, and were making a point to leave at the time to go to Liberty. The children's cancer ward was supposed to be better here – and it was. Lynn and her mother just had to learn the hard way that no matter what they did for Teddy, he would always be marked for death.

"Remember this one?" Lynn asked her mom softly, trying to break herself out of a downward spiral of thoughts.

Her mother glanced at the photo and nodded with a small smile.

"Yeah, I always thought it was funny that he wanted to be *Mulan* and you wanted to be Batman, but I wasn't about to question it." Her mom kept shuffling through photos.

"Yeah, a little boy in the hospital was just as confused. He told us both, 'you can't be *Mulan* 'cause you're a boy, and you can't be Batman 'cause you're a girl.' And Teddy looked him right in the eye and said—"

"We can be whoever we wanna be." Lynn and her mom said it at the same time, and then shared a smile.

"Badass kid," Trent muttered with a nod of approval.

Lynn smiled over at him and then set her eyes back on the photographs.

"That's not Liberty, is it?" Trent asked, looking confusedly at some of the photos.

Lynn shook her head discreetly.

"I'll always be sorry that I didn't believe you," her mother said quietly.

Lynn felt like someone had suddenly lit all the photos in front of her on fire. She looked everywhere in the room but at Trent, but she could see him from the corner of her eye with his sudden look of confusion.

"You don't… it's fine," Lynn mumbled, unsure of how to answer.

"It's not. I should have believed you the minute you said it. It shouldn't have taken Teddy to convince me."

"W—well I'm glad he did. Just leave it at that."

"But I want you to know—"

"I know, Mom!"

Lynn hadn't meant to raise her voice, but she did it out of fear. She didn't want Trent to hear this. She didn't want to listen to it either.

"I didn't mean to bring up a bad memory."

Calling being molested a 'bad memory' is like calling a stab wound a mosquito bite.

Lynn tried to push back the actual memory of the event creeping in.

"Let's just drop it, please?"

Lynn's mom nodded in agreement, and Lynn took a look at Trent, who was looking at her with furrowed brows.

"We should go back to therapy, Lynn."

"Really? D—do we have to talk about that right now?"

"I think this is a good time to talk about the idea again, but I'm not trying to rush you, okay?" Lynn's mother said, and Lynn stopped fuming for a moment.

Lynn felt a brief sense of relief. Her mother was actually listening to her today. Most days, this argument could carry on into harsher territory, because her mother knew just what to say to egg her on.

"Okay, just drop it for now," Lynn muttered and then glanced at Trent again.

He'd be concerned. He'd ask her questions about this later. She'd change the subject. That was a part of her life that he wasn't allowed to haunt yet.

The rest of the day consisted of shuffling through pictures. The two only spoke when they wanted to share a memory or needed an opinion on where to put an image in the collage. It didn't happen often after the first outburst. Neither of them was in the mood to talk after the first memory of Halloween. Instead, they quietly created their collage of pictures of Teddy with family and friends for the funeral service, and when they were finished, Lynn's mom left her alone. Lynn had made it evident to her mother that she didn't want to speak about anything else.

Lynn and Trent trudged quietly back to Lynn's room. As soon as they got in, Trent made a motion to the box of Cheez-Its still on her side table and looked over at her, raising his eyebrows suggestively. Lynn shook her head at him, and then lay down on her bed and turned on Netflix.

There wasn't an easy way to forgive someone

for what Lynn went through. Even though she'd never really blamed her mom for putting her in that situation, she never forgave her for only believing it when Teddy said he'd seen something. As though Lynn's words alone weren't enough for her. That's why Teddy was her angel: he'd saved her when no one else would.

†

"Are you okay?" Trent asked.

Lynn, now lying on her side facing her computer screen, turned to him sitting behind her. She had put on a random show as background noise and hadn't realized just how quiet she had been until he spoke. Lynn nodded to answer him, but he didn't seem very convinced.

"It's another one of those times, if I could offer you something I would, but I'm still a ghost." He smiled, but Lynn didn't have the energy to smile back after trudging up all of those memories. "You know you can talk to me about anything, Lynn. I know you think I'm trapped, no matter how much I try to convince you otherwise, but I'm here if you need me. I mean… as here as I'm gonna be."

Lynn sighed at his warm reassurance.

"It's kind of unfair. You get to pry into my life and see every secret, and I don't even know if you have a middle name. Or what your parent's names are, or if someone has given you an embarrassing nickname," Lynn mumbled, but she didn't say it with malice; she was just thinking out loud.

Of all the things he was finding out about her, a secret nickname was the least of her worries, but she wasn't about to bring up all of the other stuff he'd found out about her on his little adventure into limbo.

"My full name is, in fact, Trenton *Brian* Shawking.

But I hate my middle name, because it's my father's name, and he's a piece of shit. My mom's name is Beth. Wonderful woman. She calls me 'Trentimental' when I do something cute – like, sentimental, you know? She doesn't do it a lot. Never really got a good nickname from anyone else. Although, my best friend Adam does call me dumbass a lot, does that count?"

A small laugh escaped Lynn, and she turned over to face him and noticed his grin.

"That counts, thanks."

"You're welcome. Any other questions?" He slid down from his sitting position so that he was lying down next to her on the bed with his hands tucked underneath his head.

"Why's your father a piece of shit?"

Lynn watched as Trent tensed. His jaw locked, tightening his face's already perfect shape as he looked up at the ceiling.

"I saw him hit my mom once. He's been a piece of shit ever since."

"Oh… I'm sorry."

Trent didn't say anything else, and Lynn felt like she'd pushed a button she shouldn't have.

"I have a question for you now." He slid down further to lay on his side, mirroring her position.

Lynn gulped. The closer he got, the more her breath quickened.

"If I could get you something to make you feel better right now, what would it be?"

Lynn stared at him blankly.

"Huh?"

"Could I make you hot chocolate? Get your favourite candy bar? How about Cheez-Its? Need me to bring up another box?"

Lynn couldn't hide the red of her cheeks. There was no natural way to move now. She pursed her lips instead, suddenly realizing what he meant. He was being his usual sweet self when she needed him the most. How could she ever deserve his time, whether he was in limbo or not? She held back a grin and tried to play it cool, even though she probably looked like a giant tomato.

"I don't know... maybe an ice-cream sandwich would help?"

Trent huffed a laugh and held out his hands as if her were holding an invisible beach ball.

"What're you doing?" Lynn asked.

"This big, when I wake up. The sandwich is going to be this big. No smaller! That would be unacceptable."

That's all it took, Lynn finally let out a laugh of her own and she could swear that being haunted by Trenton Shawking was some kind of free therapy.

TUESDAY, OCTOBER 1, 2019

09:27 PM

The Shawking family often lived mundane lives. On a usual Tuesday evening, Jeremy would be hiding in his room playing a game on his PlayStation 4, yelling out obscenities to any teammates who were playing poorly. Trent, if not at a baseball game, practice, or joining his brother in a video game, would be in the basement lifting weights while blaring the Red Hot Chilli Peppers. Their mother would be watching her soap opera on the television downstairs, and the old wooden desk next to the living room that Brian once used to overwork himself while at home would still be collecting dust, as it had been ever since he'd left the house eight years ago.

Tonight, was far from typical. Trent was still in the hospital, broken on a bed, and their mother was crying while she watched her soap operas. She'd never cried watching them before, but it didn't take much to make her cry for the past weekend.

In Jeremy's case, not only was his night far from typical, but it was going terribly as well. He had run out of what little oxy he had left, and he was currently having one of the worst withdrawal headaches in the world. Whenever he stood, the room would spin, so he finally decided to lay on his bed and stay there. His forehead kept sweating even though he felt dehydrated, and he was sure the constant muscle pain he was feeling wasn't just because he was sick of sitting in that chair in Trent's hospital room.

After an hour of lying down, sweating with a dry mouth, Jeremy finally tried to stand up again. He looked at the alarm clock on his bedside table. It was time to try to get a glass of water.

He slowly made his way down the stairs. As soon as he got to the bottom, he was startled by a knock at the front door. He trudged over, silently vowing to kill the person at the door if, when he answered it, they were trying to sell him a product – or, worse, a religion, since it was much too late for that.

He got an even worse surprise when he saw Officer Lexington, whose first name he couldn't remember. As he stared through the front-door window, he assumed the officer couldn't see him, and quickly tried to get it together. After a moment of pause, he went to open the door. From the living room, his mother's voice asked who was there.

"The officer," Jeremy mumbled back.

"Good evening, Jeremy. How are you?"

"When you said we'd be hearing from you, I didn't think you'd show up at the front door," Jeremy said blankly.

Officer what's-his-face seemed to take that as a greeting, as hostile as it may have sounded.

"Well, I came to check up on you, and ask you an important question. Do you know anyone with a navy-blue truck in your family? Or anyone who is a friend, or 'enemy' of Trent's?"

"Enemy? What the hell does that mean?"

"Do you think anyone had it out for your brother for any reason?"

"Are you asking me if I think anyone wanted to kill my brother?"

"Kill is a strong word. I meant someone who has ill intentions towards him… or you?" Jeremy leaned on the door. His headache was making it impossible to stand straight.

"No, my brother is the type of dude that everyone wants to talk to, and he'll talk to anyone. If that fucker had stuck around after they hit my brother, I bet you any sort of money that Trent would wake up from his coma and forgive them. He'd probably even shake that person's hand and tell 'em, 'it hurt like hell, but thanks for the experience.'" Jeremy shook his head, knowing his brother and his forgiving nature. Jeremy knew it could cost Trent a lot one day, but he never thought it would cost him his life.

"He sounds like a stand-up guy."

"Jeremy, why didn't you tell me Officer Lexington was here?" Beth said as she rushed to the door. A blanket covered her entire body and dragged across the floor as she hurriedly shuffled over. She looked worse than Jeremy did, but only because it was more apparent that she had been crying just a second ago.

"I did."

"Well, I didn't hear you." She sighed, and the adults exchanged a brief handshake.

"Hello, Mrs. Shawking. I was just asking Jeremy here if he knew anyone in the immediate family or a friend of Trent's who may have driven a navy-blue vehicle. A truck, more specifically. It's a bit of a stretch, but we found paint transfer from the car that hit him, and we wanted to update you to see if you could help."

"I can't think of anyone who does right now, but I'll ask around." Beth furrowed her brows and wiped her nose with a tissue, as Officer Lexington scanned Jeremy's face with his eyes.

"Is that all, Officer?" Beth asked.

"For now, yes. If you think of anything else, please call me." The officer nodded to Beth, and she nodded back.

As she left, Lexington stared straight at Jeremy. The unwavering eye contact made Jeremy nervous. He nodded and went to close the door, but the officer stopped it gently with his hand.

"Does she know?" he asked, lowly.

Jeremy glared at the question.

"Know what?"

"Well, by the look of you, you're either sick or you're using." Lexington asked the question with a genuine look of concern, and Jeremy tried to close the door as fast as he could. The officer was a big man, though, and Jeremy's build was nowhere near his athletic brother's. The door barely moved. "I'm not going to bust you, Jeremy. There's no need to panic."

Jeremy's jaw unclenched, and his grip on the door did as well.

"Please know that it might be fun now, but I can tell that you're not on the 'fun' stuff. You're playing with fire. It's never too late to stop, and it's better sooner than later because you might not get a later, kid."

These simple words hit Jeremy harder than he would have expected them to. He thought he'd be cuffed or yelled at if a cop had ever found out he was using, but this guy seemed to just... get it.

Or maybe he's just trying to trick me.

"Just think about it. Call me if you need resources." He held out his card.

Jeremy looked nervously from his card to his eyes and didn't take it. Lexington sighed and put the card on the welcome mat under Jeremy's feet. Then he let the door go and turned to walk off to his car, leaving Jeremy standing at the door frozen, speechless, and still drenched in sweat.

Jeremy waited until the officer drove off to pick up his card – and his gaping mouth – off the floor. Before he turned to go inside, another car pulled into his driveway. He was scared for a moment that the officer had returned. Instead, he was caught off guard by the person who stepped out of the vehicle.

"Hi, Jeremy."

Lynn Avison was a real enigma. In the hallways at school, she always seemed so focused on getting to where she was going. Her eyes never ventured far from the path ahead of her. She could go ignored in big groups as your average-looking Caucasian brunette. Jeremy didn't know much about her and didn't care to know. There was no reason for her to be interacting with him this much, yet here she was, in his life for the third time since this terrible crash, and Jeremy couldn't understand why she kept showing up.

"Hi? What're you doing here? How do you know where I live?" For a minute, Jeremy thought about actually calling Officer Lexington, just in case this turned into a weird stalker situation.

"Um… I gotta tell you something, and I need you to be open-minded."

It was strange being familiar with her voice. He'd never really heard it at school. Since they were in different grades, they had no classes together, and she wasn't the type to randomly say hello to anyone in the hallway. Today, her voice sounded eerily calm, which made him more concerned that she might be a calculated stalker.

"What?" Jeremy suddenly felt a chill that reminded him of the visit from his father in Trent's hospital room.

"Okay, you have to promise not to run away and shut the door on me. That's already happened to me once. You gotta let me prove something to you."

Jeremy stood frozen and wide-eyed.

"Your brother Trent is, um… 'haunting' me. We found out who was driving the car that night, and we need your help to get proof. I'm trying to ease him into it, Trent, just—"

Jeremy watched as she suddenly looked to the right of her and started talking to thin air. Jeremy was growing more certain that it was time to call officer Lexington.

This chick is fucking crazy.

Jeremy turned around and quickly started walking inside.

"Juniper Park!" Lynn suddenly yelled.

Jeremy stopped with the front door wide open, and slowly turned on his heel to look back at her.

"What did you just say?" he asked in the quietest voice.

"Trent said to believe me, or he'll tell me about Juniper Park."

"Wait a damn minute. So, he didn't tell you, or he did?" Jeremy stepped out his front door, angrily slammed it shut, then started barreling towards her down the driveway.

She jolted back. He realized he'd gotten a little too close even for his liking, but if this was a prank, it was the most fucked up prank someone could pull.

"He didn't tell me anything yet, but he says if you don't help us, he'll tell me about Juniper Park." Lynn shrugged and kept looking to her right side.

Jeremy glanced where she was looking, and suddenly he imagined Trent standing there, smirking down at him like he'd won an argument – the smug grin that he loathed in this kind of situation, but would give anything to see again for real. The mirage disappeared as Jeremy slowly came to his senses. Jeremy started to shake his head in disbelief and back up towards the door again.

"I don't believe you. Maybe he told you something before, but—"

"There was a towel?" Lynn began.

"Oh my God! Trent, don't!" Jeremy hissed, and then looked to Lynn completely dumbfounded.

Surprisingly, she looked more confused than he did.

"How do you... what—" Jeremy's eyes welled, but he tried to shake it off, and glowered at Lynn. "Canyon vacation. What did he do that made Mom say she wanted to disown him?" Jeremy asked.

"Uh..." Lynn looked to her right again, as Jeremy continued to glare.

He observed her as she seemed to mouth the words 'come on.' When she cringed a second later, Jeremy didn't even have to hear the answer. He already knew it was true. Trent was here.

"He put his arm into the RV toilet to get his Power Ranger toy. He says it was disgusting, but he was a stupid kid. He also says you got him – embarrassing moment for an embarrassing moment – you win." Lynn looked like she was trying not to laugh.

Jeremy sat down on the driveway. It took too much of his energy to stand, and all of this was happening so fast.

"So... he knows who hit him? Does he remember what happened?"

"Sort of. He didn't see it, but he saw something else that led us to Ray."

"Raymond? That fuckhead? I fucking knew it was weird that he texted me," Jeremy snapped.

"He texted you?"

"Yeah, to find out where Trent was. He said he'd called Trent's phone and Trent didn't pick up, but I thought it was weird that he'd be calling him in the first place. They never really talked a lot after the whole Andy thing. I just believed him because I haven't been able to look at Trent's phone since the crash. It's busted, and it just… it hurts to look at it, or even hold it."

Jeremy rubbed his head and tried to get an image out of his mind, of Trent on the ground bleeding. Those flashes tended to happen more often when he was coming down from a high.

"Okay, so tonight, if you're up for it, we have to sneak into Dexter's junkyard and take pictures of a piece of that car – the one they hit you with – that he's hiding from Ray. Charlie Tresser is going to help us. Trent said you would, too."

"I—" Jeremy looked up at Lynn. "I'll do whatever I can." He got back up on his feet immediately and tried to stand up straight. "I'm gonna need some water first, though."

"All right, just get yourself together – we have to leave soon. We're going to go straight to Charlie's from here."

Jeremy nodded and then ran back inside to grab a water bottle. He stood in front of the garbage in his kitchen and stared at the card that Officer Lexington had just given him.

"Jer? You okay?"

His mom startled him out of his daze, and instead of throwing the card out like he planned to, he pocketed it and turned to her.

"Yeah, I'm fine. I'm going to go to the hospital tonight with one of Trent's friends. If that's okay."

"Isn't it late for you?"

"No, it's okay."

"Whatever you need to do. I can't sleep there again tonight. It's difficult." Beth's eyes were so swollen that Jeremy didn't need an explanation.

"I know, Mom, it's okay." She nodded to him and kissed him on the forehead.

"Jer, you're sweating. Take that sweater off!"

She shook her head and tugged at the collar of his dark green hoodie for emphasis. Then she turned back to the living room, and solemnly walked to the couch.

Jeremy ran back outside.

16

FEELING BRAVE

TUESDAY, OCTOBER 1, 2019

10:29 PM

As Jeremy headed into the house, Lynn and Trent hopped into the car. Trent sighed as he stared out the front window.

"After what you told me, I'm worried about him. He doesn't look good."

Lynn knew what he was talking about. Anyone could see that Jeremy looked messed up. Not just stressed, but sick from withdrawal.

"I'll text Nate to cut him off."

"Promise?"

"Promise," Lynn said with determination.

She didn't want to let Trent down anymore. Trent nodded and then turned to look at Lynn with an embarrassed half-grin.

"Do you still think... I'm as cute as a puppy after the canyon story?"

"How could I not? You were trying to save the best Power Ranger from a horrible shit canal. You're a hero." She shrugged.

Trent laughed, and Lynn giggled as Jeremy came running back to the car and swung open the front door.

"The hell you're sitting in my lap!" Trent snapped at Jeremy like he could hear him.

Lynn held her hand up to him, holding back laughter.

"Um, your brother is sitting in the front. He doesn't want you—"

"Yeah, I'd rather not sit in his lap." Jeremy grimaced and shut the door, and then jumped into the backseat.

†

The drive to Charlie's was quiet. Lynn and Trent had gotten to a point where they didn't have to speak to know what the other was thinking. They were both nervous, that was obvious, being unsure of what would happen here. It could be a picture-perfect ending or one giant mess. Neither of them was prepared for the latter, but they couldn't rule it out. Jeremy seemed very uncomfortable, like he didn't know what to say. Not to mention, Lynn was pretty sure his shakes were keeping him from talking – he must've been trying to play it cool in front of her.

When they arrived on Charlie's street, Lynn parked a couple of houses away and texted her to come meet them. A few moments later, Charlie ran out, looking like a cat burglar – dressed from head to toe in a black slimming shirt and leggings, with a dark beanie covering her red wavy hair. Lynn looked down at her dark jeans and black oversized long-sleeved top, and felt like she was underdressed. Lynn was terrified of tight-fitting shirts. She envied Charlie's confidence as she watched her open the car's front door, and before Lynn could protest, Charlie sat on Trent. Trent jumped out of the car, shaking his ghostly figure like he was trying to rid himself of goosebumps. Lynn let out a small, confused sound that didn't translate to words.

"What?" Charlie asked.

Lynn held back a laugh as Trent scowled and shook his arms out before getting into the back seat beside his brother. Jeremy was smirking. He obviously hadn't seen what happened, but he must've had some idea.

"You just… Trent was sitting there, and you made him jump. Did you feel anything?"

"Oh my God, no. I mean, it felt cold, but I just thought that was because it's cold outside. I'm sorry, should I sit in the back?" Charlie frowned and looked to the back seat.

"No, please don't sit on me again," Trent protested.

"No, it's okay," Lynn said.

Charlie shrugged and then looked to Jeremy; she seemed a little less burdened than she had earlier. Livelier even.

"Hey, Jeremy. I'm guessing you were convinced by the ghost game, too?"

"The what?" Jeremy asked, confused.

"No, we had a fun little game of trivia with their embarrassing family moments instead," Lynn said as she started up the car again.

Charlie raised a brow at the comment, but quickly moved on as another question arose.

"So, is Trent like… always… you know, if someone's *always* around, how do you do anything?"

"Yeah, just how nosy is my brother?" Jeremy mumbled.

Lynn snorted at the same time Trent did.

"He's been polite enough to give me privacy. He's trying to be a nice ghost, remember?"

Charlie shrugged at Lynn's answer, still confused.

Jeremy remained unconvinced. "Wow, he can barge into my room every other day, but the minute he has full access to a girl's, he's a gentleman."

"Damn right, dumbass," Trent replied, but Lynn noticed his tone was more arrogant than it was angry. "Apparently, I should have been searching it too," Trent muttered under his breath.

"Well, that's good. It's just weird to have someone who's *always* around," Charlie said over Trent.

"Oddly enough, I've gotten used to it." Lynn glanced back at Trent.

He flashed her a small timid grin before turning his attention to the window.

Charlie shook her head in disbelief.

"Any other questions, or are we ready to go on this mission?" Lynn asked with little to no enthusiasm.

"Ready," Charlie answered, and Jeremy nodded to Lynn in the rear-view mirror.

Lynn looked to Trent, who seemed more nervous than before, but he nodded the same way his brother had.

†

Fifteen minutes later, the group stopped down the road from the junkyard, and Charlie took a look around.

"This is a good place to park; we can walk over to the spot from here."

"All right, lead the way," Lynn said as she stopped the car and they all got out.

She tried to get over the nausea that had suddenly erupted in her stomach.

Lynn followed Charlie, with Jeremy behind Lynn. Trent tried to stay as close to Lynn as possible without running into his brother. Once they'd arrived at a part of the fence that had a rusted post, the group paused to stare at it. If anyone was just looking at this fence, it would seem pretty sturdy. The second Charlie put her hand on it, though, it opened like a wardrobe door. One by one, they walked through the gap.

Charlie looked with uncertainty at the mess in front of her. The space was cluttered with junk, but Lynn noticed almost as soon as Charlie did that there was a thin walkway between the fence and a pile of parts. Charlie waved at them to follow her toward it. Lynn assumed that this must've been the tunnel of trash she'd told them about. It really looked like a tornado had torn through this place – where Lynn expected to see the ground, there was only piles upon piles of rubble. They continued on the trail until it broke off into two paths: one through a hollow minivan shell with a detached trunk, and the other towards a clearing.

The group walked underneath the minivan shell and came out on the other side, right next to Dex's tiny house. It looked like a grimy oasis among this mess of junk. No lights were on inside, and Lynn shivered – unsure if it was from the chilly autumn night's breeze, or because they were closer to the Lion's Den than she'd ever been before. A small sconce above the back door dimly flickered, but those dark spaces that the light couldn't reach made her fear what, or who, could be hiding within them.

Charlie led them to the back of the house. Lynn was so focused on trying to be quiet that she forgot to breathe a couple of times. When they were in the dirt patch which acted as Dex's backyard, Charlie bent down to a very long – but short – basement window.

Lynn looked from the window to Jeremy, who mirrored her expression of disbelief.

"It's short, I know. But you'll get through it. If Ray can fit, you both can," Charlie whispered.

She gripped the glass and shimmied the window to the left side so there was an opening just big enough for a single person. Without warning, she slid in feet first, taking whatever dirt was at the edge of the window inside with her. Lynn grimaced and then followed suit. She brushed herself off once her feet hit the ground. Jeremy appeared beside her shortly after, and Lynn helped him wipe dirt off the back of his shoulders as he shook out his hair before looking to Trent, who was the last one to approach the window. He had taken a moment to sit on the ground; Lynn assumed he was trying to make sure he wouldn't fall through the earth, if that could even happen.

"I was going to offer to keep watch, but then I remembered I can't see fuck all past a certain poi— woah!" Trent began, but something out of Lynn's view startled him.

When he made it through the window, she widened her eyes questioningly, urging him to tell her what happened outside. He shook his head and waved the moment off, giving her the impression that it was nothing to worry about. She wished she could tell that to her now-racing heart.

"Follow me," Charlie whispered before Lynn could ask him out loud what the hell had happened.

When Lynn looked around, the darkness of the house felt even more ominous now that she stood inside. On top of that, she could have sworn she had heard something – something besides whatever had scared the wits out of Trent outside.

Lynn and Jeremy continued to follow behind Charlie. Everyone walked cautiously, careful not to make any unnecessary noise. The basement was tiny, and to make matters worse, there was a giant pool table in the middle of the room, which Lynn thought was ridiculous, since there was barely any space to play. When Lynn's hand accidentally touched the thing, a thick layer of dust was left on her fingers – clearly, it hadn't been used in years.

Charlie led them all to a narrow hallway. The floor was carpeted here, so thankfully, it was easy to be quiet. They all inched their way towards a doorway. When Lynn was close enough to see it, she noticed that the actual door was missing, as though someone had ripped it off its hinges or kicked it in.

"I think this is the only place he could put it, other than his room."

Charlie reached inside the room for a light switch and hesitantly flicked it on. Lynn held her breath – expecting some kind of alarm to go off at the same time. Realizing Dex's place wasn't that high tech, she calmly breathed out. All four of their eyes settled on a glinting piece of metal, bent out of shape, which was leaning against a boiler on the far-side of the room. It was a glossy chrome fender flare with black studs.

Trent stood gaping at it, and Lynn looked between him and the fender. It was sinking in for him now.

"I can't believe… I mean, I knew, but I just… I can't believe they left me there. They left us both there. If they had stayed, it would be easier to forgive them, but now… I don't know where to start."

Lynn scoffed. Charlie and Jeremy looked at her like she was crazy, clearly forgetting that there was a fourth person in the room who they couldn't hear.

"You don't have to forgive them, Trent. Just like you didn't have to forgive Charlie or me."

"That's my brother for you," Jeremy muttered.

"But please know that I really am sorry…" Charlie added quietly.

"Charlie, I forgave you the minute you said you'd

help," Trent sighed.

Lynn could tell he was genuine.

"He already forgave you, Charlie. Trent's the kind of guy who will forgive anybody who says they're sorry, and then he'll give them the shirt off his back." Lynn walked up to the fender and took a few pictures with her phone. "He's just too hard on himself, for no reason. You're allowed to be mad, Trent. And if you're not going to be, I'm going to be mad for you."

"You don't have to be scared of being angry, Trent. You're not Dad. You'll never be Dad," Jeremy mumbled.

"Tell him to shut up, Lynn," Trent said half-heartedly.

"I'm not telling him to shut up when I agree with him. I don't know anything about your dad other than he's a piece of shit, but you? Your name is Trent, and you are the furthest thing from a piece of shit. *You* are too nice to people who don't deserve it."

Jeremy flashed her a small, melancholy grin.

Trent sighed and Lynn wondered what he was thinking right now; she guessed it might have something to do with how frustrated he was. All he wanted to do was forgive people who almost got him killed, a concept completely lost on Lynn. She didn't understand that at all. She still didn't know how he could forgive her so easily.

After a moment of silence, Charlie nodded, signalling that it was time to leave. She turned the light off and led them into the hallway.

The four of them made their way back to the tiny room with the giant pool table. Charlie put her foot upon the table to get to the window, but Lynn suddenly noticed that something was off.

"Wait, that light outside was on when we got here," Lynn hissed as she grabbed Charlie's arm before she reached the windowsill.

Lynn bumped into Jeremy and he nearly fell over. Charlie went wide-eyed with fear and hastily motioned for them to move. Lynn's heart was racing even faster now. That light was not automatic. It'd either burnt out, or someone had turned it off, and Lynn knew none of them had touched its switch.

They all scurried over to the hallway, still making as little noise as possible.

"We're going to have to try the front door. There's no other way out unless we can crack open a window on the first floor," Charlie said under her breath.

Hearts beating and breaths stammering, they continued slowly up the stairs, trying their best not to make the old house creak.

Once up the stairs, they stood in front of the entrance to the ground floor, there was a second of silence, and Charlie let out a deep breath.

"I don't think anyone's on the other side..." she whispered, and carefully turned the doorknob.

She quickly slipped into the next room, but before the others could follow her, they heard a high-pitched squeal.

"What the hell are you doing in my house?" Dex barked.

The voice sounded close, but Lynn couldn't see him before Charlie slammed the door shut, trapping herself in with Dex on the first floor of his house.

"I was just, I—" Lynn heard Charlie stammer.

"Did Ray let you in?" Dex shouted.

Lynn didn't see what happened next, but when she heard a hollow bang, she had a bad feeling that Dex had gotten his hands on her. Jeremy tapped Lynn on the arm and leaned in close.

"Run to the back. Make noise, so he hears you. I'll sneak up on him. Got it?" Jeremy said quickly with a sudden composure she didn't know he could have.

"But Charlie—"

"We'll come back for her." Jeremy insisted.

Trent looked worriedly from his brother and then to Lynn, but quickly nodded to her.

Lynn mirrored the nod and followed Jeremy down the steps with Trent following behind. Lynn made sure to stomp, making enough noise to merit an acknowledgement from Dex.

"Who the hell is here?" Dex's voice boomed again from the other side of the door.

The sound of Dex's ranting quietened as they ran back down the short hallway and into the pool table room. Jeremy split off from her and went back to the boiler room. Without a second thought, she lifted herself up through the window with the pool table's help. There wasn't a shortage of dirt in her mouth when she got to her feet, and she viciously spat it all out before starting to run. It became very obvious that it was darker out here than before, and it was frightening not knowing where Dex could show up. She looked back to notice Trent struggling at the basement window.

"Trent, come on, what the hell?" she said, quiet but demanding.

"I don't know what's going on, just run without me. I'll figure it out," he responded, but Lynn could see the uncertainty in his eyes.

She wanted to get out of there, but she knew what would happen to Trent if she left, and she couldn't bear to put him through the pain he so desperately didn't want to feel when the darkness hit.

"I won't move. Come on."

"Avison."

The skin on Lynn's her arms erupted in goosebumps when she heard Dex's footsteps only a few feet behind her. Lynn's head whipped around and her heart sank.

"What did you do to Charlie?" Lynn's shaking

voice asked.

"I'd be more worried about yourself, sweetheart. You just broke into my house, when I already told you not to show up here. You're lucky I didn't bring my gun out."

"You're not supposed to bring a gun to a knife fight, right?" Lynn mumbled as she backed up from Dex and pulled her knife out from her shoe.

To her dismay, Lynn noticed that Trent had disappeared from the window, and she wasn't sure why.

As Dex came closer, it felt like the world was suddenly caving in. She didn't know if Jeremy would get to her in time. She knew she was alone to begin with, even when Trent was around, but now she was *really* alone with only Dex, and the single hope that maybe Jeremy would be able to sneak up on him before he hurt her. This was possibly one of the worst situations she'd ever gotten herself into.

"Feeling brave?" Dex said through gritted teeth.

"What?"

"You must be. Why else would you have come back here? For what? Do you know something that you shouldn't?"

Dex was still taking slow steps towards her, and her stomach felt queasy as she backed away.

"That's a lot of questions," Lynn said, looking him in the eyes.

In her periphery, she could see his hands. They were empty, but he was reaching for something from a pile of junk. One quick swipe, and Dex had a metal pipe in his hand; another rapid movement, and he smacked the knife out of hers, nearly crushing her thumb in the process. Lynn yelped out in pain and as she tried to back up from him, she fell backwards onto the ground. Dex's smug grin at his successful hit was more frightening than the weapon he held. Lynn scrambled away from him as fast as she could with what she now believed was a broken thumb. She didn't get far before Dex managed to pin her down.

When she went to kick and claw at him, he caught her hands and trapped them over her head. She tried to scream, but as she drew a deep breath, she saw a blur of white crash into the side of Dex and knock him right into a pile of rubble beside her. When she got a better look at the white blur, it was only Jeremy, but the cold that came off of him reminded her of Trent in that moment. Jeremy had pushed Dex off and was now struggling on the ground next to Lynn, trying to restrain him. Dex threw a punch that hit Jeremy in the chin, but Jeremy was able to move quickly enough that it wasn't a significant blow.

The two were clutching and clawing at each other as they tried to get to their feet. Jeremy swung and missed. Dex swung and hit. Blood flew from Jeremy's lip as the momentum from the hit made him roll away from Dex. In the next second, Dex was on his feet, standing over Jeremy with the pipe in his hand. He swung the pipe at Jeremy's face, but he rolled away again and whipped his leg around to kick Dex in the shin. Dex seethed and hopped on one foot a couple of times.

Lynn watched from her position on the ground, unsure of what to do, as Jeremy's demeanour changed; rather than emanating fear, Jeremy now seethed with rage. Jeremy got to his feet and threw his whole body weight at Dex, making them both hit the ground again. His balled fist came crashing down on Dex's face three times before Jeremy shook his hand out in pain. Jeremy rolled back off Dex and looked to Lynn with wide eyes. Heavy breaths were all that the two of them could produce as Dex lay unmoving on the ground. Lynn looked to Jeremy.

"Th—thanks," Lynn stuttered.

Jeremy nodded. She could tell he was shaking just as much as she was. Suddenly, a little voice in her head told her they weren't out of the woods yet.

"Trent?" she called out in her smallest voice. He was gone, and she had to remember what she promised him the last time he disappeared. "We have to go before Dex wakes up. Where's Charlie?"

Lynn and Jeremy shared a look, immediately got to their feet, and as Lynn ran to the back door, Jeremy grabbed her wrist gently and pulled her away.

"It's broken, the lock is stuck or something. I tried getting out that way, but couldn't, so that's why it took so long to jump him. I used the front door. I'm sorry, I thought I'd make it to you faster," he explained as they jogged around the front and got in.

"I'm just thankful you got to me when you did," Lynn mumbled.

Even in the darkness, it wasn't hard to navigate the small house when they got in. The light was on in the musty living room, and the two noticed a foot sticking out of the hallway. The two of them ran over to Charlie, lying on the floor in front of the basement door. With horror, Lynn realized she was unconscious. She immediately listened for breathing and checked her pulse – something she'd become accustomed to doing when taking care of Teddy. Lynn had accepted that she was terrible at protecting herself in a fight, but she knew how to resuscitate a person with her years of CPR experience. She was mentally readying herself to begin chest compressions but sighed with grateful relief when she heard Charlie's faint breaths.

"I can help you carry her," Lynn said as she looked up to Jeremy.

"It's fine, I've got her. Let's get out of here before Dex wakes up," Jeremy said under his breath and carefully cradled Charlie in his arms.

The two ran out to the car, and Lynn fumbled with her keys.

"We have to go straight to the hospital. You might have to check Charlie in if she doesn't wake up, and I know this sounds strange, but I have to go to your brother's room."

"What's wrong?"

"I can't see Trent anymore. When that happened the last two times, he said something about being in a lot of pain. Being in the dark. He said to go to his room if he disappears."

Jeremy nodded in understanding, but she could see he looked confused.

And I promised.

17

INTO OBLIVION

00:00

"I was going to offer to keep watch, but then I remembered I can't see fuck all past a certain poi—woah!" As Trent was sitting halfway through the window, his mumbling was interrupted when a giant black bird landed next to him on the ground. As it hopped closer to him, its wings shone a metallic blue in the faint light. Trent mirrored the bird's action of tilting its head and then shook his head at it. After he carefully slid himself through the window, he brushed off Lynn's concerned expression with a wave of his hand.

"Follow me," Charlie whispered.

Trent felt an uneasiness that he couldn't shake. It was hard to see the borders of his personal dark abyss around him during the night, especially in a dark room. This made the cold harder to dodge. He stayed close to Lynn as they followed Charlie.

Charlie led them to a narrow hallway in the basement, and Trent's three accomplices inched their way closer to a room at the end of the hall. The room's doorway frame looked as if someone had crashed through it at some point in time. The mental image of Dex falling through it and hurting himself made Trent snigger quietly.

"I think this is the only place he could put it other than his room," Charlie whispered as she reached inside the doorway for a switch, and hesitantly flicked it on.

The second the light turned on, Trent felt the world shift.

In his mind, he was suddenly transported to the first time he'd ever seen this fender. Two days after being dumped by Andrea, he was spending his night at a football game. A week before she'd broken up with him, he'd seen her phone over her shoulder while they were together. In the few instances of his nosiness, he'd noticed she had been sending hearts to someone other than her friends. Because he hated confrontation, he'd thought about dumping her, but couldn't decide if it was worth causing a fight or if he should suffer in silence. This internal debate didn't last long, though – Andrea had beaten him to it, dumping him first. He hadn't argued. He'd let her go easy, playing it off like it was nothing, even though it'd hurt him more than expected. He hadn't tried to convince her to stay, or asked any questions, because he hadn't wanted to know if he'd actually been cheated on.

After the football game had ended that night, Trent had hung out in the parking lot with Adam and a couple of other baseball guys. The football players were in their own circle, talking on the other side of the lot. That's when he'd noticed the flirting. Whatever conversation was going on around him was drowned out by the sound of his teeth grinding. He remembered feeling the blood rushing to his face and ears in embarrassment. He'd watched as Ray pulled at Andy's waist and whispered to her with a sly grin as she fawned over him. It was annoying, to say the least; it made him feel like his assumptions were correct. Maybe they'd been having an affair for a while – maybe they'd been flirting in front of him, and he was just blind.

As he'd watched them lean on Ray's car, snuggled up like newly-weds, all he could think about was how much he wanted to smash up one of those glossy chrome fenders with the black studs. What a fucking joke they were. He could easily take a bat to them and make them worth a fraction of whatever Ray's daddy had paid for them. He'd never act on that though.

Trent's mind suddenly snapped back to the present, where he recognized the paint colour that was scraped along the front end of the fender. Crimson red. The colour of his Ford Ranger.

Trent never wanted to succumb to anger. Anger could be volatile. *Anger* was what had boiled inside him, and made him want to use his bat for more than just the game. That awful feeling was what made his father hit his mother. Because of that, he tried to forgive Ray in his head. He wanted to make peace with this answer he'd found. Something held him back, though. Something felt so wrong about letting Ray off the hook. He couldn't just forgive this.

Ray had left him there. Broken. Him and his brother. Then Ray had hid the car and wrecked it so there wasn't any evidence. This beaten-up, glinting fender only existed because Dex wanted blackmail. If Ray had gotten his way, this wouldn't even be here right now.

Trent's mouth fell open, and he wanted to say

something, but he just didn't know where to start.

"I can't believe… I mean, I knew, but I just… I can't believe they left me there. They left us both there. If they had stayed, it would be easier to forgive them, but now… I don't know where to start."

Lynn's scoff distracted him from his internal monologue, and he looked to her. Sharp eyes. She was angry.

"You don't *have* to forgive them, Trent. Just like you didn't have to forgive Charlie or me."

"That's my brother for you," Jeremy muttered, and Trent dismissed it.

"But please know that I really am sorry…" Charlie added quietly, making earnest eye contact with thin air a few feet across from where Trent actually stood.

"Charlie, I forgave you the minute you said you'd help," Trent replied.

"He already forgave you, Charlie. Trent's the kind of guy who will forgive anybody who says they're sorry and then give them the shirt off his back." Trent watched as Lynn walked up to the piece of scrap metal and started taking pictures of it. "He's just too hard on himself, for no reason. You're allowed to be mad, Trent. And if you're not going to be, I'm going to be mad for you."

Now Trent understood. Her sharp eyes were for them. For the ones who had left him there.

"You don't have to be scared of being angry, Trent. You're not Dad. You'll never be Dad," Jeremy mumbled.

"Tell him to shut up, Lynn," Trent said.

His brother was right: he wasn't their father, but that was only because he didn't let his anger out. He was still scared of what would happen if he had.

"I'm not telling him to shut up when I agree with him. I don't know anything about your dad other than he's a piece of shit, but you? Your name is Trent, and you are the furthest thing from a piece of shit. *You* are too nice to people who don't deserve it."

If that was about her, Trent didn't want to hear any of that, either. There were only two people in this world who had ever actually angered him to the point of not being able to forgive. The first was his father, and now there was Ray. Trent shunned his anger, not wanting to express it in the only way he'd ever seen anger shown. He was afraid of what he might do if he ever got his hands on Ray.

Charlie nodded to Lynn and Jeremy, signalling that they would be leaving now, so the group retreated back to the window.

†

Charlie hoisted herself up on *the pool table.*

"Wait, that light outside was on when we got here," Lynn hissed as she grabbed Charlie's arm to pull her back down.

Trent jumped back as Lynn almost pushed Jeremy into his see-through body. Charlie went wide-eyed and nodded to the door of the room. All three of them followed her through it, still quiet but moving faster than before.

"We're going to have to try the front door. There's no other way out unless we can crack open a window on the first floor," Charlie said under her breath.

When they got up the stairs, Charlie was the first to poke her head out of the doorway. There was a second of silence, and she let out a deep breath.

"I think it's okay..." she said quietly, and cautiously walked outside.

Before anyone could follow her, she let out a squeal.

"What the hell are you doing in my house?"

Trent instinctively jumped forward and reached out to pull Charlie back in, but was quickly reminded that he was still spectral when his hand went through her arm and the door closed on it.

"I was just, I—"

"Did Ray let you in?" Dex yelled.

That was a brave move. Charlie was trying to protect Lynn and his brother, and Trent knew he would never forget his gratitude. Trent looked back to Lynn and could tell that she was ready to run. As she started down, Trent heard a bang on the other side of the door, and he hoped for the life of him that it wasn't the sound of Dex hurting Charlie.

Jeremy tapped Lynn on the arm and leaned in close to her.

"Run to the back. Make noise, so he hears you. I'll sneak up on him. Got it?" Jeremy whispered.

Trent wanted to protest, but he quickly realized there was no time, so he nodded to Lynn who seemed just as unsure of that plan.

All three of them were off like racehorses.

"Who the hell is here?" Trent heard behind him, and he turned to see the door swing open.

Trent briefly saw Dex standing in the doorway before being swallowed by the darkness. Lynn was still running, and Trent had to run to keep up with her to stay in the dim light.

When he caught up with Lynn, he watched as she maneuvered herself out of the window. Trent reached his hands out to the edge of the window to follow Lynn outside, but couldn't seem to plant them on anything – they kept disappearing into the wall. When Lynn looked back at him, he tried not to look nervous, but he knew he was a terrible actor.

"Trent, come on, what the hell?"

"I don't know what's going on, just run without me. I'll figure it out." Even he could hear the shakiness in his own voice.

"I won't move. Come on," were the last muffled

words Trent heard before he was completely engulfed in darkness.

A switch which controlled his entire world had been turned off. His light source was out of reach now. The cold was quick to catch his skin.

All of a sudden, he could feel his limbs again. His head felt like an avalanche had hit it, and he cried out in pain as he fell to his knees. This dark place wasn't weightless anymore. For a moment, Trent couldn't decipher what was happening to him – what he was feeling – until eventually, it dawned on him: he was back in his body, and all of it was broken. He was being forced to stand the cold of the arctic with only the t-shirt and jeans he'd arrived here with. He reached out in search of something, anything solid, and to his surprise, felt a wall in front of him. He moved his hands up the surface slowly – not just out of fear, but because he could barely move while in so much pain.

He felt the ledge of the windowsill, and this time it was solid. His hands weren't going through it like they had been before. Trent pulled himself up; even with the weight of the world on his shoulders, he knew he had to get back to Lynn. He exerted all his energy, but he just couldn't lift himself that far. He didn't have the strength. He stumbled back and slammed into something behind him.

The pool table, he thought to himself. He felt around in the darkness and lifted one leg to get on top of it, and then another. He faced the direction where he knew Lynn was; her light was shining close. When he reached out for the windowsill this time, he could feel it solid under his hands, and it took every ounce of strength he had left to push himself up and out of the window.

He came into the light to find Dex on top of Lynn. Without thinking, he threw himself into Dex. He thought he would feel the crash of a tackle and was shocked that he felt like he was falling into a pool of water instead. Trent dove headfirst back into the abyss. His lungs felt like they were going to burst, and his limbs felt sore and weighed down, like he was swimming in tar again, and just as suddenly as he felt everything before, he now felt nothing at all.

Time had stopped.

He couldn't feel any pain anymore.

No senses were afforded to him until he slowly opened his eyes, and all at once, his senses flooded back. Trent found himself lying face first in dewy grass. He could feel it on his cheek and in his hands. The cold wet had quickly sunk into his clothes, and he could suddenly feel his skin. He got to his feet slowly, disoriented. The smell of rain in the air was a pleasant yet confusing surprise.

In the distance, the land was flat and went on for what looked like miles. Further, there was a body of water, still but moving, and he could see the flares of light bounce off the small waves. The sky was a collision of dark purple and red brush strokes, but where there should have been clouds, there was a rolling fog instead. The dark fog he'd become so accustomed to. A flash of lightning in the distance made him start walking towards the water. The lightning felt familiar. He trudged along the cold, wet grass towards the spectacle.

Trent was both perplexed and delighted that he could feel his whole body again. He didn't feel as light as air anymore. He breathed in the cold, and it stung his lungs in a familiar way, like he was standing outside on a frigid Autumn night. The wet grass had soaked through his sneakers and made his shoes feel like soppy pools. Any other day, he would hate the feeling of wearing wet socks, but right now, he was just grateful to be feeling anything. A wind picked up and hit his skin to make goosebumps erupt on the back of his neck.

The confusion of where he was nagged at him as he continued to walk. He had only counted a few steps in his head, but it felt like he'd been walking for hours.

"Lynn?" he finally called out.

"Welcome."

The unexpected sound of another voice made him stop abruptly, and he turned to look for where it had come from. Seemingly out of thin air, a wooden bench with a man sat upon it appeared behind him. To Trent's surprise, the stranger looked like Trent's father, but his eyes were different. They looked more delicate than his father's. If Trent hadn't known better, he could've sworn he was looking in a mirror that transported him thirty years into the future. Something in Trent's gut told him he didn't have to fear this man, but the goosebumps which now coated his arms warned him to be careful.

"Who are you?" Trent asked.

The man gestured for Trent to take a seat beside him, but Trent stayed glaring at him in place.

"We've met before. It was raining then," the man said as he looked out into the distance.

A loud crack of thunder made Trent look in the same direction. Lightning struck again on the horizon, and a flood of memories suddenly came back to him. One, in particular, hurt the most. The night Teddy died.

"Are you the one who spoke to Teddy?" Trent asked as he slowly turned his head back.

He smiled. "Precisely."

Trent felt an overwhelming sadness. It suddenly dawned on him what this moment might mean. Perhaps this was his time to choose.

"What is this place?" Trent asked as he cautiously

took a seat next to the man, keeping a fair distance between them on the bench.

"I like to call it the Middle, but there are a lot of names for it. Limbo, Oblivion, Purgatory. People can be creative." The man smiled as he continued to look out into the horizon.

His expression was oddly familiar to Trent, as if he'd seen this man's face a million times before.

"Are you God?" The words were shaky as his voice trembled with uncertainty.

The man laughed lightly.

"No, I have another name. But don't worry – I'm harmless."

Trent stared at him, caught in a daze as the man spoke again.

"I know you have a lot of questions for me, and before you ask, you couldn't have saved Teddy. Everyone knew he had to leave. Lynn, more than anyone. More importantly, you can't stay in this place for too long."

As the words washed over him, Trent felt a sudden relief from the immense guilt he had felt for not saving Teddy that night. But only seconds later, something caught Trent's attention from the corner of his eye. He looked around, and the dark rolling fog seemed closer than it was before. Trent scratched the back of his neck as his eyes darted around the surreal atmosphere.

"Would you like to go back to the body now?" the man continued.

"The body?" Trent seemed offended by the question. "The body? I assume you mean my body? Yes, I would like to go back to *my* body now. This body! Trent grabbed at his chest.

Now that he could feel himself whole again, he wasn't going to let that slip through his fingers.

"Do you remember where the body was last?" the

man asked.

Trent thought for a moment. Why had he asked like that? As if there were another body he would go back to? There was only one he wanted to live in – the only one he felt whole in.

"My body is in the hospital. It's a few days after the crash. I remember being a ghost and trying to get out of the basement window. When I finally did, I tried to push Dex off Lynn… and now I'm here. Is Lynn okay?"

The man nodded and smiled again.

He replied, "Good. A warning, then." Trent's brow furrowed, and the man looked into Trent's eyes as he continued, "I will have to take more memories from you: memories of this place, of the crash, and of Lynn. You have escaped the darkness, and you have saved her from it, but the darkness is relentless. They believe they're owed."

"Wait, hold on, *more* memories owed? What do you—

"I'm giving you a choice, Trent. I know what is ahead of you. If you choose to go back to the body now, your life will end in a worse way later. Are you sure you want to go back, now?"

"Worse? Worse than a car crash as a teenager? Worse than cancer at eleven? What more could you possibly do to me or Lynn?"

"Please, believe me when I say worse. I need an answer, Trent. You need to be sure."

Trent scoffed at the man. He was getting more infuriating by the second.

"So, let me get this strange verbal contract straight. If I go back to my body now, I won't remember this? I won't remember Lynn. I won't remember that you warned me I would die in a worse way. But if I die now, if I don't go back to my body, I'll just… die? With the memory of Lynn? What happens when I die?"

The man sighed heavily, and when he spoke next,

Trent noticed his voice had lost the confidence it once had.

"I can't tell you what happens when you die."

Trent's teeth clenched.

"If I go back, Jeremy will remember what happened when I was a ghost, he'll have to tell me about Lynn! Or Lynn will tell me herself!"

The man stayed quiet. He simply kept his eyes on the horizon as Trent searched the man's face for any hint of emotion. As much as Trent was sure of his own statement, the man's look of hardened empathy made Trent doubt himself. It's like he wanted to tell Trent everything, but something was stopping him, or perhaps someone.

"Jeremy will tell me what happened here… won't he?"

"I can't answer that."

"But—" Trent sighed in frustration and ran a hand through his hair. He felt like pulling it out.

The rolling fog was much too close now. The sun in the distance was falling into the water faster than he expected, setting at a rate which he'd never witnessed in his life. The darkness was caving in, and he had no light to run toward. Nothing felt real right now except for his body, and even then, he felt he could lose that at any moment if he made the wrong decision.

Was this what death is?

A trip into oblivion?

A one-way ticket into the darkness he loathed so much, just to have it swallow him for eternity?

Trent didn't want to find out, but he also didn't want to go back and forget who Lynn was. To not know how caring she was to those she loved, her tenacious attitude, or what her favourite movies were. He didn't want to forget her eyes, gentle and sharp as they could be. All at once, he felt so angry, and he wasn't scared to be mad in this place. There was no one here who he could hurt by accident, except maybe this idiot on the bench beside him.

"I don't want to die, and I don't want to forget her! Why is this happening?" Trent got up and began to pace.

"I can't answer that."

Not only did this man look like his father, but he was starting to remind Trent of him too. The worst parts of him. Fickle and vacant.

"Well then, what good is a warning if I'm not going to remember it, or this place, when I go back?"

The man's eyes widened slightly.

"Everyone remembers the Middle. Everyone. I can only keep memories for so long."

Trent huffed in a confusing bit of relief. It was nice to know he would remember at some point, but the only question was—

"How long? How long before I remember Lynn?" Trent asked.

Trent noticed the man smirk, and suddenly felt as if the man had stolen that smirk off of Trent's very own face.

"I can't—"

"Answer that." Trent rolled his eyes as he finished the man's sentence for him.

"So, are you sure that you want to go back to the body now?"

The dark rolling fog was starting to inch closer to Trent, pestering him to make a choice. Instead of being scared of it now, he shooed it away with his hand like an annoying acquaintance. There was no thinking about it anymore. He knew from the very beginning what he wanted. He felt a pain in his heart, or maybe it was his soul, knowing that Lynn had guessed correctly that he would have to forget her, and realizing the pain she would feel when he spoke to her like a stranger. But no matter what, he had to go back. She promised that she would try to make him remember. He promised her that he wouldn't die if he had a choice.

"Pull the lever, Kronk."

WEDNESDAY, OCTOBER 2, 2019

12:34 AM

All at once, Trent's nerves were on fire. He breathed in and felt something strange in his mouth. His head was pounding.

Where the fuck am I?

"Oh my God. Trent?"

Jeremy? Is that you? Where are you?

Trent slowly opened his eyes. He emitted a gurgling sound when he tried to speak. Taking in the room around him was overwhelming. Trent could see Jeremy, who was talking to someone on the phone, and a strange shape of bright, blurred light. As his eyes tried to focus on the bright spot, it became less intense, and the room came into focus. He tried to take a deep breath to calm himself, but it was so painful and sharp that he winced. The blurred light beside Jeremy began to burn so bright he had to close his eyes again, and Trent felt like he was missing something – like he had lost something other than his consciousness.

Which, after a moment, he lost again.

WEDNESDAY, OCTOBER 2, 2019

06:56 AM

The next time he awoke, the pain wasn't as overwhelming. Instead, his body ached as though it were the morning after a particularly strenuous baseball game.

246

"Did I get hit or something?" his voice croaked.

When he opened his eyes, he saw Jeremy lean in from his left side.

"Well..." His brother paused, and Trent noticed Jeremy's eyes look over at his mother, who Trent realized was on his right.

There was a third figure in the room: a man in a white coat. Trent squinted, trying to bring the man's features into focus, but everything was blurry.

"Hello, Trent. I don't mean to overwhelm you. My name is Doctor Rimari, and you are in Liberty Hospital. Speak slow; you have a partial collapse of the lung. If you feel it's hard to breathe when you speak, you can write something on that board there on the side table instead. What's the last thing you remember?"

Trent had to think for a moment. There was a dull, throbbing pain in his head, making concentration difficult. The doctor's face was coming in a little clearer. Brown eyes, slicked back hair, and a bronze complexion that made Trent think he might've just returned from a vacation in Cancun.

"I remember being at Adam's house before a game. I think it was a playoff..." Trent croaked and furrowed his brows, trying to recall which game it was.

Jeremy's brow furrowed as well.

"Playoffs were a month ago," Jeremy said quietly to the doctor, and the doctor nodded in response.

Trent felt like he had gotten an answer wrong on a test and, in his embarrassment, looked to his mom, whose eyes looked worn out, red and puffy. Trent didn't ask out loud, but the doctor seemed to understand what he wanted to ask next.

"You were in a car wreck. You fractured your skull, broke an arm, and a few ribs on your left side, which is why it hurts to breathe or talk right now. You fell into a coma after the anesthetic. Quite a short one, although you had us scared for a minute. You bounce back quick, kid."

Trent's eyes grew wide.

"You've been out for four days. I expected some memory loss. We'll need to catch you up to speed slowly. I'll have a specialist come in, but in the meantime, we'll get you more medication for the pain."

Trent nodded at the doctor, and then looked at the tired faces of his family.

"What day is it?"

Beth grabbed her son's hand and kissed it, tears running from her eyes. Trent looked to his brother for an answer.

"It's Wednesday, October 2nd."

"October? But… playoffs? What happened?"

"Playoffs are over. You guys won, Trent. I don't know if this is a good time to tell you, but a scout for junior rep came out to see you play. He loved you, and they're still working out an offer for next season. I don't know how this will affect that, but…"

Trent was shocked. His dreams were being held out to him on a silver platter, but for some reason, all he felt was sorrow.

"Did someone die?" he croaked.

"What, honey? No one died!" his mother answered with a weak smile. "You're fine, you're going to be fine. You're awake." She smiled, and Trent shook his head and looked down at his cast.

That took his breath away. *That's why my arm hurts so much.*

"W—what happened?"

Jeremy sighed deeply. Trent felt like his brother was searching his eyes for the memory Trent just couldn't find in his own head.

"Hit and run. There's an officer you might meet. No suspects yet, but they think they know the colour of the car. Navy blue," Jeremy explained, and Trent nodded his head slowly.

"And... you're sure no one died?" he asked his mom again.

She shook her head and gave him another kiss on the back of his hand. When he laid his head back, she gently stroked his hair – at least, the small amount which wasn't wrapped up in his head bandage – away from his face. There was so much going on in Trent's mind. He didn't even know what to ask next.

✝

The next two weeks went by in a hazy blur. The first person to visit Trent from school after he woke up was Adam, who was so overjoyed to see Trent awake that he started singing a terrible rendition of *Hallelujah* the first time he visited. Trent met with specialist after specialist. He was put through so many tests that he felt like the hospital was worse than school. He met with detectives who seemed like they knew something that they couldn't tell him. Talking, breathing, it was all so painful, but as time went by, he did feel like he was getting better.

Through all this healing, though, a new kind of pain erupted inside of him.

He felt a strange yearning, like he was missing something. He wondered if it was the memory loss, but the feeling didn't change once he started remembering things. Shortly after waking, memories began flooding back: the first month of school. He started to remember some of his playoff games. He remembered boring, mundane moments: what he had for dinner three weeks ago, when he got a card in the mail from his grandmother in Florida.

The more memories that came back, the better he felt, but something was always missing.

Like a word he often used was no longer a part of his vocabulary.

18

LYNN MARIE

WEDNESDAY, OCTOBER 2, 2019

12:26 AM

Once in the car, Lynn sped Jeremy and Charlie to the hospital. Even though the drive went by faster than usual, the millions of thoughts in her head made it feel like an hour had passed. She'd promised Trent the next time he disappeared that she'd get to his room so he wouldn't be stuck in the darkness. With what he'd just done for her, however he had done it, she was prepared to fight anyone who would hold her back from getting to him now. She was sure that it wasn't only Jeremy who had knocked Dex off of her. She had felt an arctic wind sweep by as Jeremy hurled toward him. Her entire body was still shaking from watching the whole fight, and she was scared that Dex would wake up and come after them in some shape or form.

"Did you feel anything weird when I pushed Dex?" Jeremy suddenly asked.

Lynn went wide-eyed at his question.

"Did you... did you see what I saw?" Lynn asked as her panic turned her thoughts into a vortex, and she didn't know how to explain to him exactly what she had seen.

"When I jumped, I was freezing. I didn't see anything, but it felt like it wasn't me. It felt like... I don't know. It was weird." Jeremy shook his head and nervously ran a hand through his hair.

Lynn recognised this trademark Shawking move.

"What do you think happened?"

Lynn took a moment before answering.

"I don't know, but I'm hoping whatever it is, it's good."

Jeremy nodded in silent agreement.

"What the hell happened?" Charlie suddenly moaned from the back seat.

Lynn and Jeremy both jumped, startled, and turned to see Charlie waking up.

"Are you okay? We didn't see what happened to you," Jeremy explained to her as Lynn set her eyes back on the road.

"Yeah, just the back of my head hurts a little. Dex pushed me into the wall. Where are we going? What happened?" Charlie breathed as she rubbed the back of her head.

"We're going to the hospital; I can't see Trent. The last two times this happened, he got pulled back to his room or something, so I have to get there."

"You might want to get your head checked, too," Jeremy added, and Charlie shook her head at him.

"It's okay, I just faint easily. Ask Lynn; I almost passed out in my driveway when she convinced me Trent was a ghost."

Jeremy looked to Lynn, and she shrugged in

agreement. Charlie rested her head back on the seat for the rest of the drive.

✝

Once they arrived at Liberty, Jeremy, Lynn and Charlie made their way to Trent's hospital room. The group kept their heads down and walked close to the walls; they realised that a dishevelled group of teenagers might look a little suspicious if they were seen rushing around in the middle of the night.

"Excuse me," the man at the desk stopped them with his stern voice. "It's too late for three visitors in one room. Now, I know you're someone's brother on this floor, and I've seen you before, but not usually in ICU," he said as he looked from Jeremy to Lynn. "Family only, please."

Both of the girls looked to Jeremy, and he cleared his throat.

"Uh, yeah, she's my sister though. Can't she at least come in?"

Lynn did her best not to react to Jeremy's white lie. The man at the desk looked skeptically from one to the other.

"I don't know—"

"We'll be quiet – it's not like we're going in there to party, you know?" Lynn added before the man could protest.

He sighed, then nodded in the direction of the room, begrudgingly motioning for them to go in. Jeremy gave Charlie a look, and she took a seat next to the receptionist's desk.

Once they entered the room, Lynn noticed Jeremy wince at the sight of Trent's body. Jeremy looked over at Lynn for an answer.

"I don't... I don't see him," she stuttered, but she didn't hear that drawn-out beeping noise of his machine either.

That had to be a good sign, right? Lynn's eyes searched every part of the room. She didn't want to look at Trent's body.

"Oh my God. Trent?"

Jeremy was looking at his brother now, and Lynn finally let her eyes settle on Trent too. She was shocked to see that Trent's eyes were open. She felt elated – he was awake! Trent's eyelids were heavy, but he managed to register that people were in the room. He looked sluggishly, comfortably, at Jeremy, and then he winced at the sight of Lynn. Lynn instantly felt her stomach drop. Something told her that he had no idea who he was looking at. She had guessed that this might happen, and she had imagined how it might hurt, but none of her premonitions could prepare her for how bad she felt right now.

"Mom, he's waking up, you need to get here!" Jeremy exclaimed into his phone.

Lynn heard his mother's voice on the other end of the call, loud and excited, before he hung up. Jeremy started frantically hitting a button to call in a nurse. Trent had passed out just as quickly as he'd woken up, but Lynn could see how determined Jeremy was to let everyone know that his brother did open his eyes and seemed lucid for ten seconds. Lynn turned to him.

"Jer... can you... I—"

"What is it?" Jeremy asked, and the concern in his eyes made her hate what she had to say next.

"I can't be here when he wakes up."

"But you should be—"

"Just listen, Jer. I *can't* be here. If he doesn't remember me, I can't handle that right now. I'm going to go to the police with what I have. Can you please just keep me updated? Let me know what happens? I need to know that he's safe. And…" Lynn looked down at her feet. "…I'm going to talk to Charlie about this – I think we can all agree that we can't tell him everything that happened right away, you know? It's going to be too overwhelming. We need to keep this between the three of us. Okay?"

Jeremy looked like he wanted to protest but didn't know how to. He sighed and then gave Lynn his phone.

"I need your number, then."

Lynn took it from him and put it in.

"You'll be able to get home, right? I'm going to drive Charlie home and tell her in the car."

Jeremy nodded in response. Lynn took a deep breath before she continued.

"That's not the only reason I want you to text me. I want you to text me every single time you think about texting Nate. I don't want you to text him anymore, got it?"

Jeremy looked confused for a second, but then his eyes lit up with understanding.

"Shit – that's why Nate knows you. Lynn, it's not what you think."

"Jeremy, it's what I know." Lynn closed her eyes, thinking that not looking him in the eyes would soften the blow of what she was going to say to him next. "I'm the reason your brother is here." Even though she had closed her eyes when she said it, it didn't soften the blow of shame she felt in her stomach. Lynn opened her eyes and grimaced at the ground.

"You owed Nate money. I asked him to deal with it, and you know what he did? He told Ray, and Ray did this. He wanted to scare you that night, I'm sure of it. I don't think he wanted *this* to happen, but it did, and he clearly doesn't give a shit what happens to other people when he wants to scare them. I can't... I'm not going to be like them anymore. I can't do it anymore. I need you to know how fucking sorry I am that this ever happened to you and your brother." Lynn was determined to not choke on her words; she was going to say her piece, no matter how difficult. "Even if you need more help than I can give you, I will stop at nothing to help you. Trent didn't know about any of this until he got dropped into my life, and maybe this is—" Lynn winced at the reminder of a conversation between her and Trent. "Maybe this is the reason. When he wakes up, I don't think he will remember anything from this, and I know you'll want to keep it that way. I do, too. When he wakes up, he won't know what you've done, and he doesn't have to. This was a horrible accident that was all my fault, and I'll pay for it. But I'm also going to make sure Ray pays for it. Okay?"

Jeremy stood frozen in place. He seemed embarrassed, but also angry. He had every right to be, and Lynn thought he'd be more upset than he was right now, but she could tell that he was holding something back.

He nodded his head, and Lynn glared at him.

"I'm serious. I know you barely know me, but you need to know that I care about your brother more than anything and…" Lynn's shoulders suddenly untensed, and she slumped, defeated.

Her determined speech was exhausting, but only because she couldn't hold back the sadness of knowing that Trent would probably wake up without knowing her.

"I'm going to make sure that I keep my promises to him. Whether or not he remembers them," she finished.

Jeremy's small moment of anger quickly subsided.

"I've been trying to stop."

"I know, Jeremy. You don't have to make excuses with me. Just tell me the truth. When it gets bad, I will help you. Got it?"

Jeremy nodded in relief. The small amount of embarrassment he showed seemed to subside as well.

"Remember. Text me. Any update you can, anytime you have the urge to text Nate. Text me instead. G*ot it*?" Lynn persisted.

"Got it," Jeremy finally agreed, and then Lynn left the room to catch up with Charlie.

As Lynn walked away from the room, she could hear Jeremy on the phone telling someone else that Trent had awakened.

"Did I hear that right? Is Trent awake?" Charlie stood as she saw Lynn walk down the hallway towards her. Lynn nodded.

"He woke up for a few seconds, and Jeremy called his mom. I need to get to the police station now, but I'm taking you home first."

Charlie nodded and quietly followed Lynn back to her car.

"I know we have to go to the cops about this, but what do you think Ray will do to us once he finds out? He already threatened me the first time I told him we should tell the cops," Charlie asked as she got into the front seat of Lynn's car.

Lynn didn't know how to answer. They weren't idiots. Lynn and Charlie both knew that Dex would tell Ray what had happened tonight, and that they'd both be furious. Lynn could only hope that, maybe, they wouldn't believe she'd actually go to the police.

"I don't think he'll find out," she lied. "At least, I know neither of us is going to tell him. Maybe he won't find out."

Charlie stared at Lynn disbelievingly from the passenger seat. Lynn tried to ignore the look as she pulled out of the hospital's garage.

"Okay, maybe, I don't know. All I know is that I have to go to the cops tonight. I'm too scared Dex will kill me in my sleep, so the cops have to know before that happens. You know?"

This time, Charlie didn't know how to answer. She just rubbed her forehead with an open palm and sighed.

It didn't take them very long to get to Charlie's house, and Charlie took a deep breath before turning to Lynn and giving her a hug. Lynn tensed awkwardly. This was way more physical contact than she was used to, but it wasn't as scary as she had worked it up to be in her head. She felt safe with Charlie now.

"I'm going to text you tomorrow to ask you what happened, and to make sure you're alive," Charlie told her before she got out of the car.

It would have been a funny joke if it weren't true. Once she'd made sure Charlie got into her house safely, Lynn headed straight for the police station.

WEDNESDAY, OCTOBER 2, 2019

01:10 AM

As Lynn pulled up to the local police station, she suddenly felt her heart pounding against her chest. She'd never been this scared in her life, but she knew she had to do this. She had to get out of the car and tell someone what she knew. Trying to muster the emotional strength to get out of the car made her realize how exhausted she really was; she hadn't had a good night's sleep in a long time.

When she walked into the foyer, she took an awkwardly long look around the walls and floor. They were all white and pristinely clean. She spotted the secretary, who was absentmindedly scrolling through her phone with palpable boredom. When Lynn finally shuffled over to the front desk, the woman's gaze flicked up at her. Her eyes grew wide instantly, and she immediately put her phone down. They were both silent as the secretary gaped at Lynn in shock. The woman's sudden and dramatic change of expression reminded Lynn that she probably looked extremely alarming right now, all filthy and frenzied from the night's events.

"I know its late, but I need to speak to someone about the hit and run on Trent Shawking."

The receptionist closed her mouth, furrowed her brow, and tilted her head before pointing behind Lynn, inviting her to take a seat. Her nails clicked away on the keyboard.

"Shawking is spelled S-h-a-w-k-i-n-g?"

Lynn nodded in response, then took a seat.

"Looks like that's Lexington's case. I'll call him. He usually works nights. Are you okay with waiting, or do you need to be somewhere?"

This is probably the safest place for me right now.

"I can wait," Lynn mumbled.

The receptionist nodded and then picked up the phone to make a call. A few muffled words were exchanged, and then the phone call ended with a swift click.

"He's on his way," she assured her, and Lynn was left to her thoughts.

She couldn't help but wonder if Dex was out there looking for her. The worst-case scenarios played out in her imagination: Dex coming into the foyer with a gun pointed straight at her head; Dex waiting at her house while her family, visiting for Teddy's funeral, were asleep and vulnerable. The thought of Teddy's funeral reminded her that she hadn't checked her phone in hours. When she opened it, her heart sank yet again.

Lynn Marie. Where are you?
I'm not mad, I just need to

know that you're safe.
Please, just text me.

Lynn felt disappointed in herself. Her mother seemed to actually be trying for once; normally, her mother would become angry instantly over an ignored text, but this time, she only seemed concerned. She had already lost one child, and now she was worried about the safety of the other.

I'm sorry if this wakes
you. I'm safe. I'll be
home soon. I promise.

I wasn't sleeping.
Too worried. I love you.

Lynn hesitated before typing it back. Then she took a deep breath.

I love you too.

After hitting send, Lynn revisited a small detail from her worst-case scenarios which she had been trying to ignore. Tomorrow, she would have to attend Teddy's funeral. As this realisation settled in, the idea of going home seemed scarier than waiting to talk to this officer. Maybe she'd even prefer to face Dex. Just as she was beginning to spiral into a state of total panic, a deep voice broke her out of her thoughts.

"Hey, Kat, what happened?"

A tall black man entered the foyer and addressed the receptionist. He was dressed rather nicely: sky blue button-up shirt, black dress pants, polished shoes, and his cologne smelled expensive. As the man approached her, Lynn noted that she was a stark contrast in style and hygiene right now, with dirt from the junkyard still clinging to her hair and clothes. He didn't seem to care, though. The receptionist nodded at Lynn, and Lexington held out a hand for her to shake.

"Hi, I'm Officer Lexington. You are?"

"L—Lynn Avison." Lynn paused awkwardly before shaking his hand. She thought officers wore a police uniform.

"I hear you know something about Trent's case?"

Lynn couldn't find the words, so she forced her hand to unlock her phone and show him the photos she'd taken just hours before. Lexington looked her up and down quizzically.

"I didn't want to bring it with me because I thought that might make it worse, but I needed to show you something before I just told you a long-winded story that would only get me into trouble," Lynn said slowly, and Lexington nodded at her to follow him.

Lexington led her down a small hallway to an extremely tidy office. All of the paperwork on his desk was organized into neat piles, and the shelves were free from the grey layer of dust which often covered her shelves at home. The room smelled strongly of his cologne, with a subtle hint of rose; the red flower sat on his desk in a vase. Lexington pointed to the chair opposite his, and Lynn took a hesitant seat.

"So, did you want to start from the beginning?"

"Um—"

Oh, right, I'm going to have to explain myself.

The thought scared Lynn. There were things she wanted to say, and some things she wasn't sure she could say without running into a wall that had to be explained with 'a ghost told me.'

"Let's start with your full name and age. I'm going to record this," he said, his fingers resting on his computer's keyboard.

Lynn's stomach twisted in knots as she glanced at her phone, which he had placed between them.

"My name is Lynn Avison, I'm seventeen. I know that Ray Hurley, uh, Raymond Hurley, was driving the car that hit Trent Shawking."

"Were you there?"

"No, but this picture on my phone is a picture of his pickup truck's broken fender. I know Ray's cousin Dexter broke up the rest of the truck to hide evidence the night after it happened, and then he kept this piece in his house to use as blackmail against Ray."

"How do you know all this?"

"So… this is where I incriminate myself, and I need your help to keep me from rotting in jail."

Lexington let out a confused chuckle, though Lynn gave no indication that she was joking.

"I…" Lynn stopped and looked down at her feet for a moment. She wanted to look the man in the eye when she admitted her crimes, but knew she couldn't. With a large inhale, she continued, "I collect for Raymond Hurley. I started about two years ago. I was the new kid at school. I was awkward, I guess – I kept to myself. He started talking to me and found out about my situation with my brother. Teddy was sick and we moved here thinking this hospital, Liberty, would help him. Ray told me I could make a lot of money if I helped him do something, and that something was collecting oxy. I didn't move much product at a time; there were always small packages that someone would leave for me on the roof at Liberty, and I'd have to bring it to someone else, who would then bring it to Raymond. I'm not going to collect for him anymore. I can't, and I'm turning myself in so I can take him down with me. This dude is a fucking asshole, and the fact that he thought he could hit Trent and get away with it really pisses me off! So, even if he doesn't go down, at least I'll go down knowing that someone knows the fucking truth!"

Lynn finally dared to look the officer in the eye, and was surprised to find that he didn't look shocked, but slightly amused at her passionate ramblings.

"So, what now?" she finished.

"What now?" he parroted.

"Yeah, what now?" Lynn asked, annoyed.

She felt like maybe he wasn't taking this seriously.

"As theatrical as that was – and believe me, I enjoyed every second of it – it's a confession, and as easy as it would be to put cuffs on you, I don't think that would solve the problem. We need more evidence to put cuffs on Ray."

"Okay, then what do we do to put cuffs on him?"

"Keep quiet. Don't tell anyone else what you just told me, and let my investigation continue. I'm going to ask you to keep collecting for him if he asks you, unless you made a show of telling him that you were coming to the police, but I doubt that you did. So, thank you, Lynn Avison, for a new lead. I'll be in contact."

Lynn didn't know how to respond. Her face was frozen in an expression which seemed to ask: what the hell was this man talking about?

"But... aren't I in trouble? What's going to happen to me?"

Lexington's smug smirk suddenly softened into a genuine grin.

"I don't know yet, but you did ask me to help you not rot in jail, and I'd like to. You just have to cooperate. We'll be in contact."

Lynn sat, dumbstruck, and watched as the gentleman got up from his chair and held the door open for her.

"So, if that's all for the night, you're free to go, and I'm going to give you my card. I'll need you to send me that picture—"

"Yeah, about being free to go, I'm kind of scared that Dex will kill me in my sleep. I just escaped from his junkyard and came straight here."

"*Escaped*? It's a junkyard, not a lair."

"Well, it kind of looks like one, and he did try and attack me while I was there, so what other word do you think I should use?"

Lexington rubbed his forehead with his hand. Lynn couldn't tell if he was holding back a sigh or a laugh. He dug around in his pocket for something and produced a copy of his card. She stared at it.

"I don't think this is going to be an effective weapon to use against Dexter Hurley if he decides to come after me. The dude almost broke my thumb with a metal pipe."

Lexington snorted, but his face immediately became serious when he looked at the blotchy purple hand she was holding up.

"Did you need someone to look at that?"

How battered to do I have to be for someone to take me seriously around here?

"No, I'll be fine – but if he hits me in the head next time, I doubt I'll be able to tell you about it after."

Lexington let out a small dubious laugh, and Lynn still couldn't see what was so funny.

"Lynn, you have what I like to call a payout. It isn't exactly blackmail until you need it to be. With a broken thumb, we could charge him for assault, but it wouldn't do much in the long run. If need be, I'm talking in the worst-case scenario, we can threaten Dexter with this picture. If he gets you to collect for him again, just do it and pretend like nothing's happening, but then call me directly. We need to collect more evidence. If he threatens you, or tries to harm you – even if you see him lurking around a little too close – I can be anywhere in this town within five minutes. Even if you think you see his shadow, I'll come running. That man works hard, not smart. I wouldn't be so scared of him. His uncle, yes. But honestly, he's probably crying somewhere right now if he knows you have evidence, not plotting to kill you. Dexter is the runt of the Hurley family."

Lynn furrowed her brows at him, and Lexington again urged her to take his card with a subtle hand movement.

"Use my number to send that picture by the way, not my work e-mail."

Lynn finally took it, shoving it into the pocket of her jeans.

"Really? You can't let me borrow a gun or something?" Lynn mumbled.

This time she was joking, but only partly.

"Borrow a gun? Yeah, why don't you take mine? While you're at it, take my badge, too. I won't need it anymore, anyway, if my commander hears about you 'borrowing' my gun." Lexington let out a short laugh, but Lynn didn't have the energy to return it. She still didn't feel very safe, but Lexington seemed all right. It didn't hurt that he dressed well, too.

WEDNESDAY, OCTOBER 2, 2019

$$02{:}03_{\text{PM}}$$

At Teddy's funeral, Lynn sat in the front row, between her mother and her Aunt Marie. She kept her eyes on the casket's baby blue cloak, which reached the floor. Sometimes her eyes would drift off to the many bouquets of flowers set around him. She'd even caught herself counting and keeping track of every different kind of shoe that everyone was wearing in the funeral home. Anything to distract her from actually looking at her brother lying in his casket.

After all she'd seen, Lynn had begun to think of people's bodies as nothing more than physical vessels. This new understanding was really disturbing, but in a way, it kind of helped. Lynn grew up in a religious family, but they never really attended church. Her mother sort of gave up on that when Teddy became really sick. Most people would fall back on religion in a time like that, but Lynn and her mother relied more on the hospital and the hope they were given by science. Lynn took comfort now in knowing that Teddy was somewhere else, not in pain. The idea of 'souls' never really clicked until Trent's ghost was dropped on her head, and even with that experience, she didn't understand half of what had actually gone on. Lynn started to loathe the fact that maybe Trent was right about him disrupting her life with his ghostly presence for 'a reason'.

Maybe *this* was the reason. To accept death as it was. Time running out for our bodies. *Only* our bodies. There would always be an inevitable end to our physical selves, but what makes us unique, the things that make us who we are— never really die. Lynn had had a genuine experience with a ghost. Teddy's passage to the other side had been revealed to her by a surprisingly sweet boy in one of the worst circumstances of his life. Although the specifics of death remained a mystery, this whole experience made it easier to let go of Teddy because she knew now that everyone was more than just their bodies. In some way, the spirit persists long after their physical bodies have given out. It was made very clear to her that her physical form and her soul were two separate things. The more she thought about this, the less she felt trapped in her body, which she'd grown to despise over the years. She realized that the person who invaded her body so long ago had only hurt her shell. He had not harmed her soul. Her soul was resilient, and she was determined to make her soul as strong as Trent's, with all its stubbornness to live.

These thoughts kept her from crying, although she must have looked insanely numb to her family members. Lynn's mother hadn't stopped crying since the beginning of the service.

†

An hour into the wake, when there weren't many new visitors anymore, Lynn decided she had to leave the room. She walked outside of the funeral home, into the parking lot, and breathed in the fall air. It was just cold enough to make her shiver, and the nostalgia of a biting chill made her miss someone.

Lynn looked out to the trees behind the funeral home and imagined Trent standing beside her. If he were still here as a ghost, he'd try to make some joke to lighten the mood, call her Lynny, and grin that stupid grin of his. She'd roll her eyes at him or join in the banter, and she'd feel like she wasn't so alone in the world anymore.

She'd never thought there'd come a time in her life when she actually wanted to be haunted by a ghost.

Lynn pulled her phone out of her pocket and opened the picture of the fender, but before she could take a better look at it, she was startled.

"Lynn Marie," a sing-song voice sighed.

Lynn jumped slightly at the voice, and turned to see her Aunt Marie who was hugging herself tightly as protection against the cold breeze. As she leaned against the wall, she sullenly smiled at her niece.

"Why're you smiling at a funeral?" Lynn asked her aunt, but her interrogation was light-hearted.

"That's all I know how to do, Marie Two," Marie answered with a shrug, and Lynn softened at the throwback to one of her old nicknames.

"Well, that's no fun, Marie One," Lynn answered back.

The pair looked out to the parking lot and

watched a large black bird swoop down from above the funeral home and land somewhere among the mess of parked cars.

"You ready to move back to Logan? If you're willing, you and your mom can stay with me until you find a new place."

Lynn unexpectedly felt offended by the question. Four days ago, she would have said yes in a heartbeat. Now, she had to think about it. Did she want to go back to Logan, the place she called her real home, or did she want to stay here and chase a ghost?

"I don't know, honestly. I have to think about it." Lynn shrugged.

"Hm, okay, kid – just let your mom or me know. You know, she sent me out here to talk to you about it. She can get a little scared to talk to you sometimes."

"She's scared of me?"

Lynn was hurt by that, but when she saw her aunt smile and shake her head, she figured she understood wrong.

"No, she's not scared *of* you. She's scared to talk to you about some things. She tells me she messed up bad, and she doesn't know how to fix it."

"Oh."

"Yeah, well, I know what it is, and I know it's hard to forgive, but you two need to work together if you wanna stay here with just the two of you, right? If you want to come back to Logan, you'll have me to take some of that burden off you. Okay, Marie Two?"

Lynn stared at her Aunt Marie, wanting to answer her but having a hard time, her stomach in knots. Aunt Marie nodded and raised an arm to Lynn, beckoning her to come back inside. When Lynn got close enough, her aunt wrapped her arm around her shoulders.

†

Teddy's funeral service went by too slowly. Or maybe it only felt that way because Lynn kept checking her phone with every single minute that passed. The extended family visited, and she hugged people she had forgotten she'd known. She and her mother had moved from Logan to Heatherdale only two years ago, but they'd never really seen much of her family before that. All of the family who attended the funeral were from her mom's side. Lynn's biological father died when she was young, and obviously never knew Teddy. Her mother had remarried to a man named Henry.

Henry not only turned into a deadbeat, but he also demonized Lynn and her mom to his whole family because, in his eyes, Lynn was a liar. Lynn had told Henry that his best friend from high school, who Henry had invited over every Saturday night, had a way of making her very uncomfortable. At the time, when she explained what he did, no one believed her. They wrote it off as Henry's friend 'playing a joke'.

The tension after her confession had left Lynn, and by extension Teddy, entirely estranged from Henry and those close to him. No matter what she did or said, she knew she would always be a liar to them – even when her claim was proven. She knew there was no turning back, no making amends; she just wanted to forget about that part of her life, especially today. She was already dealing with too much.

She held her breath the whole time at the funeral, thinking that anyone from Teddy's father's side could show up, and she'd have to be shamed by their eyes on her. But no one from Teddy's side of the family showed up to the funeral, not even his own father. Lynn was sure her mother had told him that Teddy was dead, but she wondered now if she had also told Henry to stay away, or if he'd chosen to himself.

✝

By six in the evening, Lynn was in the car with her mother going home when her phone went off. A message from Charlie.

**Hey Lynn
Wanna get something to
eat with me tonight?**

Lynn felt scared and relieved all at once. Relieved, because now she could stop thinking about the funeral for two seconds and go somewhere else, but scared because she wasn't used to having friends anymore. She had spent two years being anti-social; she was shy to begin with, and had been inducted into the Heatherdale drug scene before she'd ever made any actual friends. Suddenly, the idea of trying to socialise made her nervous.

Sure, what time?

**Is in half an hour okay?
Burger Monk?**

Ok.

Jeremy's coming too.

Lynn sighed. Why did Charlie have to mention that detail afterwards? Lynn probably would've said no if she'd known Jeremy was coming. It's not that she didn't want to talk to him – she told him to text her whenever he needed help – but right now, Jeremy was just an awful reminder of his brother not being around anymore. That was especially hard to think about today, when Lynn needed Trent the most.

"Mom, I'm going to go out with a couple of friends tonight, if that's okay."

"Okay. Just remember to text me, please."

That was surprisingly easy. Lynn's Aunt Marie was right; her mother seemed scared to talk to Lynn about anything right now. Lynn decided to take that as a blessing in disguise. They'd speak to each other only when they had to. Maybe fewer arguments would arise this way.

As soon as they got home, Lynn's mother went to the front door, and Lynn noticed her fumbling with her keys for longer than usual. In Lynn's mind, she saw Trent from the corner of her eye, nodding towards her mom like he had when Charlie needed a hug. That had been entirely his idea – Lynn was never a hugger, and she'd been very reluctant to offer Charlie an open arm. Today was different, though. Without thinking, Lynn ran up behind her mom and wrapped her arms around her, holding on until her mother turned around and gave her a kiss on the top of her head.

"Love you, Mom."

"Love you too, Lynny," her mother replied.

There was something oddly comforting in that. The only two people who'd ever used that nickname were gone, and she thought she'd never hear it again. It was the first time her mother had used it instead of Lynn Marie.

19

BUNGEE JUMPING

WEDNESDAY, OCTOBER 2, 2019

06:36 PM

The first person who Lynn set her eyes on was Jeremy. He must've noticed her car pull into the parking lot of Burger Monk before Charlie did, because he was already staring at her through the window of the restaurant when she got out of her car.

Great. Can't turn back now.

The two were sitting next to the front window at a table. Both of them already had half-empty glasses of soft drinks. She wondered how long they'd been waiting and what they'd been talking about in the time it had taken her to get there. She had a fairly good guess.

Lynn sighed and entered the restaurant, slowing her pace before she sat down.

"Hey," she breathed, then took a seat next to Charlie in the booth across from Jeremy.

"Hey, Lynn," Charlie said, and Jeremy nodded to her.

They both had an intense look in their eyes. Lynn raised a brow and looked back and forth between them.

"So, is there a specific reason you wanted to do this, or are we trying to force a friendship over our shared traumatic and paranormal experience?" Lynn didn't know how to turn her cynical mind off sometimes, and she could tell neither of them found what she said very funny.

"Well… there's a couple of things. I just found out something that I thought you should know. Mel told me she saw Trent's…" Charlie looked around to make sure no one was looking, and then mouthed the word 'ghost.'

"Wait, what?" Lynn went wide-eyed and sat up in the booth.

Her heart started hammering against her chest.

"Yeah, well, Mel was in the car with me when we… you know… when Ray…" Charlie mouthed the word 'hit', "Trent, and she told me just yesterday that she saw Trent when it happened as a…" Charlie mouthed the word 'ghost' for a second time, "and she couldn't tell me *then* because she had a panic attack. The last three days, she's been having a mental breakdown about it, and she finally spilled. And I had to tell her what happened to you to make her feel less crazy."

"Wait, you told her? How well do you even know this girl?" Lynn huffed in frustration.

"Lynn, she's my girlfriend – didn't you know? She was a wreck, and I love her, I had to tell her. She almost tried to… It was just important that I tell her. I'm sorry. I know it wasn't my place, but I had to help her."

Charlie cut herself off before she went into too much detail, but Lynn had gotten the idea.

"So, now Mel knows?"

"She knows enough. She knew about Trent in the first place anyway, so I just told her about our encounter so she wouldn't feel so alone. But Ray doesn't know that you went to the cops. You did go to the cops, right? We wanted to ask you what happened when you went to the station."

The edge in Charlie's voice revealed the subtext of her question: when Lynn went to the station, whose names did she give out?

"I talked to this guy named Lexington, and before you ask – no I didn't give him anyone else's name but Ray and Dex."

"Lexington – he's the officer on Trent's case," Jeremy interjected, and Charlie looked relieved.

"Yeah, he said that what I told him could get me thrown in jail, but he wants Ray in cuffs more than me. I sent him the pictures that I took of the fender. He also told me not to be afraid of Dex, but I'm almost sure he and Ray are planning something to keep me quiet. Once they figure out what they want to do with me, I'm probably done for. I don't want to collect for them anymore, but Lexington told me to. I mean, Ray hasn't asked me for anything lately – he just threatened me the night before the three of us went to the junkyard, and I haven't heard from him or Nate since. Usually, I'd hear from Nate looking for a pickup, but I just haven't. I was thinking of leaving Heatherdale before anything else happens."

"What? How're you going to leave?" Charlie asked.

"The only reason I got involved with this shit in the first place was because my mom and I always planned on moving back to Logan after we'd worked through my brother's remission, or... if he ended up dying here, then we'd move back anyway. I always knew I didn't have a future here. Now that Teddy's..." Lynn hated the word but knew she had to grow accustomed to saying it. "Now that he's dead, Mom is ready to leave. My aunt says we can stay with her, and I might have to take her up on the offer."

Lynn looked to Jeremy, who looked a little more scared than Lynn had expected.

"But you can't leave..." Jeremy said, and Lynn sighed as she realized she would be breaking the promise she made to Trent *and* Jeremy if she left.

This is why she didn't want to make friends here. She didn't want to let anyone down when she had to walk away.

"Jer, I'm sorry. To tell you the truth, I don't want to go. I want..." Lynn sighed with frustration this time. She didn't want to admit this to them, but the world's weight was still crashing down on her shoulders, and she just couldn't take it anymore. "I want to stay here and talk to Trent. I want him to remember me, but I'm scared that even if he does remember me, it won't be like it was. I want to stay and help you Jer, and I think you're cool, and I want to be your friend Charlie, but I dug myself a hole I don't know how to get out of and if I have the option to run from it, I have to. Don't I?"

The two of them stared at her. The look of confused concern on their faces was comforting, but she was nervous of what they'd say. There was only one other person she'd poured her heart out to like this before, and he didn't even remember her.

"You fell in love with him, didn't you?"

Lynn didn't have to answer Charlie's question. It seemed like Charlie already knew the answer when Lynn looked down at her hands, interlocked on the table.

"Fucking hell, my brother doesn't even get rejected

in the afterlife," Jeremy muttered under his breath, and both Lynn and Charlie gave him an odd look.

Jeremy rolled his eyes and sighed.

"Lynn, just stay here, please. We'll look out for each other. We'll make sure we're not alone all the time. We'll keep doing what the officer tells us to do. We *will* get Ray for this, but you need to stay," he said.

His eyes reminded her of Trent's. He had the same determination, but while Trent's was as strong as a forest fire, Jeremy's was the flame of a candle. Lynn could tell he doubted himself, but he was trying hard to make a compelling argument.

"I'm with Jeremy on this one. You need to do what feels right, not what feels safe. If you feel like you need to stay here, you need to stay here. And... I think you're cool too." Charlie smiled, and Lynn let herself relax a little.

Even with everything going on, it was nice to have a couple of people looking out for her now.

"Okay, so what's the plan then?" Jeremy asked, and Lynn looked up at him blankly.

"The plan? What plan? We're not breaking into another junkyard, are we?"

Jeremy grinned lightly and shook his head at the comment.

"No, but I think we need Trent to remember what happened. I know you said it was a bad idea, but how will we hide this shit from him? I agree we shouldn't tell him everything at once, but we need to warm him up to it, and tell him bits and pieces over like... like a year or something."

Lynn's instincts told her to put up a fight, but she could see Charlie nodding enthusiastically.

"I don't know." Lynn breathed in deeply.

What if that part of him is gone forever? What if there's no way to get it back, and I'm quite literally chasing a ghost?

"Okay, well let's not agree on that right now. Let's see what happens, you know? What if he starts remembering things on his own? It's not like we're going to gaslight him and tell him it isn't true. We'll be the memory referees and just kind of go with it," Charlie said with a shrug.

Lynn looked to Jeremy, who was returning Charlie's previous nods of agreement. Maybe it was just because Lynn was emotionally exhausted, or because she was sick of arguing, but she offered them a defeated shrug in agreement.

"So, how's he doing anyway?" Lynn asked Jeremy.

"He's pretty lucid now, and they put him on a rehabilitation plan. You know what was weird? When he woke up, he asked if someone had died. Maybe he remembered your brother? Sorry to hear about that, by the way." Jeremy awkwardly looked down at his hands on the table.

There was something strange about his expression. Like he felt guilty that Lynn had helped his brother live and there was nothing he could do for her.

Lynn covered her face with her hands.

"Oh my God," her muffled voice said, "...maybe he does remember."

It may have been the worst part about their time together, but the fact that he might be remembering Teddy gave Lynn a bit more hope.

"Yeah, maybe. The doctor told him he could be back to school in two or three weeks. If you're not going to visit him, you should at least be the first person to talk to him when he comes back." Jeremy shrugged.

Lynn uncovered her face and glared at Jeremy for a moment. He pursed his lips and raised his eyebrows expectantly, clearly waiting for a rebuttal.

"Fine. I'll do it. But only if you buy me a

Neapolitan milkshake."

Lynn was sort of kidding, and sort of not. All she knew right now is that she was sick of being so hard on herself, and tired of always expecting the worst. She kept fighting with the thought that maybe Trent wasn't supposed to remember her, because that was part of her cosmic punishment. But Jeremy was only asking her to talk to him, and she was too exhausted to disagree anymore.

In response to Lynn's request, Jeremy pulled his wallet out of his back pocket, slapped it on the table overdramatically, and dragged it with him as he headed to the ordering counter. The two girls watched as he ordered the milkshake with no change in his demeanour. Meanwhile, they were quietly laughing at the table.

"Deal," Jeremy said as he set the milkshake down in front of her and took a seat across from them again.

"Wait, I said maybe I'd do it—"

"No, you didn't. You said you'd do it, and the milkshake seals it. I'm his witness, and now technically a memory referee," Charlie shot back.

"Charlie, I thought we were cool," Lynn mumbled jokingly, and then took a sip from the straw.

"I grew up with Trent," said Jeremy. "You're going to have to be more stubborn than that to win any argument with me."

Lynn pulled a face at him, lacking a better comeback.

For the next two hours, the three talked about what they might do in a range of hypothetical situations, including dangerous run-ins with Dexter or Ray, or Trent remembering certain moments from his existence as a ghost. As the chatter continued, it dawned on Lynn that she finally, for the first time in Heatherdale, felt like she fit in somewhere. It had happened in the strangest circumstance, but it still felt great. Maybe she had been alone needlessly; maybe she had been hiding from everyone for no reason. None of that really mattered anymore, though – she was just happy that she had people to talk to after her brother's funeral.

This was a new kind of white noise.

SUNDAY, OCTOBER 20, 2019

08:16 AM

The next two weeks were hard. Lynn's mother regularly talked about whether or not they were going back to Logan. Lynn kept making it clear that she didn't want to leave anymore, but her mother kept pushing. Lynn's mother wasn't being as understanding as her Aunt Marie made her seem, but Lynn could understand her mom's insistence. Heatherdale had become the sight of a horrible memory for their family, and her mom wanted to leave that memory behind.

On the bright side, her mother wasn't arguing with her. They were having actual discussions, and disagreements weren't met with raised voices; they were met with valid points. Her mother's points included: they would spend less money on living expenses in Logan, Lynn would be able to go back to her friends there, and they'd be near family when Lynn's mother needed her family the most. They were all excellent points, and Lynn felt selfish for continuously saying no. This feeling was only made worse because Lynn couldn't really tell her mother why she wanted to stay.

Though she couldn't discuss it with her mother, Lynn would question her reasoning over and over again. It was making the prospect of going to school and not seeing Trent for the next two weeks a bit harder, but Charlie and Jeremy made it bearable. The three were becoming inseparable, and she quite liked that. Mel started hanging out with them too, and to her surprise, Lynn grew comfortable around her quickly.

One night during those two weeks, Lynn spent an hour explaining to Charlie that she might have to go back on her deal with Jeremy. Her reasoning was the same as it has always been: she didn't think she deserved to talk to Trent after what she'd done to him in the first place. Charlie spent the rest of that night telling her different. While Charlie argued her point, Lynn felt angry that she'd never spoken to Charlie before; she really was an excellent friend. At one point in their debate, Charlie got Mel in on the conversation, and the two of them spent hours crushing every doubt that Lynn threw their way.

Finally, on October 20th, the moment came when Jeremy sent a warning text in the group chat that Trent would be coming to school the next day, and Lynn was required to hold up her end of the deal. Lynn became so nervous that she thought about not even showing up. Every day Trent hadn't been in, she'd imagined running into him around a corner, or seeing him in math class. This was sort of a coping mechanism for Lynn. Every afternoon at three o'clock, she'd remember that she had to go to the hospital to see Teddy – then she'd quickly realize she no longer had that responsibility. It was like a reflex; her mind just couldn't shut it off. It made her feel like shit every time it happened, so she'd try to cope by imagining a ghostly mirage of Trent smirking at her in the school hallways. It worked in the first week. But by the second, it began to make her feel worse, as she realized she was mourning for two people, even though one wasn't even dead.

The thing that surprised her the most was that Raymond Hurley hadn't approached her for anything. Maybe he'd realized her brother was dead and assumed she'd be unwilling to help him with anything ever again. Alternatively, maybe he'd been waiting to get her alone so he could threaten her again, and this idea made Lynn much more grateful for her new friends and their commitment to the buddy system – at school, and outside of it.

MONDAY, OCTOBER 21, 2019

08:12 AM

If your car gets totalled, the first day back at school feels kind of embarrassing. It wasn't because Trent had to be driven there by his mom, but because he hated not having his own ride. His mom was wonderful, and he loved her, and anyone who made him feel bad about that could go fuck themselves.

Jeremy walked with him to his locker and made sure he could remember his code.

"You don't have to babysit me," Trent mumbled as his first attempt at opening his padlock failed.

"I'm not. It's fun to watch you struggle." Jeremy crossed his arms over his chest as he leaned on the locker next to Trent's.

"Yeah sure." Trent sighed and let the padlock smack into his locker as he dropped it in frustration.

"Do you want me to tell you the code already, or did you wanna try one last time?" Jeremy asked.

Trent's demeanor switched from sad to determined in one second. He wouldn't let this lock beat him yet.

"I know the code, man, but there's a trick to it I'm forgetting, and I think it's because I can't use my arm," he muttered.

Now, he was awkwardly using both hands with his body pressed against the locker. He tried to get his left arm to participate, even though it was in a cast on a sling. All the struggling seemed to work, though, and he smiled smugly over to his brother, but then frowned. Jeremy had been texting someone and hadn't even witnessed Trent's accomplishment.

"You owe me twenty bucks," Trent demanded.

"I didn't bet that," Jeremy said as he looked up from his phone.

"You still owe me out of principle."

"What?"

"Exactly."

Jeremy rolled his eyes.

"Okay, here's where we part ways. You're going to English. Room—"

"Room twenty-one, third floor. That, I can remember."

"Good. If you need me, text me."

Trent nodded to his brother and then watched as he walked off. Seemingly out of nowhere, an incredible loneliness sunk in. He felt lost for just a moment, as though Jeremy had left him in a dark forest he'd never seen before, and not in the brightly lit hallways of his high school. Trent stared into his locker at books and oddities he could only vaguely remember, and eventually picked up his English textbook. He hoped this was all he had to bring. He didn't want to have to come back to this locker in twenty minutes and struggle with the lock again without his brother by his side. As he closed his locker, he couldn't shake the feeling that he was lost, even though he knew where he was going. He figured the terrible loneliness and disorientation was made worse because he hadn't run into Adam yet. His friend had promised to meet him at lunch later, though, which helped a little.

As Trent turned to walk to class, he felt a breeze, which carried the pleasant smell of coconuts. He looked over at the girl approaching him.

She seemed nervous.

Short, brown hair, and big, beautiful brown eyes. He always really liked girls with pretty eyelashes. If he'd remembered correctly, this girl was slightly new to his school. Every time he'd passed her in the hallway or seen her in his math class, she seemed focused on something else. Like she didn't have time for anyone. Now she looked like she was anxious to talk to him. Trent felt a little worried – he wondered if he should remember her. Maybe they spoke in the last month, and he hadn't remembered? Getting a skull fracture was a pretty good excuse, so he didn't know why he felt as nervous as he did now. He tried his best to remember her name, and it suddenly came to him faster than he expected.

Lynn?

"Hi."

MONDAY, OCTOBER 21, 2019

08:18AM

Jeremy: I'm leaving him here. You better talk to him. Or I'm never buying you a milkshake again Avison.

Charlie: LYNN JUST LIKE

WE PRACTICED!!!!

Mel: But don't use Charlie's cheesy line.

Charlie: It wasn't that bad, was it? :(

Jeremy: Ye, it was worse.

Jeremy's first text made all of the butterflies in Lynn's stomach take flight and try to escape. It was showtime; the hallway was her stage, and her group chat was the audience. The first few steps she took towards Trent were easy. He wasn't even looking at her, and the locker door was hiding his face. His ocean blue eyes couldn't drown her in nerves yet. When he closed his locker, though, her nerves raged. That was her cue.

"Hi." It took everything inside of Lynn not to choke on that first word.

Trent's eyes fell on her and widened slightly.

"Uh, hi," he answered with a tilt of his head.

The initial feeling of rejection sunk into the pit of Lynn's stomach like a costly ring falling into a deep, dark lake to be lost forever, but she pushed past the horrible feeling.

"Good to see you in school again. I heard what happened. Are you, uh, are you feeling better?"

Trent grinned and looked at his feet. Lynn swooned at the sight of his smile, which she had missed for the past fortnight.

"Yeah, I'm not good as new yet," Trent wiggled the fingers on his broken arm, "but I'll manage. Thanks. You're Lynn, right?"

Lynn nodded to him. The question she wanted to ask next made her feel sick to her stomach, like she'd eaten a bad takeout burger with a side order of pure fear. Trent's eyes were still as mesmerizing as ever.

She'd grown accustomed to just how spellbinding they were, but after not seeing them in a while, they struck her anew.

Lynn took note of the black beanie on his head. She could tell he'd gotten a buzzcut so that the rest of his hair would match where he'd had it cut for the surgery. It was strange to see him without his long hair, which she'd grown so used to watching him rake his hands through.

"Um," she scratched her forehead and couldn't look him in the eyes anymore. "Do you think you'd like... wanna hang out or something, when you're feeling up to it?"

Lynn braced for impact.

Rejection was pretty new to her. She'd never been asked out, and she'd never dared to ask anyone else out. This new territory was frightening, but she couldn't turn back now. Lynn could tell he hesitated before answering, but she wasn't sure it was because he wanted to reject her. He looked as if he was simply mulling over the idea. After what had felt like several hours to Lynn, but was only a few seconds, he finally shrugged.

"Sure. What would you want to do?"

Those big, innocent eyes focused on hers now, and she couldn't look away no matter how anxious they were making her.

"I don't know. We could like," she gulped, hating how obviously nervous she was, "eat ice cream sandwiches and watch Disney movies, or go... bungee jumping, maybe? When you feel better, of course." She shrugged as she pointed to his cast.

Trent went from a little confused to totally flabbergasted, and she watched as his smug smirk snuck across his face. In his awe of her bold request, he leaned on his locker, bumping the pained shoulder and immediately making a face before standing upright.

Lynn bit her lip to hold back a laugh.

"Y—yeah, I would love to go... bungee jumping with you. Once I'm better." Trent agreed to it like it was just an ordinary request, but Lynn could tell he was in utter shock that she'd asked. "So, can I have your number? I'll tell you when I'm feeling up to – you know – bungee jumping. Or like, just going out to get something to eat." He finished with a smile, and Lynn reached out to take his phone.

She touched his hand and smiled at the warmth. That was different.

When Lynn finished punching in her number, she nodded at him warmly before slowly turning away to walk through a set of doors towards the nearest staircase. Her phone went off immediately.

Hey Lynn, not up to bungee jumping yet but when do you wanna get something to eat? Tonight?

Lynn beamed at the message and turned to see him through the door's window, looking back at her with a broad, stupid grin. She felt sick and happy, and had to look away from him quickly to hide the fact that she was smiling like an idiot as she texted back.

Sure, around 6?

When she reached the bottom of the stairs, her smile faded quickly, and her happy-sick feeling turned into a terrible, unadulterated nausea.

Raymond Hurley smiled manically at her at the bottom of the stairs.

Two weeks ago, she had accidentally left a knife in Dex's backyard. Now, Raymond was waiting for her, a few feet away, holding that same knife in his hand.

THANK YOU

Thank you so much for supporting this book.
Your Deadly Decisions will continue in book two.

Visit www.knpantarotto.com for more information.

Manufactured by Amazon.ca
Bolton, ON